Twisted Tales from the Big Fail

Twisted Tales from the Big Fail

E Lloyd Kelly

CONTENTS

Twisted Tales from the Big Fail   1

1   Die Kingdom Come   2

2   Lucky You, Lucy.   10

3   Fatman's Doggy Pup Got Picked Up   32

4   Foul Winds Came Rushing In   42

5   I'm Going to See the King   52

6   Border Crash   61

7   Sheamus' Story   69

8   Go West, My Son   88

9   He Raised Me   107

10   Finding a Way Out   123

11   What About This Peace   142

12   Fire Sale on Falsehoods Beams   159

13   Sacrificial Lambs   166

14   My Way, or the Higher Ways   177

15   The Nanny   186

16   Billie B Leave and the Wong Brothers   214

17   Die Will is Done   223

18   Click This Case, and Step In   228

Extras 238

Twisted Tales from the Big Fail

Book 2, Real Inky Trails Series.

Description

Two thousand years ago, the mighty Cekko people ruled the land. This is according to the KD's measuring instruments and how such records were kept in Kingsland. The scepter has been passed to these, a ruthless clan of murderers and thieves who are now in command, and the entire Kingsland world is just about to feel the caring habits under the right hand of their peace and passivity. One man and his dog from the past are left walking the path, hoping to find a remnant of the ancient kinds, but...

Note: this story is told from a Carib-Jamericanadian perspective, in a richly blended language-mix of nonsense-talk, sensational spellings, double entendre, poetry, and Jamaican patois. Yes, wordplay is the order of the day around here. Yeah, man, a Jamaica yaad mi come from, sorry, I meant to say, I'm Jamaican born and bred, okay?

Die Kingdom Come

Here comes Blister, yes, after the real work is done, mister. This is his moment to come into the shine, always. Now, let the real jobbing workout begin, because you're about to run headlong into him. Here's a little something you might need to know about him before heading in. So, put away that gadget thing and lend me the pit of the hearing in your hand-me-down headphones here, stuffing the sort of hearing that may remain in your ear.

Tall and thin and young and ugly, the boy from Lucky Hill Road comes towards me. Bow-legged baggy pants, casually walking, good enough to break it up on the cup of a dark king, or brown. Any shade of hue you may hang them on is sound and good enough for you down home. It will sit as comfy as his rocking chair, leaning against his backbone, covered up under the shadows of you. If and when one is to be starting right there at the first fight scene in Mountain View, "sight, Hingh?"

"Yeah, man, you're all in."

"Okay." Just in time to get a chance to see Lucy's lifeline itself, strung up and running off towards the end of the beating belt. But look, look at the scenes through the lens of this thing. Gone is he, going off towards the living room first and foremost, kid Nii. Look, he's going inside now, to go and shelf himself on the bunking sin ting, or something, if you prefer it when it's said that way. After ticking off the first act of the evening and marking it as complete, Ted... I mean, as completely as he possibly could. The act of trying to secure some food that he needed, you know, like, badly. Then, when he was done washing the bedpan, he did what he usually does: a night slam. Sliding under the covering cloth satisfied with knowing he could still find his bedding. The one in the gloom atop the ladder head leaned and hung headlong and half dead against the head of somebody else's sleeping room. Pulling it in and hanging up his feet headlong against the other brother's buffoonery.

Well, not quite that soon, Miles is quite a guy, don't call him that though, I'll tell you why. That name has remained for the family, and I, yes, that would be me. Everybody else around these parts on the dusty farm belt calls him Robbie Sly, or Robert Sylvester when he's with the official's irregular, uppity guy in the crib next door. But he's not as rough and tumble when going down the aisles as this Lucy one, and I am, when he's the one always carried along in his finest style. Nowhere else to go this time, though, Dorian, except to bed down in his dorm room with him. No need to argue with anyone this evening, not even with Slim. Not when one sees him being so meager and thin within the body framed by design sin. As compared to the brother below him on the underside low limb of the bunking sin Ting. Yes, that same thing that you sometimes call something, or another. He's a real bother, though, just like any other younger brother that you might know; always trying to prevent Slim from getting his shut-eye in. Look, he's nicely covered up now under the darkling. Cut the talking, because, in a drowsy waking-up moment, tomorrow is coming, and who's to tell what platter will be served up to him and his papa when times are becoming so uncertain on these properties on the farming acres?

What a name, though, who in the KD's names his sonny little boy baby Lucy like that lady named Dulce? Then expects him to go out on duty, and have fun on tonight's latest sleuths of showdowns, doing so in comfort and beauty to go and tell-say on the streets of her hometown? No, it won't happen, not as it's now showing on TV down-home weekly, Yuh sei mi?

"Yes, I can see you, but…"

"I know, I know." He can surely pack a hail of a lot of tiny little peanut punches though, and a masterful power-packed nutria-bar chord of an upper cutter wrist tick type of knee-bumping kick back king scheme slight below.

"Don't you mean 'slightly' below?"

"Yes, the below-the-knee caps scene is what I mean, seen?"

"Seen."

Yeah, man, that would be him, blowing off his brother like the whistle-blowers' Rastafar-I of a friend's right hand dem... I mean, them, where the hurt is slower than them, the most. Well, both memes are the same thing, of course. Both of his arms are good to use on your corpse, yes, they're there and bearing with the hang-ups, right there where the hurt is slower than them, the most. He then went out walking along the path to go somewhere with the other men the following morning and ended up planting a tree knee deep up another man... oh, sheet! Wait a minute, that doesn't sound right. Sorry, man, I meant to say it this way. He ended up on the farm the following morning, plowing and planting corn. That's when he ended up planting a tree knee-deep in Mister Groener's man-made mountain of blabber mouths, no end of long-winded, never-ending chats about boxes, now, carry on.

"Um? What's this, chats about what?"

"About someone or another, or something else that was not yours nor his brother's. Mouthing off their choruses of talks, blabbering on with the words coming in wrong from below the clutter near the gutter post that spouts the dripping sort down the way to the north..."

"Coast, right?"

"Well, of course, you're really bright."

"Trying to go out and look at the incoming boats, I suppose?"

"But of course, yes," that's what brought him and these petty little guest goats in contact this morning, without even so much as a warning. He couldn't quite say why, but they're there now, look. There they are, hiding out on the hidden path now, are they, or trying to hide, routing them and their dirty ends way too close to home this time around today. So close that they almost wanted to stop and stay. But 'Nay,' said another naked little brat, like his little big brother is said to have got a lot of, still walking somewhere there on the lot."

"Go away," his old man said to them from far away, and out of their hearing. But got a mouthful of nothing nests to say today too, is this one over here leading the crew, and who really knew what to do in such a situation, like, more nothingness, yes. Before Lucy inadvertently ran into them, but since he never really knew anything, for sure, you can bet on this one too, and win. Like, that he didn't know how it was all going to end, no. He didn't know the real pain that was about to come falling upon him and all the rest of them, Dames and all, not before...

"What, before what?"

Before the ugly man brought the scrabbling ram to the end of its shining, by slamming it on somebody and his buddies behind the scenes, kind of timing. Well, he's not all that ugly, just as seen in his mode of dressing when he's dressed up in his clothes on his tall and scrawny frame, and thing and ting, like that hole in the bucket near the sink. Well, at least, he was trying out his hand at a slam dunk because he wanted to own his bunk.

"You owe me one, my friend," the intruder said to him under his grin, "and it's pay-up time now, hahahahaa."

"I owe you "nuttn" and I'm nobody's friend," came the refrain to plow through the grain, damaging the entire harvest for them, again. While hitting up against him and his name tag pin. Look, there it is. Right there beside his lapel button, but it was "nuttn", nothing at all. Just boxed in there near the empty shell locked down under his sheep's skin, where all the hard feelings stopped and grew. Yes, the soft ones were there too, no doubt. Parts of at least one-half of them will be swimming in a frosty ditched-out heaven, soon. Dishing out something near and dear to the hut's out-posting sticks sometime before noon-ish. After ten, my friend, if you need to be fed with a spoon like me and Alfred (dem), or else...

"Or else what?"

"What the fork?" Came Fatty's remarks. "No, go fork that? I mean, park. Go, park that part and come back again, let's talk fox, like the falling rain." As I was saying, it'll be dished out of the pots and into someone's mouthful of talk, soon.

"Well, where's he now, the fat man of a ram and his cousins like cows?"

"Look, that's him right there, sitting in the gloom right over there under that tiny tree house room with the rest of his goons." Can you see them?

"Yes."

"Yeah, man." That's where he's planning to shack up his new home with a few guest rooms, I'm sure. Someone else's efforts at making room for more, like, for the coming boom, somehow, yes. After them should come the reborn, yes, the one that's coming into the birth house of thorns to sit down at the usual address, Norm, kiss the wishbone. Such coming things had so far brought them nothing but glooming something sin ting, like, yawning on the false alarm, Hingh (or true).

"Um," yeah, that is the one truth that someone else is now hastening to run headlong into, right?"

"Yes, that is the truth, mi yute, you're really bright. I'm talking to the youth over there by the shoot, spreading them wide to either side and trying not to get too many watery droplets on his booth. Up until this break of the latest last morning sleuth of slates that came popping out of someone's pants foot. But wait, what the heck does he care about anyone? "Look, he's coming again today," little brother heard him say, "so get prepared, or go away."

"Where, where should I go, west?"

"Yes, I'm sure, since you seemed to consider it best before, like, the expiry date. Better than all the rest, Gord, even the Ape."

The end was fast falling on them all, wrapped up warm in their old-timers' evening gowns and waiting in the hall for the comers to come running into them and to cull, sorry, I meant to say, call. But they'd still have enough fighting will left within their gall, I mean, gut, within their guts. At least one of them did, if not all; one never knows for sure what metal they're made of, you know, since they hardly ever bother to go, yes, that's what I'm talking about, Sir Beau, war. They hardly ever go to war. Not until or unless they're pushed too far, which is just about what is being pissed off, sorry, I meant to say, passed off. Yes, what is being passed off to them through the bar right about now is a situation where they'll be forced to show how it's done, so look. This is it.

The swivel-faced old man was sitting and watching to see if food was getting ready to find a place on their shelves to sit in... He looked on as grudgingly as he could stuff in the tin can and shook his topmost top end up at the new real guards' man and his men coming on down towards him, sitting on his thin in Hingston. Those whose noses were quickly turning up again to watch their eyes looking down the road as roses grew on him and his kind of thin lines, lining him, as usual. "Have you seen any of them yet, my pal?"

"No."

"Look nuh man, look nuh, there they are, those who are walking along right there with somebody whose gal friend bare bar... um, did I say that right?"

"I don't care, ma-hite. *Mi nuh... mi nuh eeven knoah har like that at all.*"

"I already know that you don't know her, and that's not all." They're coming anyway and closing in on us, to get close enough to where lucky Lucy is standing up as if on duty. He's standing on another mound thing and waiting for something like..."

"Like, like what, the bus?"

"Yes, I think, or some other such thing," while taking a wide-eyed stare at the glutonous, there. Trying to come in and gut ten of them and us, squares, to go over and cook up a roast again, rare. While the old man mumbled the worst thing he could stumble upon, cursing the hurting out of his system on their blameless bottoms, good and proper. All of them are now on this side of the plain land — Papa. "This is going to be the new source of somebody's pain." So complained the ancient name who was sitting there within a shaky frame. Just a few too many walking feet away from them, those who are not too meek, but coming in to leak before...

"Now, leave that kid alone," he growled, "and go about your business." He said this with his voice rising just a tad bit above his hearing (spit). Still knee-deep in his scorn of them to get it through their thick heads quickly. But then, what he didn't know was that the kid was their only business to show there this time around the hoe, machetes, and ground forks. All the peasant farming tools that were scattered haphazardly about the yard, Leigh. Scratching was happening too, under three or four of the hens' claws in their shoes. Those who were getting ready for the draw to sweep the yard clean. Trying to come up with some food for their beautiful new age chicks and..."

"And what, and the mean, right?"

"Yes, you too, mi lawd, oh yes, My Lord, what else did you expect, a reward?" Well, that would have been before he... (the old man, not me) dropped in on things that didn't belong to him. As seen through the eyes of the rowdy bunch of stinks, and got dragged into the mixing bin kind of thing for their added reckoning.

"You," said the fat head, "like all the rest of peasants in this rat's nest, head-on, are the cause of this one." He said this to the old man's fistful of further chagrin, and Ned's. While Miles slyly slid out from behind the hut of a shed that they called a house with a few too many beds, and ran away towards the south-south-west. The old man was skillfully helping him out by shaking his furlong of first-timers' fists for way too long in front of the intruders and their eyelash strands for their liking. Like, like hammering it with the hammer stick at the fat one's headpan still, as if he were a Viking. Still fixed hated... I mean, fixated on this little bit of a walking stick, bearing with his overweight self. Like this little bit that I'm holding in my fist. Meanwhile, the old man's head slowly moved back up from where it had fallen almost to get the round of his chin propped up on the hanging down spot on his stick's uppermost end, before they came. But the bunch of intruding slimy ends is now all riding in and turned on against the side wind. "Wow!" While mocking the ending of each note of his song upon the tips of a drawn-out sliver of a tongue in return. Amen.

"Get out of my '*waey*,'" came the fat man's response to disobey. Because, to them, everything remained unchanged from the new bad normal types of playing of the game that came falling on the old-timer and all of his kinds of lame, it would have seemed, yes. As all the people like these in this space of mine, eh, were beginning to see these things, Ray.

"Oh, please."

"Yes, I know all about these, but..." As seen through the eyes of Fatty Big Bratty and his kind of friend, Li Mess. They're there, eking out a living on next to nothing in recent times, at his new address. It was as if it were always raining on mankind. But, to them, like, to the fat man and his friends, it's just the new playing fields witnessing the next new players committing new criminal deals of the day-oh, playing them for fool hitch nests again, oh. I mean, "ish," like, foolishness.

With nothing left except leftover pain and broken scraps of eggshells for them, coming from the latest hatchets they'd salvaged and sold, to get it on them. On crash and carry away, of their everything. Just as easily as chicken and chips in their pockets on payday, that is worth as much to them as a pocket full of hay. "Nothing" is probably a better word to say about what's coming off them to us, as if it's a game. Well, as it pertains to those from the other side of the aisle, I'm sure it is. Like, nothing but a game. But what is just a joke to a mischievous little kid's mouse means death to the weaklings in the rat's house. As seen through this old man's gaze and his cache of a kid's knave, like these are. Just bush frogs to them, we are, who are being played as a game, which is just about to get started to blow up in flames, right about now. Somebody there knew that much about the score, anyhow.

2

Lucky You, Lucy.

Lucy was a beauty when it came to doing his duty. Somebody and his bunch of rowdies sliding in and around my daddy's paddy must have known that much already about the youth, ee!

"Lucky you, old man," said the fat, low one, "you're about to get a front-seat view of this one. You'll soon get to see him at work for a quarter of the feet in your pants end up touching the dirt." But of course, he wanted to say, for a quarter of the fee in advance. All paid up and brought in, or two, wrapped up in romance. "Two quarters will still do. Well, if you want," he continued to blabber like an ant. Lick the sheet out of the little crawlers too many feet, you know.

"Two pennies' worth of your skin is a good and handy little purse for a senior's discount price on you and your worth, right?" He said this again and continued in spite… He grinned and winked at him twice, but… How Slim had managed to get in so deeply and readying to be skinned nice and neatly, again, he didn't quite know the reason for his name. How he hadn't noticed them earlier was beyond him and his program. He's usually as alert and quick to elude the predators' gripping, hurting habits as a wild deer, or rabbit running up into him while he's wearing his crocodile skin shirt, like this one, right here, in the dirt.

But it would have appeared as if those skunks over there, unfit, came in unawares to him like the late shift at evening at 6, up against the wind. That could explain why they managed to avoid the bulk of the stink from hitting him near the sinkhole. Even before they ever got to see him. Growl. Now, though, um, never mind, oh, I'm gone, just moving along.

"Are you going to show or what?" The fat man redirected his attention back to the boy's hand from the old man's cap, as he tossed the ask at him fast.

"What, show what?" The boy croaked out the notes from the depths of the pot in his throat. Yes, that deep spot where his last meager meal was stored up. "Oh, that," he continued and glanced up at the swipe pad in the claws of a duce bag of a swindle for a head of his, complete with two fat Aces to look at our faces. Still standing there in the places where a man's gaze should have been placed, Sis, lusting hard and looking on in awe at the daisies. As the young man growled out another verse of his song's notes from the pages of oats.

"Shouldn't you be the one to show, though? I thought you were the ones dropping in on us, no?"

"There is no 'us,' buddy, not as it pertains to you and your old pops over there. Everything belongs to us, the real us," he said, "Even the crops and the hairs, and that cache of hens laying on eggs over there too." He said this whilst spreading his stinking finger across his friend's face in a linear motion. Like, as if it was the front window blades needing to be wiped cleaner than your shades, B Leigh Ocean. To get them rid of their sins to be saved, in the ocean, you know, but no. That was designed to show them up for dinner, like, showing off the thing that they wanted the most at the time, for getting a bit further away from turning thinner, by not doing the diet dine. Like, on food, like, it was like too many days of them being away from the crumbs falling off the table that you'd spread before them nice and good, I'm sure.

"Okay," he said. Just as the fat man tossed the heel of his palm on the backside of his almshouse thing. Yes, the thing that he carries around for an arm most of the time, Most High Hingh, and which was known to disrupt the calm everywhere he goes around town. Look, it's turned up now to face a cup filled to the brim with his new old-time not-so-friendly companion's face within, in haste. To remind him how it's done, you know, just in case.

"Swipe," he said. Lucy obeyed the command and reached out his arm, swiping it in a slightly Zaro-like zig-zagging motion to try and redirect the big man's scanning gaze from the oversized clothing that he wears on his blades. Those same ones that were hanging on him there at the time and shaking as if in dread. Afraid of what the clock was striking the day to have them say whenever they said things about him, and the condition of his permission to stay within. Or go back to the old man's cabin for further scrubbing, perhaps.

Out comes the gadget stretching towards him, and fretting was up in somebody's face, chatting. It was coming from the kit that was tucked under his armpit, the funky place where it was put in what smells like stinky old …it, sheet, um, shirt, or some other such thing, plentiful as dirt, dumpling.

"What the fork is going on here?" Fatman queried his ask in alarming fear, while squeezing his eye skin almost to a shut-in, trying to zero in on the queue slot there, I mean. The dial had lost control of all the heart it had in its hold upon the vial in his ole… Coming in the form of splitting the hue in its dialing shoot into two, or too many little pieces for its good, you know. The gumption to stay put had gone capote and was wobbling its way all over the face of the day. From six to six, probably. Then flipping across the zipping to drag the darkest part of the night, Ted evening, in. Via the same ways and means committee that committed yet more sin than he on me. Like, ten thousand times per minute, I'd say.

Meanwhile, the lone hide guide standing before their eyes was hoping that the second time around was going to be a lot better than the first. Will it? Sit, take a seat on this long bench of mine, and allow your eyes to shine in deeply. Yes, I'll tell you about that, and this, Leigh, of course, if even a little bit off course.

"What, about what, the first encounter of sorts?"

"Yes. It was like this." Slim and skinned, Lucy was in for a beauty of a whipping he wasn't going to be forgetting any time soon, mi yuty. Yes, my youth. Got himself into a ruckus with the wrong pack of hog husk goons from the other side of the loom. He did put on a good show that time, though. Too good if you'd bothered to ask me about mine,

"Oh!"

Yes, I know, opinion is considered a thing gone wrong, gone the way of a crime scorned these last days long, gone are they. But still, if you'd bothered to ask as to how it was to go a swayed so fast on nulled blades of haystack grass, I would have told you more than that, and fast. Six of them were a bit too much for the young kid to go touching his stick at the end in good stead and avoiding the hard luck of smelling the residue of the muck mugging when he gets back home to the inn and his bed. Oh, look, the bugs are buzzing again, at his ear on the nether side of his forehead. …Or more like, if, if he's lucky enough. He wasn't even done training his Pop's legs yet about how to stand up for very long, but yes, I'm coming to that. They spread him out on a batter board and beat the living daylights out of his trailer load of clothes. But the gods were on the kid's side of the waterlogged road a bit, it would have seemed to this sneaky little snitch I'd supposed, and the mean one too, like this. Despite the jellybeans that were left in the yellow stitched threads on the seams of his baggy jeans, he'd gotten a bit of wind still in.

"Or was… wasn't it, under it?"

"Probably there, my brother, yes, over yonder, sit." He still has a few good friends around by then, too, including a big little brother who was always as good in a fight as his last pair of running shoes might have been. "True." But still, all of them together were good enough for him to weather the storm, not you. They picked him up and dragged him home. That was when…

In the meantime, though, back over there is where we must go, because… The big man still wanted to know, "What the hail is going on, what's wrong with the thin man's horn? "Sorry," he said, "I meant to say, 'arm,' with your arm. What's wrong with it, whiz kid?" Which was the same one-tooth speech of his, come to think of it, in this biz pan kind of kneeze. Horn or arm, at least he had some on, for the time being. "What's wrong with your arm? Have you been messing around with the chip monk under your skin bump, the one that we put there last month? Have you tampered with it? You'd better not," the big man's knuckled, finger-fisting tricks had a hit song scored on the fore-shoulder of the kid's hand above the pit that he carries under it towards the boulder.

"Ah-woo!" I heard him call out to me and you.

"But-but, why?"

"Why, what, why did I not answer back?"

"No, why did he allow his guards to fall so hard in front of their eyes once more, mi lawd, and so firmly on the flat?"

"We probably won't get to the 'know' part on that corn bump of a guy's pop e-show sort of jerking cord cap, but…" This would have happened after the question that the fat man was asking got past his last string, by sliding out past the half-skinned bulging neckline under his teeth, less a jawbone of mine. It then got into the habit of irritating the young man's earings, small pits, and eat, I mean, hit, and hit upon his last nerve endings at the end of the week.

"It's just about to harm you, that's what's wrong with it," he said to the big youth buck and… and, and now, look, he's seeing red. He's acting like a brat instead of a man, resisting his bedpan again, against his mom's command. Wanted to squirt a little extra work for her and them, you know, on another patch of stinky-smelling, stained-up car pet in the back of the van that she'd owned, amen, now, go. "Is he gone?"

"No."

"Well, let's continue along with the song, anyhow," so he seemed to have said to the young man, as it would have seemed to this sneaky little someone looking ahead in the program. As seen through his longing eyes as he looked in through a flashback to the home of my… I mean his… his home. The home of his childhood dreamy lullabies habits alone, but the impact of such a big talk seemed to us to have hit hard against the shortest inside track of the big shot's hot spot. Jerking the worst thing out of him and the other bigger kids than him, along with their hatless head-tops, those that were quickly pulled closer in. Coming in and up from around the back sort of spread, to get up a head or seven from where they had been dicing for leaven, I think. While I was sitting there and watching Lucy-Slim spreading out the proper formation for someone's deathbed "ding" by dimension. Acted as if they were jumping back out of a sweet little snort of a nap they were on, you know. Perhaps trying to pacify the big man's wrath alone, well, let's leave it "a loan" so that they won't have to live on water and bread alone. This, along with the hard-hitting speech, would have stirred the big man's path just as fast as the rest of 'the brat pack.' Up to the boiling point of the cooking pot, you know, if it wasn't up north near a lost cart already, Hugh-go. Might as well join the bandwagon train now and go." Because, yes, the rush roast was on the tablecloth somehow, somewhere.

"Sit, sit down," was what I heard. "Yes, have a seat over here," he said to the herd, "and eat." So, they each took a plate amounting to about seven or eight and ate their steaming little pieces of hate away. Well, they wanted to do that, right away, but the big man's biggest temper was about to be proven wrong again, Sir. It happened when he swung a fisted fan like a heavy right hand at the slim one's eye, risking a head-on bond dead companion, yes. Just as rich as the I-Man's hard-hitting armband that came to him and you from the wrestling federation. Rich enough to hit upon a kickback money laundering plot at the big man's but tux, I mean, buttons. Button galore and a-plenty, and badges that he had on

him and his empty, something, sorry man, sorry for
getting that one wrong. But he couldn't say "nuttn" Mister
bad man Hodges, nothing at all that is. Not even what
hand it was that came back, hitting upon him one, two,
three, like, seven thousand times seven a day, like me.
Nor could he say from whence it had come to hit the pop
charts' shortest path to every part of him home, really
fast. To get him on his journey up and in against the rest
of the gnomes in the rat pack, like him, and them. Those
at whom I'm pointing out the way to the Jones Town
types of problem math tick men in the line, ahead of
them, man! It was like, like, sixty times six, hits after
stunningly amazing hits. Boy! That DJ sure has a good
ear for an eye, I couldn't afford not to buy. Neither could
his wonderful wandering friends there with aim, I mean,
him, yes. They were there with him and watching the
fixing good and properly, before. All of them were now
spinning around him and lined up in circles surrounding
the property's door. Searching for the rest of his keyed-in
door pins too, and the battery to activate the key to try
and pop the gate for their entry in, and to get through for
me, fast, perhaps. Like, in ones and twos, at last, my
pops. It was just about to fence and frame him in, on you
and your… Yes, they were trying to see the ghost wind
that came in, blowing them down the thin line to the
ground floor. Flooding them with yet some more and
waxing him and them bruised and round like… no, sorry, I

meant to say, brown. Bruised and brown like, as brown as Buju's browning's dumplings.

"What, shop?"

"Stop that, because a loving deer was responsible for that applause, not you and all your faults."

They were just about to learn some more about the wonderful one's door full of new songs, filling someone's long pockets of feelings for themselves. Everyone of them fell.

"On the path to hell?"

"Yes, my dear sister Nell, to go and check out the new-look Club Inferno as well, before the return trip back home-oh."

"Where, where does she live?"

"Back over these South Sounding spheres here with Hugo and the kids." He who usually goes on the west bay end of the bend and stays there a bit too long, like, all night sometimes, at one of Kelly's bars again.

"But, but did it happen at all?"

"Wait nuh, man, wait, follow me closely along around the gate, you'll see the waterfall." It should have been an easy piece of cheese whiz, please, like, please Mom, please, to please him by holding him tightly, squeezing, and taking away his car keys, Hingh. But some e-how or another, Wee Pow must have been his brother, because… It was not turning out and over the engine as they'd planned it to be… wing on the brother's stinging ask him about it when he's finished singing, not me. Like, something was about to be waxed and polished to a shine with hide looking a lot like mine. "Yes?" "Yes. Wink and shout 'yes,' and amen, again."

"Oh, c'mon," he said, but. "Not like the first time, not like the first time. This is the second time around and – "Oh!"

"Yeah, that, the first fight-night time. Want to hear some more?"

"Yeah, man, what happened? Tell me, you poor poor…"

"In three little words, I'll agree to it being heard, he lost it." He would have lost the first part of the two-part series on a miss-op with the walk past me, as I was passing along the hearse key rings of the Kiwis to get him home in it for meat, me, at the corner. If it went to the big boss? Of course, yuh sei mi?

"Yeah, man! I can see you, but I'm still hoarse from laughing so hard at your horse-E. Hugh."

"Well, you may just as easily ignore this one at once, okay, mi cous?"

"Yes, of course, my cousin."

That's what would have caused the extra cache of homework tasks-eh? The one his dad didn't want to be talking to me about so fast, Ray. But, because his father was a bad asset, of a man, one who was asking me about his kid's kneecaps at the time – "Oh c'mon…"

"Yeah, I'll tell you squats about that if you don't mind, mind you." Not just the greatest and best general surgeon was he, around those parts in the country of the third land east of the waste indeed. Yes indeed, he was, but that's where it was and still is, before all that was gone away from the worldly count three, as it was to become known to them and me, my kids, at the same time.

But he was also a hail of a handyman with the proper tools of the trade in his left hand. Or even the improper right one, which is usually what he gets to fall back on, bright man. Yes, man. The left hand is the next one that he tends to use best, Sam. So, when his son was dragged back home to him with a bag full of broken bones within, acting as if the old ones were still whole and lined up properly in his beaten-down skin, you know what? Dad lit up his smoking pipe wide and bright. Then got inside the musky hut to work that night, and many others were to follow him through to the daylight. Working on rendering him a bit heavier than light and slim, so he could take on the heavyweight champs next time, not just the light ones, and fight it out to the win. He was lending him some support in getting the new bones in, you know… "Despite…" "No doubt, yes, I already know how that one would have turned out, Ma-hite."

All he wanted from him in return was never to let him see him beaten down like that old engine mound out back amongst the beetle bugs, again. Not after he'd gone through all that pain, bruises, and muscle strain, excuse me, please. Now, though, go, get out of the rain. Because, as the flash scenes were to be seen showing up in his father's overactive brain, "I hope he's learned how to master the pain, that's the only thing that still worries me a lot," his papa mumbled under his thoughts, but… This was the time to show his pops and the rest of them all how far he's come away from that fall, yes, manly men. He was about to fall on them like the falling rain coming in to call. Look at the scene again, yeah, man, you can see the rerun via this little tin bump of a program thing that I am in on the lump sum and reminiscing, yes, it has a companion within that's recording everything. Come, my darling, stand by him, I mean, me. Come a bit closer to me and see; one, two, three times in, and then it happened, look. Every time the big man gets back into his lying habits of lying down on the ground like this. Acting, you know, acting as if he's blowing up and rolling off a tantrum-throwing fit of rabbit sheets from the background. His warships, the mayors, and the other one without the named swayers' hot comb. Those who were targeted for no other purpose than to show off this one ounce of Players Lite (or none, Drunk-a-lot) as the main focus, back home. All for distraction, you know, but. It was also the act of them trying to teach Slim a lesser lesson than him, "You know what I mean, right?"

"Right."

"Yes, man, you're really bright, but…" Fatman was (a moment later) getting dragged up off the pavement crater, by the helping hands of two or three of his own braver men than me. Braver than he would have been by then, if you can still c mi… I mean, can you see me? If you see me say "sure and amen."

"Sure, and amen."

"Ten Q, now, let's roll this circus of a show all the way home, and in on you." While another handyman was brushing off the rear-end parts of his knee pants, you know what I mean, Champ?

"Yes."

"Yes, yes, the new pieces of sheet E kind of cloth he was trying to place his waste things on fast, right?"

"Yes, I agree." And which was to then be handed off to the rest of the clean clan's men to weep on, because. Can't have the big man standing in front of a stranger leaner person than I am in… to perform with dirt on his underarm pants, thing. Like, while acting as if he's got barbed wire in his… wait a minute, Aunt Enid, no, settle and cease. Sue is who I meant to do, to say, and, sorry, remember her? "Yes." Well, don't ever react to her, because that one can't do that, we don't want her kind of servicing shoe n sock, so tell me, can you, like, dig it?

"No, it wasn't me who planted it."

"Okay, leave it a loan, I'd say, and go." So that the kid may be able to purchase and pay for whatever he may owe, or even June.

"Oh no-o…"

"Yes, it can surely fit in my room." Meanwhile, the Slim and thin of a "sin" Ting, still being a child in sin. Lucy has the profile of one who was born to defile everybody and everything. Everything he touches tends to spoil in front of me, not him. But they didn't know much about the rest of the power shots that he had hidden in his stash of sack shots. So what they were about to see for the first time on that morning, drawn at the draft line, was fine, like this.

The young one's right-hand e-man's fist was quicker than this silky sand on which the eye-man stands tall and stiffer. Just like this spin fan in my hand, on an e-zee zip lock bag with sharp spike heels on. Spinning around him like a bladed hand and dangling from handling another Anglin girlfriend from a long time gone.

"Where, down to the west end of the pond?"

"Yes, like, 'down, in Montego Bay,' where she and her lovely nest came from to sojourn and stay. Oh oh oh oh, ugh, oh man, remember how much you loved that woman?"

"Yeah man, but, but…"

"That's enough, because – "He was activating his plans to land the fat man back where he came from, yes?"

"Yes, the fat one is who I'm placing all of the blame for this talking sin Ting on." He landed him shaking like jelly on his newly leased piece of land-dead ground provisions, Nellie. That's when the rest of the men entered the ring as was the planned program, Hingh, again, and did to me what friends did for him; going along with him to the end, Hingh. Well, they were trying to, that was the plan as intended by you, not him. But that was when those who were a moment ago standing by him and looking at him low, down there where he came from, like, from down below the elbow of each man's hand (me down, to the toe) as he was coming in from the cold ground that was fast and furious, at becoming his deathbed that night. A flat rock band hit was his pillow too, just like a big beloved darling, darling, darling, please consider me nuh man, so he said, but. Not on this day, they were going to get exactly what was coming their way, mi bred. They were to then brave the bruising caves of the spinning blades and run into the grave. Just by trying to try and see if they could save the fatling knave a fat chance at learning how to act and behave, like me, even. But his pride would not agree to be denied, not by me or anyone else this side of Eden. Because he wouldn't have had any of it left on the losing side of the kays to the west of me and my sea through, all season. So he fanned all seven of them off the kid's leaven and sent him towards the end, like a pen pinned pan his scarf above the navel, again, king.

"Where, in heaven?"

"Yes, where you were and keeping the records just like the capable scribe that you are, you know, like…" Like, just like the same devil of a one that they were with, in the brawl wash pan, all six. They then went squabbling for the last skin off him, while asking about his belongings they wanted. Would have happened while they were going through their soon-coming-to-them pant pocket full of strawberry-brewed broth pulled in from their minds on open-mouthed talks of it, and whining. Trying to decide who will be the merry one taking off with it to get home as fast as his food kicks knees can… can, can you allow me, please? Allow me to ask a lot more questions like these, please, like… about what it will mean for us to have these.

"Yes, ninety seconds more."

"Ten Q, for sure." Having it to themselves is what they needed most, you know, like, whenever they're done with him and you, like, licking it up against the pillar and then posting it. Yeah, I know, this is more than a little bit screwed up for you, of course, but…

"This one is mine, though," said the kid to them in a very de voice vine low. "Almost as low as where their heads were at the time, no?"

"Yes, very near and dear to where the hem of their gourmet pants was when they were coming in from far too many chances at stopping at those chatterbox doors on the way south for more. It sounds like crying to them."

"And 'har?'"

"Yes, Sir, I think you're talking about 'her,' the lady over there by the Front Door, but no. No good at all was the result of that crawl." But then, they hobbled up and down the bend to go do an about-town turnaround for him and them. Trying out their winning arm at turning things around for the fat one on a tentative stance, as shown. "Can you still, like, see?"

"Yes, carry on, carry on for me."

"Okay then, let's confess, I mean, continue, to tin you in a tight lid can, if nothing else, Canute, as you already know that I definitely can." Look, Fatman is now facing off again with the kid in the way too big pants for his pumps and pride fame at a dance from way back then. But that same one who a moment ago had lied when he told himself so, saying that he could right the wrong on this other side of the pond, south of Benbow, came back to apologize with the sharp point of the hidden knives. But the brute of a trite wasn't very nice, took to tumbling down on the kid's very life-ending. After the gig with way too many wives and the chopsticks that were his other man's bride's mending added yet a bit more clicks on the scaled-up slab of meat. Weighing him down heavily on the poor pickney, yes, yes, my child. Eventually, he gets a stronghold on the kid "ding" under him, wobbly. He was readying himself to step into the suit, gladly. The belt, and boots, too, the one that was way too big for the kid's "foots of" shoes that he wears on his feet, whenever he's out talking blues to the melodious songs and beats. Just like a world-class wrestling king of a champ does and sings the notes wrong, my cousin, Boaz. Like, when seen in the news from above the tell-lie vision. Pinning the kid "ding" dangling dung under him and the rest of his mal-handling lump sum of something from way downtown. Summing it all up to a laughing, winning showdown for him and his cronies' companions to take back home to the inn. "Yes, man," said someone else, "good thing." Got him right where he wanted him, he thought, as seen via his eyes popping out of his stinking sackcloth of an unthinking skin part. But he was not too big on winning the smart, so it would have seemed to someone looking on from afar. As seen via the tallying upper score ring too, of this inning on the scoreboard to tally up in the view, because… He lost, he was in for his last belting of the sort from a kid with a lot of help from the string swimming from somewhere around his heart, and wing. Have those types of string Hingh sin ting on almost all body parts of him, as a matter of "far…" I mean, fact. Parting from every port on the north, while one is on the way out the back. Kiddo might be thin and slim oh, but he packs tons of lethal punches within his funny bones of jokes. Jokes were popping out like puffs of smoke while he was punching off some splitting images of skin-toning bump-ups. Now, somebody is about to find the punchline within his mouth froth, none such as I'm given out of…

"This one last laugh is mine," said the waxed and polished to a shiny kid.

"No kidding."

"Yes, that's also what he was heard saying out there that evening." This is probably the best time to use something of my own doing on him, thought the kid from within, like, from somewhere around those parts where his heart hurts, him. He then took a liking to getting some wetting on pairs of pants matching his wayward companions'. While watching the rest of the rowdy bunch of romance ticks' onions, yes, those types of ticks crawling all over the onion pits were the nuances that lost it. While they were laughing off their last kicks at the winning chances of having it all, Sis, if nothing else. By now, the big man was exhausted, but he was happy because, look-Mass Kidd, he's got the kid pinned under him, and having a whale of a time squeezing the last Kacie and the sunshine bandage that he was handed, out of him. Squeezed everything it was dealing out, you know, off him as quickly as it came in. "No matter where the bucket chooses this time to stop this lifeline of mine," he said. Like, like, if even to drop him and his reasons bare and prime here, on the deathbed of mine. "I'm sure that…" Yes, he was more than half sure that he would be coming out on more of the top than that of thine. But, as seen from behind a patch of dirty old greying hair on the pork barrel of swine, that's not how he was seeing the signs at this rather critical point, look. He's not laughing quite as often anymore. Surely, not as much fasting is coming off him as his pastor was asking him to do before, but…

Taking a chance at taunting Slim with what they wanted, were the rest of the crew of saints now freed from sin to rawtid. Look, now they're cheering everything out of Fatty while prodding him along the edge of the Allan Bamboo wagon, within. That was the place to start a good bit of something, even before they would go in for the final kick-off of the "dumb thing" to finish up the act at the kill Hingh off of the prang from the back lands' parts of the bunking.

But the kid was still willing, still able, and still had some skills left under his table at the naval-based stable of a pentalene's vest of the indies, I mean, his knee, left under his knees, west of the bird's nest. It was there beside the right one, too, yes, the right knee is what we're talking about for free, and true, I guess. The very best of such was free for them to get their kicks on and off me, and you too if you were found hanging around with those clowns while passing through on the way down towards the sea, but… The big man's big bag of seeds will soon be able to say "Abblle," please, please, please, at least one more time before these.

"Before what?"

Before he'll be able to give the rest of his buddies an insight as to how some things feel right, just after swallowing one's sneeze along with the Pride brand of rice and peas he'd just gone into for a sumptuous bite, of these. Yes, these types of super rice seeds came as no surprise, kids. The groin wasn't mine, but his, but it was where Slim landed his kids, I mean, knees, his kind of kid knees. Which were a lot smaller than these, look nuh, look nuh man. You know what I mean, right?

"Yes, mi know, I know what you're saying, but go away fast because those legs of his will apply the parking brakes on your own horse, ask King partly because…"

"Yes, I know, they're made of metallic scraps, flexible sheets of something looking a lot like steel glass, and a leather cloth of some sort of sheepskin part was the bag fencing and framing them in, all of his new body parts were there within, so…" After he was done delivering the pack of power, he rolled him over the raspberry patch of mixing powder and slid out from under his two-piece shuddering shoulder blades. Those that were covered by some sort of bearded heads of hair, the powder kegs too, yes, they must have been there, because… Dusting was happening, somebody was shaking and dropping a lot of the rusting off his half-big, broad-boned bed frame and skin, showering the kid with the muskiest kind of dusting, before the rest of the brat pack of handling beholders like rats from the sewer, storing path, covered up under your asphalt down the path near the soft shoulder, ran back to their places on the softer shoulders of a downtrodden boss, and into the task of helping him grow older. Then took to launching another soldier of an attacking pushover on the but tux of the little brat soever. But they could not save her. Because Slim was way too fast for him, and they put together to catch the balldest point of Miss Piggy's "Ointe!" meant for two pints of seven men's pens, now void of the ink, click… I mean, inclination within them. He was so inclined to climb up and out from under the boat, and the other men's too, as they were about to shout "Yes! Yes, woo!" all those other old apartments, too, fell off most of the brother's men onto you, and now his marked marksman must go and ask for one of those, them. Like, an insight as to how to repent and get four "give nest" from their wrong I'd supposed, because.

Lucky Lucy then hopped further upon two of the other men's rotten little things, looking a lot like you rats' pushover stew to them and him. Just like columns on the canyon's horizon, he went. Up a column or two walls, he meant, and sat ten feet taller than them. But on a branch up a carefully measured length from the descent. Was there taking a nap and readying to go watch the rest of the argument from his hammock, as they tumbled hard to the fullest length where they fell and dropped; Bud-duff, Slim's two thumbs went up. He went off, kicking, screaming, and laughing, too. Kicking the hell out of the screaming little brats' stinking smell; rotten as… well, I can't quite remember who, but… All the rest of the healing, too, fell out of their sack full of, yes, hard feelings, please. Because the kid, unlike the rest of the thieves in the cribs, was not just doing his job for fees. Watch the scenes again if you don't believe. Boy! He was spinning around all of these and wheeling their hardest feeling away, as each one tumbled on the full fall yet further down the wall and away. To go and get settled in nicely into the usual routine near the splendid waterfall in Old Carron Hall that day.

"You mean…?"

"No, look at it and see for yourself, where I lean; not like the first time, "not like the first time," he said while pointing a finger pointedly at each of their heads, no, not mine. "That's not how it's going to end this time at all, Mister Hall."

"We're even now, I guess," he said to the corpses now at rest on their regular dirty beds, or were they?

"No, not all of them," as I was to have heard it "tell-say."

As time and circumstances would have remained too many days, or as it would have pretended to relay such things to you in some strange little ways. He glanced back over the shoulders to behold eight humanoid frames below her lying there, and telling yet more lies on him again, as I was to hear.

"He-he, he wasn't even there when they came falling in!" she said, in a bewildered gaze at her friends and away from him and Fatty's men, still lying there, in bed. For the first time, Lucy was more than happy to hear her (or anyone else, for that matter) say that someone was willing to swear on his honor that day. And take up for the rather bad grammar on even a small part of a brother's ask King way too many questions, man. Happened while he was turning around to walk away. Because he may be small, yes, but his new legs are stronger and taller than they all, I guess. And as fast as a piston blast from the lightning bolt's past, past me, the ball, please. Yes, that ball, the one that he, who is a saint, threw last Saturday night at the community hall near the football field, for you all. Saw him spinning that web of de feet off every one of those thieves, while walking away, just like a propeller-eh, on air, even. To go and deliver the invitation to you fellows that day. "Leave him alone," some protesters were heard trying to say. So, here we go, walking away. Yeah, man. Wordplay is the order of the day around here.

3

Fatman's Doggy Pup Got Picked Up

It was on the day of the raid; they were as cruel as hail, not even a newborn baby was spared the nail. "We're on the king's business here, friend, go back over there and get it done," he said to the young man who was just about to lose his nerve on seeing the bloodshed. It was obvious to him that they were all dead, well, not quite. The people were dead; they were more than sure. But if there were any who would have escaped the sword, the blazing huts that were inflamed and all up in her arms over it again, would have taken care of that little bit towards them and their claim on the overload. Even this far away from the smoldering site, Ma-hite, the heat was almost unbearable for him to take a bite.

The smell of burning flesh weighed heavily on the night air he was forced to breathe out there. "But that dog..." Yes, man, shook him up hard. "She had a hell of a lot of heart, that was for sure a smart one," he said. Not just her, but her puppies, too. She almost bit somebody's foot out of their loaned shoe.

They were real men of war; their mercy was dirty. Everywhere they went in those days, they took a broom with them, or thirty, to sweep the landscape clean of them. Fatman was young and ambitious then; he was numbered amongst them as ten. One notch down behind him was Dedimus, his friend. His trigger-happy finger ring tools took too many cups of the vicious tea with his breakfast foods in those days, like "biscuits and cheese, please." Those whom he was eating greedily among the rest of the thieves. But this time, um, never mind me and my...

The dog fought hard to protect, not just the people in the yard, but her cache of beautiful pups, too. Until Fatty got himself a bit too close to being bitten up like you, so he took them out for dinner with the ravenous scavengers flying in with the pick-up truck for the lifting of the corpses, sooner or later. The dog howled and squeaked out a grunting bark more, then dropped on the ground (dead), floored like Rory's bed. But she wasn't done with all that said, she dragged her hind half, the part that had lost the ability to support her upstanding doggy corpse in her frame, anymore. Went and dragged it over by the lifeless body of a man and lay there with him beside the door, barely breathing, until she wasn't anymore. The remaining puppy didn't know that, though, she wanted to nurse her bad self with the sack full of a mother's tender loving care, like so. The same motherly one that's usually got the juicy treats of milk that would not flow anymore for her there. Must have touched the fat man's heartstrings from somewhere around the back door part of him, or nearby. He walked over and picked up the little pup, patted it down for a while, and rubbed it. Then bedded her down on the inner crooks of his arm and walked back towards the rest of the no-talking brat pack, near the horses. Fingering his ration canteen and stuffing something into the puppy's mouth against the tongue within the door of the teething part, Sis.

Talking conversations may resume after the dark king, yes, mi Sisdren, my sister knew them. But as of now, Fatty and his doggy show are riding the inside row, going somewhat on the slow-footed nest back to the other side of town from whence they came riding in on this leg of the destructive game. None has been able to tear Fatty and his dog puppy apart since, but then again.

Those were good times, as seen through the eyes of those warring kinds. The promise was shining upon their eyes so brightly that they almost went blind. Come to think of it, they did. So blinded were they by the light up ahead of the way that none of them saw when the dial shifted. But it did; they were not to be spared the wrath of the sicklies. None of them knew for sure what came first, but the thermostat was turned on and up. Getting the fire burning, hotter and hotter each day, so that the haves wanted to be in the boots of the have-nots, so I heard someone say. Started at, or somewhere around the same time as when the foul wind started blowing in, in line. They knew there and then that something had gone wrong; nothing was going to be the same again for them, Mr. Man... Ugh, mankind, come along. Then there were the young men, those who had somewhat of a brain left to their names. They, too, knew that their times and fortune had changed. So, they decided to do something more than just complain, and that was when the fraternity was born.

Then comes the moment to start the work on the torment by the full length of the long-term alms (house) men. Those who would have heard about the efforts of the young scouts, so they set out on the step-by-step incremental movements, to try and protect their worth from them. "No matter what the cost was to be." Even though it meant the separation of a man from his son, permanently, down his asked, I mean, as asked. Which was what many of them chose to do, Sis, to get the excess flesh to lose some weight and take the burden off the long journeying legs of the KD's age. Although they were sure that they would not be removed from the crosswalk king paths they'd chosen for their own feet. With all that protection that they were given and would have had from the sage's mighty ones to eat, yes, the savior's bag of meat was what did it, and they being so very good, in all their ways and practices. Always on their best behavior, as they knew they should. Go ask the chief of a savior, if you don't believe me, Mister Wood. Fatty and his bratty companion, though, those few who'd managed to survive the first attack on their but tux and grew to become strong and still able to go along. They were in prime positions to have been able to see. They saw not just what was going on above, but also where such a road was leading them to go walking it on with love, for themselves and me. Well, those who would have been found mighty lucky enough to be able to even walk at all or stand up on the rough and tough old grass in front of me, in the yard.

In this, the new broken-down and loosened hell hut that is just about to come forth, or even the forty-fourth of an eighth. So, they decided to skip town, well, two of them came walking down, same as I did. Dedimus, and Sheamus with his doggy pup, my kid. Just as soon as they were able to slide down on the side gig from under their eyelids and get out of their regular stare-down notices. Always looking down their suspicion on him and the rest of them and us, eh, without even so much as a sound system for us to go play, and dance with a fat thing (or Slim) at our favorite spot in the club at Constant Spring. It came about in this wise.

Old men sat down together at the last round table of leather to talk about silk one night. As smooth as death bills, they were, "Right, Will?"

"Right."

"Well, not quite, just those two bigger bosses than the I-man, plus a walk-pass kid secretly eyeing them while moving along, okay?"

"Okay."

The chief wanted to talk to him and discuss matters that were near and dear to their heartstring. Happened when the weatherman was asked in. After he did his duties and was found suited for their greatest and best results to suit me and "my knees, mi yuty." At least, so they thought at the time. When they finally got up again from the dining, the pain they had planned for the rest of the multitude of lame mankind to dine in, stepped right out the door with them and into active applications to rein on prime time, Hingh. All the select tools that were needed to score the job well and good, and which were stored away from ancient times under the eyelid and dead "ding" down deeds down the noses of fools, like mine. Along with the staring eyewear of the blind who'd said roses weren't cool. Came into the stadium that day to play ball with the real players of thine, like fools, and went all the way to the swimming pool. The celebration of freedom was the latter of the last one taking a knee down, deep into the we-dumbs, yes man, such ones, once again. That's all there was to it, my friend. The former ones, too, came walking right back into view, those who, according to them and you, and as to how such things were viewed via their high-rise elitist eye views. Those, too, were to see us out there forming alliances and positioning the war machines for them, in the high sciences. While foolish farmers were still farming yet more, like forty thousand fools than were allowed in their schools that were given to them often, and for that very reason. But, what's up with that, like, with so few little stools at the bar counter for them to sit on and announce her in season, and all? Somebody was trying to prove that very point to whoever was found faking the lying reason and called. Trying to show how much they were hip and cool, you know. So, they instituted an IQ testing system, mi Breda man, believe him or me, that's him right there with the Nedda-one, or someone another. It was to determine if I owe you anything, unfair though it was, as said. All designed (it would have seemed) to determine who must go to their places in the line-in, or who may remain within their skin that I'm in with mine on the rim at the Bed Ward water springs. The test itself was to prove that you're smart as hail (or not). If you take the test at all and get nailed to the blood clot, that's it, it means that you didn't do the math, Sis, nor your due dilly gents that you should have wheeled him in on this. That's what he meant, kids, not as of yet. Hence, you would have had no defense against the cleansing sent... tens of thousands of arguments that were to be the next thing sent from them. To you and all other demented saints on the queue, and those who will soon be coming in their defense on two or three.

Did it not come? Yes, it did. In the form of the plague, bug-borne diseases. The most dangerous diseases. Sent more billions to an earlier sleep-in, in their grave-digging site, than him. Seen?

"Yeah, man, mi see it, I can see much more than his teeth, and him and..."

"Stop the pointing, you must always keep the fingering within the house on the ninth skin, don't you know that already?"

"Yes, I know, but..."

"But nothing, go sit over there on your as... because the evening is coming fast." Even coming from amongst those two who were sure that they knew a lot more than you, who were brave enough to have asked, therefore, they were also sure that they would be saved from the flu. Because they were behaved enough to have been washed in the sure pass-over saving potions of, guess who? Yes, the sage. The one who was the worst of the knaves, even. But they were not as clean as they should have been, so it would have seemed to mean, because... Now, only those who were favored by the queen for whatever reason they should not have been are left in some villages, few and far between.

"Who, between whom?"

"Between you, her, and him, along with the rest of them." Yes, the king's men, who else did you expect it to have meant but him and them? That is why these naked eyes are now rolling in, on the journeying thing. Going along on my wrong side and passing you by, trying to find a place to settle down and get to belong to someone. Like him and I, before the bigger half of the Rat Pack, are all written off and tossed out to Rastafar-I. To make way for the restart that didn't come from the eye to look at me. Well, that was his plan at the start, but his plan was disrupted by an ask... of an attack out of the mask of a sneaking, sneeze attack. The one that caught him off guard. A few familiar faces were to meet up in some rather strange places along the way out. Hence, the source of this story is on these pages of Ore Ritz biscuits, made of oats, ee. It was in the making room fermenting for a long time. Like, from thousands upon thousands of years down the thin line, to the sinks. Long enough for many to outgrow and forget about the protection that they were known to have gotten when such were given on a hand up and out by the great one, and they would have had it baked in on them before the king's reasons came, and take dumb. Sorry, I meant to say, them, to take them.

"But, but, why, how come?"

"Why, what?"

"How did they get to override them so fast?"

Because over time, they would have developed agencies within the underside of their ancient aging skin line that were not able to withstand the onslaught of the ravages upon the cloth to make their clothes to wash pan, to go and wash them clean, in it. Probably via some antidotes that were given to them in the other people's feeding that they needed more than anything else in the Kingsland world at the time, I mean, to eat. Because they had given up on ever doing anything for themselves by then, not too neat. Such was not placed there by the real super maker bosses of protection causes kinds of saline care kids, as you'd claimed. No, but by that of the very plague-maker sort, they thought that they were made able to stave off without even so much as a second dose of freedom of thought like this. The sort that came from further back up north, let alone a mouthful of chats and playing hopscotch, in their family line, dark and almost wiped out. While they were there, watching the timeline disappear and passing them by over here and eying my wine, through their bottled beer. How did we get to see so far back through their eyes, though, my dear? Pass me a secure light-up for my piped-up smoking gear and take a seat below. You're about to hear some things that will grind your molars from within for weeks of mouth... ten you know, on ends. Or no.

For a very long time, the idea would have crossed somebody's already made-up mind. It had somehow popped through the window and sidestepped the blinds. Wise old guys thought to themselves that the entire Kingsland world could be theirs to help, and theirs alone. His common, her wealth, too, was made very content at home with you, where he could do whatever he felt like. To all those within his family bloodline, bones, and skin tones, he'd promised to pass it with all of the hammering sticks down, alright? Yes, to some close friends on the trail back home ends, and in too, no? "True." He, therefore, set out on the mission to meticulously plan it out and strategize the roundabouts on the road from Porus, on through to poor ole me and you. Adding it all up to become the "poor us" as we're now known. Most of this was done to figure out how to faze out all the rest of the goods for noting the old brutes, of folks' kin, kinds of guys like dust, and dump them on cigarette butts, but in the ashtrays of most of the overworked and burned-out husks. All the waste of space ones, too, such as that one standing by you, as he and his clan were seeing them through by way of their uppity eyes, Sister Grace, yes, that's who. Speaking of ice, they knew right there and then that their own eyes would not gaze upon them. Nor prepare a stare upon their skins to harm them, you know. Like, the eventual first prize winner who wins, and gets to store up the darned prize within the jars below, our dinner. Since they already knew that they would not have been likely to be living within their timelines anymore, by then. But they also knew that their descent, danced down the line thin, like this said Lance Singh sin ting, something else, would. Like, would have made it all the way there and stayed good, to be living down there in their stead, and playing their regular kinds of ball games with their hardwoods, mi bred. So, for several generations down, even further than timelines are now known. They knew that their descendants would be looking back and praising the sheets out of their names in nightgowns and languages that they may not be able to understand the games in sounds. (Give me a sandwich, please). Not enough to be able to go complain, anyway. "This," they said at the time, "is a cause for the ages worth dying for." So, they did, but not before they wrote it down in the pages. Things that some of the others did, like not bother to engage in, such as... well, not even so much as to read any such darn thing, not on your horse (or theirs). Not that those kinds of writings of the right things were intended for them and their unlikely kind of eyes and skin to shine on. But they continued riding throughout the ages while their eyes were still able to see the ladies with an I man. Writing in those books and parchment pages that were meant for the eyes of only them and their kids, to dine on. Those within the bloodline races of their homeborn heart men, and their kind of kings. So that they, and they only, would know what to do, and how to do it to get it done. So it was for tens of thousands of years down the thin line home spheres, until just around this time, right here, as it was beginning to be seen happening there in the open square of the KD's world, a place called Kingsland, my girl.

In the meantime, though, others were walking slowly (or fast) and admiring the roses as just colorful blades of worthless grass. While these rather beautiful things were growing and blooming the Rastafar-I out from the dark ages. The other man and his clan, though, were studying the hail out of everything and everyone, no? "Yes." Hear this. All that their eyes came dropping a wooden cross upon, those eyes would have been gazing upon them and their kind, too. But they thought that these were just their adoring admirers looking at them as beautiful Hybrids on the lids of men like you. Eye lighting the good nests of them and their friends as they were coming in, to gaze upon you and me again, like... like daisies. In the early days, that is. I mean, there was no lack of energy in the veins of those enemies, those who knew how to gain by misbehaving with me, while enslaving me. Misbehaving was what they did, getting into all manner of mischief. Since the big man wasn't known to be passing up on an opportunity that he was given, that was what he did before evening. He reached out his arm and armed a stout bottle that was accustomed to support the brother's spout, and rattled... it. Then took a supporting role upon each opportunity he was given to study the scrolls sent down from Mount Haven in a bottle, to him. He studied everything that was thrown at him in those days. In part, or in the old cloth that he was (wrapped in), in his effort to learn how they worked and to try and get them to work for him. Even the most feared vices, as was seen through his far-reaching eyes, Sis, yes, mi Sister in... He used them as whatever tool or weapon he could crack a win out of. Something that he could use to get his objectives on our butts, leftovers from the cigarettes, in the ashtrays. The plague virus was one such agent that he must have crawled upon, Dave's Gents, "the duck man." He studied it and then rid himself of the rest of the pygmies' health, only to use them as unpaid help. All and everyone were rid of it when he chased it out of his land, dead grips. Well, not quite, because... Yes, the cure was found and acted upon fast, and all around you're asked. All for the betterment of everyone in the studying type of class, clowns.
But then, when that was done, he stored up the knowledge he'd found

of it, as well as the samples that were left in the pocket under his handling armpits. After wrapping them up nicely in his fist, he stored them all up securely in the magician's "cup this," he said, "and hide it under the bed. Or better yet, in the deepest degrees of freeze that you and yours can squeeze under the sandy sea of his, and yours." Even in storage rooms that he would have built on his cold land, dead loom, or in the land of those other friends of his, not the buffoons. "Said speed mi goon." Scared the daylights out of many of his buddies' tights, like, those who didn't agree with it "*oite*?"

"Yeah, man, oh please, but..." Yes, man, don't ever forget the message; wordplay is still the order of the day around here.

4

Foul Winds Came Rushing In

Angry wind, that foul thing again. They would not listen to the warning, because they did not take it seriously enough to get the heart warmed, Hingh. But then came the ice age to reach its limits — Norm in... and the melting icy cold war men were to start them off storming. Many shrugged it off the arm, Hingh, and called it all fake pan and a farce, false timing, too, coming at us, at last, until the rotten winds started blowing in faster than him. "Who?" Just like a lightning bolt load of something, or even someone. One who's sane like... "Like who?" "You, no?" "Yes, like... like that thing." Like...

"What, farthing?"

"Yes, aren't you smart, Hingh? How did you guess that one so fast, um? I mean, yes. It was like a stale, outdated Ford, and it would have caught them in its wake fast. Look, now they're busily running around in class, like, whenever..."

"When what?"

"Like, whenever they happen to hear the sound coming on down the chime chrome. Yes, that, as you'd guessed." Yes, that's the sound of the man, working on his tasks to get you going, home, or something. The one sound that was signaling the coming in of the mighty, rushing foully winds, maybe. Look at them riding the waves like palm-ember boughs, and brave when tossed to and from the windy enclave.

After watching the Earth grind and come to a screeching halt, Ted stopped. "What now?" They'd asked, "What are the options going forward from here to that?"

"To what?"

"That."

"What, what? tell me, nuh, man?"

"Okay, man, listen up, and you'll see who I'm hearing it from." It's like, like, you hearing it declared that it was your fault, Sly, silly head, Sylvester "the investor guy." Yes, it's you I'm talking to, mister, sir, oh my. What if you should hear it asked of you, "Which direction do we go from here, my dear?" Pass me the salt, right there. Huh-huh, still tastes like something is missing, it's your fault; need a dash of something, I'd say.

"Why not try dashing? You know, like, like dashing it away?"

Okay, "Bud-duff," comes the sound of the "thud up," as it dropped.

"Hey! I didn't mean it that way. What are we... I mean, you. What are you going to eat now?"

"Nothing. Anyway..."

Look... Somebody is sulking, but... "Do we even know, though? Should we continue along as if we know, like, walking on the same path as before, to go? Or do we turn around and take another look out the back door and over our shoulder, ring ground, just to be sure?" The young man wanted to know more, but... (Sound; what happened to the sound? *Huh-huh. Mi nuh like dis eno*).

"No, I really don't like things like these either, but..." "...Just to see if we might have made a wrong turn somewhere along the way home, I mean, like, while coming over here, since this is not our home sphere," he was heard saying this to his friend's interest, there. "We've got some decisions to make here, folks," he said, "if I'm allowed to say squat about that, peradventure we may find the right way back. We cannot say that we haven't been warned off. Did you know that there are other people in this worldly farmhouse, though? People who live their lives and behave quite differently from me, and that one with the eyes? Even you on the knife stand, by the beehive? Yes, oh yes, man, and him too, that same Stevie go slow, yes, go on, see him through." No? Well, I do believe, I guess. Of course, it's so, yes. Um, what a mess! I think we can do well with oats... these sorts of blabbermouth ends, yes?

"Yes."

Well, they expect different results than ours from what they do and work towards. Like, like... Those other types of outcomes, going towards you and your cards, you know?

"Said speed, mi Lawd. Oh, yes, my lord, where should I go for the work?"

"Well, not so much the work, but 'think.'" They were there thinking up the outcomes they wanted to drink, like white rum or whiskey in the sink. While you were busily working to enrich and empower them to "rawtid" Skink, the just-comers came in with Brinks, to go carrying off the remaining copper and zinc. Meanwhile, you were there enticing the hell out of them and him, Aunt Enid, and Clair.

"To go buy and sell?"

"Well, what else? Beware, though, profits from such activities are getting really scarce over here, too." While you were doing these, though, he has all the time in the world to sit by himself, shaking his girls' toe... toes below the knees, and twirling. Like, his fingers and thumbs around the girl's cotton-picking plum-plum for the pudding he wanted to put the oil in, for some... You know, of course. Or to get together with the other girl and have some fun. Or even worse than that, gnome's comb, like, with other like-minded persons as him and I did for some, sin. Or was it son, their sons? Whichever was to come, they were sipping on murder, sorry, I meant to say, red rum, those that were quickly coming off the shelf, down home. Then, when they were done, each one got up and went back home, but not to just sit down, no, but to think up other outcomes of wealth, power, and Dominion.

What do these entities have in common? Well, I will tell you two, or just one. Yeah, maybe that "one" so that you may understand, easier, since easier is yours, always. They have, at one time or another, been advocating for the same one thing for the brother. For quite a long time, as a matter of fact, and finding...

"What fault?"

"Yes, that was when I saw them, and you, while you were out there talking…"

"Fark?"

"I'm sure that's what you're going to say to Mister Smart as…"

"Who, Leroy?"

"Yes, I must confess," but… "Why?" You'd asked. It's because I would have heard some of you while talking on the phone line, coming through. This one in particular, no, not you, but that one, your brother. I was eavesdropping on his end of the chat room, and that's when I heard it, coming through. On the one hand, he was telling you… telling the hell out of a mouthful of nothing to bother you. But still, while a child would have lied when she'd hoped, prayed, and cried…" She was there trying hard to speak some response out of the others of you guys' chords on this side, at once. Oh, my Lord, advance, step up, man, move up, and make way for the others to get on the long bench and sit down, okay? Now let's continue on, small up yuh self nuh man, or move around the back, and… And she was trying to get your reactions to the message they were bringing through their eyes scan, real hard too. Telling you to take a glance and get bringing in on the bringer's balance, Singh, of the sheaves to the yard as shipped in, to you. It was the same with the game chord, too, but it was not to be forthcoming on you, or even off, that would have been smart, but "Clear off," you'd said, because… It was like… like flashcards at hearts. Gart's funks kills music; it's a new device, learn to use it. On the one hand, she got (for the most part) mostly denial, and the Euphrates of sorts, great rivers like these are, thou art. The message they came bringing in was this song for us to sing.

"We've got to change the way we're going about doing things, or nothing, like, not doing anything at all that's worth doing." The way we are going, they say, is unsustainable as things are now showing to Wayne Able and Sue Hingh, okay? But we shrugged it off our shoulders, bark and continued to talk, going to the same leveled-up startled Bart beat, dancing to the beating of the constant Kette drumming on our feet, but now. Look at what's coming, can you see it? Yeah, it's coming down on all of us, like we are. Just a little reminder here for you, my dear, super-star. A thing I'd like to share, or two. Want to hear?

"Yes, ask who?"

Okay, smart you. I want to share it now and say this to you, so that you may hear if you didn't already know the news. But that's just like a showbiz shoe because, such a one door full of wonderful things, we all know that you already know the tidings. But let's go all the way through and get to the show with you, at the drive-ins.

In some anointed years ago, like, let's say, in 2992, away from here, and you. Some world scientists put their feet in front of them and kicked off their shoes. To comfort themselves as they chit-chat and report something to cook in the teapots, you know, of booze. Something that was supposed to place the calls on the Kingsland's world leaders of sorts to… Now, pay close attention to this sort of text in bold remarks. It's true and smart. Please, listen.

World leaders, it says, not people of the world, nor thieves like you, my girl, except at shirking the work thing when feathering your beds, of pearls, okay?

"Okay."

But, there's a significant difference here, Frieda Mackay, as it says. They called on leaders to act, which, for the most part, means the elites up at the top. Like, the politicians and corporate leaders leading the pack… stand out from that, short-distance tribal roundtable talk. While you were left around the back, talking a lot more about that… yes. "Act now," they say, to save the planet Tory system, and our way of life, you know, it's in. "Yay. Isn't that nice?"

"Don't say."

"Okay! I won't, Faye, but may I have a cube or two of ice?"

"No problem, man, here. Nice, eh!"

"Thank you for the beer." Hmm, this thing is really nice, but…

"Carry on, carry on, on the nicer thing about which you were chatting up a storm."

Hardly anyone bopped an eyelid a little bit faster than you, or I did, when I was seen going at top speeds down at the violent ends of the rapids, and felt as if I couldn't breathe. Let alone sneak a peek at the report to read. The one they'd put together and sent a strong force from them to give meat to whomever, take heed.

Fast forward 25 years, when other scientific seers and futuristic shapers revisited the issue, to inquire and say, Amen, sure. This has got to be the best and most opportunistic TikTok door. Isn't it?

"No, but..."

"I know, I know, it probably included many of the same old Lii ore than Dow." I could have easily complained and placed such blame on the Hi-yah man's door. No, not you, there, they're hearing from the liar, core, but. Snore on good and proper, on them: the original blame heads game, yes, those, too, they were there yet again that time with you, no? However, as was expected by the all-knowing and the clever. The findings were that the situation was by far worse than ever, my kind kids, and could not be ignored much longer than it already is, mi bredda pickneys. For sure, to our curse, we continue to reverse the hearse for the shaggy man's wonderful verse and curse the cure they're bringing in first. Many well-thinking people, kind of thinkers, took to linking it to their indoor, hearty fingers, pointing. Yes, they were, not you, though, you're a beginner, though all anointed. Some of the ill-thinking drinking no thinkers sort, too, got smart. Even as smart as you are, aren't you?

"No."

I know, no one can ever blame me and you on that sort of showtime snowshoe. As may be seen, showing off you now, and me too, yes. Talking to... You know who, shame on you. "Or is it we, us two?"

"Mi nuh knoah-man, I really don't know."

"I know, you never knew anything about such things, or how they would go. They, though, those over there, they knew." So, they took it to heart that time around the park and decided to act on what they'd found, out back. Well, on at least one aspect of the plan in the pan tea frock sort of clit... I mean, clothes made from this piece of cloth. Some among them at the time were about ten or nine, but they were eyeing the dollar wine. Like, 5 cents, ten cents, a dollar, or something else, another. All the way ahead of the lineman's brother as a dancing partner. They were making it their lifelong mission-stick... No, not mine, nor yours, Nerdy Nick, not this time. The mission was to address the undressed and then be sure not to rest for a minute longer than that of thine, as already said. Not until things change back around to normal customers, round like... mi bread end, on buttered oats.

 Speaking of normal, "New normal," they say, but the new normal was never the normal anyway. So, when you're back from the shock attack that you'll get from sipping the cup, which of their "norms" are you going to hang on to, to ease yourself up? Anyway, look, take a look over this way, and listen up. Now, we are looking at the bookings and seeing some changes taking place before our feisty front doors, where we were cooking the goose eggs. While Sadie was savoring the food and licking her finger ring plate white, like yours, yes, mi bred. As our auntie was saying the grace twice, even. Meanwhile, our very blue eyes, or whatever other color they were found to be, were denied for being too wise, then were opened wide to stare down her guts, trying to see... Well, not wide enough to be facing the game in this space, to be getting it plain and straight. As straight as ever, it was in our lives as lived in this space, and the way we live it. Whether any of those groups or individuals with one less tooth directly have anything to do with these current scuds over here sitting in the booths. Those things too, that are happening to the youths, like, gal pickneys topless suits, are up for the bait. Like, arguing these things out with you and all eight. Yes, in your face, pal. I'm sure that the debate is going on somewhere down the interstate, about the gal. Go on, do a street race to get there in first place, and find out for yourself what such things are based on. But the conditions those scientists ticked man Delians were slick enough to have found and documented for the many millions and us to act upon the ground un-amended. While wearing the white bib open front down, as they often did, and which would have prompted those actors to act then... sit down, yes Enid, and wait your turn, as they did, up until...

These things haven't changed until now, my kid. At least not for the better mint purposes, no way how. "Mi rathid!" "Yes." Everything has ground to a screeching halt, Ted, stop, don't talk so much.

What now. Where do we go from here to that, yes, the gold rush? That is the question to ponder, my dear, don't stop to slander, about them culling off the deer on door rust, beware. But if one were to look a bit closer at the book lists of facts in the toaster. One might notice that the current actors crowding out this chapter of the shopping blocks here in the nooks' outer, and whose names are coming up top to take a look at the poster, girls. Girls like sand, to match everyone. Hey, you there in the stack king high heel shoes and stock Hingh the stuffer, aren't you one of those magician class of blameless crooks who stole the sucker from around my banana?

"No."

"Are you sure? Are you telling me the truth? Weren't you the one, or one of those who tried to wake us up with the alarm clock last night at the booth, no?"

"No."

I could have sworn that you were, but since you said no, what else can I do but go, no? No one from the common people's cranny and nook is bothering to turn around and take a look. Those kinds, though, were the ones who had studied the signs and raised the alarm about what was going on the first time we saw the crooks come and go. They looked at it and got to see what needed to be done, or to be changed, if we were to save ourselves before the worst comes. Like, before we're all done and gone back home, to change our gowns and sit back down again, if the Kingsland world is to remain in a good state and be sustained. On top of that, the desired effect they had argued for in the chat is the obvious spinning offshoot behind the current driverless car shoot, down the track. The one that just got booted past me, the glass, my youth. Yes, thank you for the ten Q, like. Like, as it pertains to the situation on the factory floor, at the bar, in truth. Yet no one speaks a snoring sobering word about it anymore than tits, I mean, ticks, like, TikTok shoots.

"Oh, shoots."

"Yes, my lord, some of them will be shot soon.

"You mean it, like, literally?"

"Yes, my youth, yes, yuh feel mi? That's what I mean, shots were flying, and they will, again, if I'm not lying (down), but..." Too occupied are we with what's currently hitting the poor of the week, like me, humble and meek, and you, too, yes, see?

"Yes, I can see it now, 'I'm blessed.'"

"I know, you are very blessed to have been able to see anything, like her. Or even Wayne Able, sipping tea, as it occurred." So preoccupied are we (you and me, even now) that our eyes are never able to see the score. Just like her, at the ballroom door. We've forgotten way too quickly, but... One thing I know, and it's for sure and thickly. Far fewer babies, like peopled pickney, will be coming through the bore to be graciously gracing these shores, and hopping in like children through our closed-up school door, as before, like weekly. Not in ways as such things used to be, come meet me at the corner, down my avenue. Come in, man, meet the metal pan the Batman way before I close this door, ram, eh. Don't forget that I've got to socialize a measured distance away from my other girls and their moms, Faye. Anyhow, let's carry Ann on our shoulders some more, since she has no feet of her own to walk on the floor. Not after we're done fixing the cure for free, which requires us, manly bores like me, to socialize the distance far away from Clor, and she, who's walking there across the street, by meat, I mean, me. Because when scientists are done with this cure, they can take a long-distance breather line tour, to go on a world-class tourist tick of an uproar and toast a sip with El Freda once more. One that was taken from the lower end of the freezer, on the door, perhaps. "Yes, I'm sure, mi pops." Or go out with her and do a bit more than that. Like, go somewhere on the seashore and see if they can, Seymore, in a tin can. Well, you already know what a yam... Come with me to the marketplace, where I am going to buy some dried yellow yams. Because their most difficult job, "Bing" task, would have been done at last, by my brother, Bob Whitehorse, of course. While they were busily doing the other one tooth, cast, sip, sit, and sip it. Man, don't gulp it down, you're asked. Sip it, like this. Yeah, that's it, the world-class habits. At last, the KD's world was saved from extinction by the vice of overpup... Hugh, lay shun. This was done by no one when they weren't even looking on. They did not understand what was going wrong. Because they were forced to quit the investigation, fast, to go and work on a more urgent sit...sit, you Haitian of class, highly classified, and all that. In all the best things, as they were related to the Kingsland on the upper rocks. But one that just happened to have popped in and up out of the gray sand e-thermos, to de-mask it, as he must. One that could only be handled by their capable hands, e Mass man Cleveland, what's your name again? Yes, you. Thank you, man. Happened while they were busily saving the lives of people who were like flies and weevils, facing imminent demise, and all. Like we, Orville, yes, you little devil you, and bee from the hives. "Oh, no!" Yeah, man, disheveled is he. "Like me?"

"No, not quite so, you're from the top row, extraordinary." But more like, so they, these very people, let's say it, with ease. So they may remain atop the overly popped-up, you lated earthly, soiled up vehicle topsoil clay, and stay as fertile as they may. Making babies and giving birth to your child, okay? "Okay." "Yeah, man." The gods were working on their chief cause, my child, all day. That of the magician types. Because now they're back to see the applause, and it's looking bright; the Kingsland world is no longer in danger of the pause, yeah, right. That will be all, Ma-hite.

5

I'm Going to See the King

"I know all that there is to know about the birds and the bees already, please," he said, "please. Don't waste my time on sheets like these." "Yes, yes, I know, Your Majesty, but we're not talking about those sorts of wonderful stories to pass the time away here with Ma's best tea in the doorway, not today. Today we're talking about the wolves, the bears, the tigers, and the deer. They have their stories to tell us, too, no?"

"Chief, my patience is not without its limits, you know?"

"I know, I know, I'm coming to it. Remember what would have happened to the whitetail deer in the park over there, and the moose population in Royse's burial Park near the dam?"

"Damn, can't you hear? Come on, man, speak up fast, and let's get it on with your air..."

"Remember how well they fared out, how about those stray dogs in your Souci salad? What was to become of the rest of them in the den, by the end of the ballads?"

"What are you getting at, Chief? I have a feeling that this one is going to be deep, really deep."

"A little bit of some things, you know, are quite nice to have the pleasure of dumping your eyes on sometimes, just to take a glance at, and go. Like, like, dumplings and wine, with cheese, no?"

"No, please, no thank you."

"Okay, but, but too much can sometimes become a bit, you know, like, too much, right — "What, what're you getting at?"

"Not much, just a thought, freely."

Meanwhile, the chief, who had been there juggling his balls pointedly up and down the roomy air for what seemed to be a predetermined number of tosses. As seen through the eyes of that porter guy who just walked past them, sitting there, tall Sis, on their high horses. After placing each in a jar across from him on the nightstand again, the chief carried on with his performance of the "Strandy" game. When he was done with his balls, he took up the pouch with his marbles and began to roll them from hand to hand before adding those also to the ordeals, in the jar. The jar that was already filled with tennis balls, as you are. Each marble rolled and slid through every available crack, crevasse, and air pocket crease to find a settlement feet, Sis, of their outstanding affairs in the proper or most suited place for them in the jarred air, to sit. Hesitantly, the chief councilor heaved forward and a bit to the right of him and picked up the smallest sandbag from among the rest of the puffed-up and sulking duce or three bags in its place beside the goblets of water. Or whatever else the liquid contents might have been in them and spilling over into the saucer, under them. He untied the baggy knot on his bag of sandy little beads he'd got (ten) while spacing out his words slowly like this.

Now, after seeing the king's countenance take a tumble down the slide with an ounce of ease. He continued to try to get it done with the quickest of speed. "All these elements round about us," he said, while waving his right hand across the face of the tables that were already spread, with various material compounds sitting there around a round of beer, about them, as said. "All these things are infinite, but as for this? How much space do we have left in here for these to escape?" He reached across to the other table, where the jar, now (seemingly) full to the brim with tar-studied Sable, and all the other things that were thrown in and still able were.

That was when the king slapped his palms in a half-loud thud "Ding" alarm on the armrest of the chair he'd been sitting on and heaved himself forward toward the door, then stopped just long enough to stare at the chief's face stuffing, or toward it some more. The chief himself, a moment later, stopped the sharing out of his mouthful of talk about safer, before raising himself out of his seat in front of the king's feet. The king, after finishing the act of getting up and out of the seat and walking towards the door stick... thing, still holding on to the door now partially ajar, with him. Went on to sing; I think you've used up all of your attendance calls for the next, what, I don't know, how about, five years, perhaps? "Not to worry, though," he said, "I should be able to find a summons form somewhere around if I need to see you for any reason, mi bred, or just to call you in for whatever it is that may be found in your arm by then, good evening." He then walked away, leaving the door pushed back wide open that way.

But he was back there again the following day, rubbing his palms and plating his fingers and thumbs like, like... this way. Pop, pop. "So, how shall we go about getting this done? Any suggestions?" The king wanted to know more sounds from his sons than that one. So, he pulled harder at the councilor's right, left-hand dead brother and cracked the elbow bone down under. That was what brought back the speech to his tongue, now grown a bit longer. "Waaaheeh!" He exclaimed, but then. Look, he's about to explain. "Look, he said, see those gooselike birds out there floating on the pond, remember what happened with them from way back then?"

"Yes, there weren't so many of them in the beginning, though."

"Well, that's the point, and no, not quite that far back. We won't have to go that far as to get us to the beginning of the avatars' first acts, but... Remember how they were almost wiped out and hunted to extinction?"

"Yes, I remember that December, as well as you, my redeemed son." "Gulp!"

"That's why we had to come up with a plan of solution, good enough to save at least some of them from — "How did they manage to bounce back so quickly from that one?"

"Well, since you'd asked, I'll tell you," Put on your mask, man. Why do you always take these unnecessary risks during an attack, such as this? Go cover up your asthmatic, a... um, as you're asked, and come back.

"Yes, great to have you back." It was because of the plan, don't you remember? We came up with the plan and put it into active execution by November. Did it well enough to have brought a remnant of the species back to this, their original habitation spot, and then watched the Poobirds like a geezerly goose population from over there on the other sandy wetland, got up on their feet and stood on the stand. They bounced back and grew quickly into another contingency plan. One where they had to have been prevented from breeding so exponentially, ever again."

"You mean that was 'your' doing, it was you who came up with the miracle fix that quelled the rapid increase of the pooing?"

"Yes, well, not just me, but us. It was due to the effort of all of us in the goat house you're in — "Oh!"

"Yes, don't forget that 'you'd' given us the instructions so to do first, and your blessings too, afterward."

"So, what exactly did 'you' do to come up with such dramatic results for 'you'?"

"We'd tackled it from several angles, the entry point of the problem being the birth rate triangle, that was our first gate to handle, because... Far too many baby chicks were being hatched and brought into it. Yes, into the ever-growing family problem of the ...hit, with far too few natural predators to maintain a balanced population of them, yes, those cute little chicks. Doing so by doing them a favor while smiling up at them, and twitching. At the same time, the food supply to keep them occupied in their habitat-wide... was dwindling fast before our very eyes, and yes, theirs too. Though they could not seem to see it all the way through. So, we couldn't just sit around and watch; we came up with a plan to reduce the rate of the hatch. The hatchlings crammed and entering every year needed a reduction to maintain this. It was way too grand, as great as that was."

"How did you manage to do that?"

"We did it by doctoring the eggs that they laid and then mounting upon the nests to try and bring to the hatch for yet another batch to 'shegg, parade.' Well, they did their part in the process as usual. If you'd bothered to ask the new gal, she would have told you not to beg, but yes. They laid a hefty batch the following year as well, but that was it for them, not you. Not many chicks were coming to the hatch after we were done with doctoring them up fast."

"How, by what means or method?"

"By way of the process of heat and cold."

"You mean..." Look, the half-asking king is now pointing his finger ring towards the side wing, nook.

"Yes, we went out and collected those eggs of theirs while they were out and weren't looking nearby, to avoid getting ourselves into a geese-like Poobird beak of a whooping treat, yuh see it, in my eye?"

"Yes, I can see it."

"Then we took them to the heat by hard boiling them for several minutes. Then, cold freeze them for months on end to ensure what's left in it, until next season when they return to the region to eat, mate, and cover the nest for chicks to bring to the hatch, again. Wait, we're not done yet. We then go in and replace the fresh cache of eggs that they'd just laid with the treated ones now under their legs. Mother Goose was soon left in wonder and bewilderment that could have been meant for the fending at the gander king's head atop the neck's fullest length, as if asking what went wrong with him. 'Dah! O-Cho, o-Cho,' said the would-be fada of a not-fathering-anymore brother of a gander. He probably won't get another. You know, like, another chance at a chick to color him father, with, and to get up on a fly-mount upward and take to the sky. So that he may be able to teach it how to fly a proper V-shaped line south of the border to winter there in style."

"My, oh my."

Meanwhile, with all that setting of the goose half of a poo bird on the nest for the nestlings she wanted to get. She was sitting and betting on it, yes, but... Mother Goose would have been lucky if she were rewarded with one young chick of a poobird looking like a gooseling from the other worlds, like, even one chick to take back to the pond quickly to meet the new girl. That would have been the yield from the very last egg she'd managed to drop on the bed, I mean, batch, on the batch of dead. Which was what they began to say and said after the raiders would have dumped the cache of spoiled to death-bed ones on her and left. Not to worry about her neighborly goosey enemy of a show-off girlfriend, though. Because the same fate would have befallen her and the rest of her grudging companions, who have always been trying to one-up her effort at the show-off parade out there on the commons. "Oh?" "Yes." But that was still not enough for us, we had to do something about the gander Prof of a poo birdy boss. He who would have been more than happy to go in and work off his ask me no more questions on another number one hit song in such a bad, lucky situation for him, usually. Not this time, though, because we'd served up a portion for him and his asking part string that he wasn't expecting, nor was he aware of it. Did it by way of the never-ending supply of food he needed to be good, before he would have gone out and pooed on the other guy's plate of woodland shrubs on which he was feeding bugs, "He's such a tug!" We'd gotten him to agree to this by re-engineering the supply of the grass he'd always wanted to eat without stopping or bothering to ask for it, so to speak. The tasty treat he liked to reap from off the peat was what did it. Though he wouldn't have known that much, did he ever know anything worth knowing, though? Anyway, no, Hingh, no. Didn't know that what he'd found to be so inviting and irresistibly intoxicating to do a bite-in with the other gander fellows two bits, you know. Like, while licking it up against his chap's stick and dripping rabbits' sheets off his beak, as time passed them by, still fast asleep, was not the real thing that he should have been doing with the other Gander ring bossy guys, one shoe in.

But with all that energy now welling up in him fast, he had to find a new hobby or an outlet to work at last. As for the wife and mother, though? After spending far too much time sitting on the nest that would not be bringing her any chicks to the hatch anytime soon. Mother goose of a poobird lady came back looking up at the pop's brother gander man's cap, in amazement. "Look at that." He suddenly appeared to her as if he didn't want anything more to do with her and the rest of the lot because he'd found far grander things to do with his life and times than that. Far better than to be chasing chicks like her around all these vines on the lot. But he couldn't say from whence such good luck had come upon him to shine the Jonny Cooper brush of a rap pack. Not knowing such a thing as that because... No one had bothered to tell him that the man who feeds him and you is the one who gets to decide whether you're fattened up for the cooking pot of stew or to go out working on other batches of chicks for the hatch. Look at that mask, yes, you. Stop asking around, man, we're all good and done, go on through. Gwaan, galong nuh man.

...

So, what makes you think that you're so much different from the dough, though? Oh, dear guard, no, you're not.

Well, not when the conditions over there are the same as they are over here, these past years. Certainly, not when the overseer's guy commanding his friend and I is the same alibi everywhere — "As you and I, right?"

"Well, of course, go on and lie as much as you want, ma-hite, and boast." One thing is for sure, my best friend's Aunt from Mount Calm's coast. When they're done with managing the hail out of the campgrounds near Mount Angus Towns, across from Gayle.

There'll be as much doe left around your pockets' row as the number of bucks it will cost them to pay for that wreck. Heck, wanna know more? "Yes."

Well, go on and stick your neck out at the doe as much as you may know how to.

You'll soon get to know a lot more fabulous things to do than you should have ever had any need to. Because, when Halls said and done, Als' guns will be aiming at you in Aymial Town, where they'd come, and you will be there thinking that it was their business affairs, alone. Yes, my good gnome, go right on home, Homey, because everybody is heading home to take down your hometown, to the ground, ee.

Yes, like grinding ground dead grass, in a nice round dead number that they may be able to fit firmly on your ass, Berry (or not).

Whilst firmly fitting it into their cockpit concept of what is good, "govern" meant, for them and their brothers' arguments, yes. Not you and yours, though. Because, from the back door, you saw them coming when they first came in, and thought it was their Cranium alone that they were aiming the takedown at. "Rightly so," was what little concern you showed "off" your show-off self, Hugo.

So, to your Cranial door at the Browns Town seasonal four squares, leads all those heavily laden roads. No need to obey the codes, you were from amongst the good ones, you'd supposed. But did you even bother to wonder, or to toss an ask over yonder? Like, just to inquire about it from a brother who might have known the answer, did you?

Couldn't you have gone in and asked the gnomes' combs about him? Like, "Tell me, Sir. How come the whole pack of friendly combat ants could not get their reins on the dumb nut's hands?" I mean, they weren't able to get their hands on their rogue friend's arms, eh, while wriggling the bumps away. To make him not do the wrong whack attack on their allied neighbor in the pack, eh.

"Yes, 'twas breaking something on the poor man's harmless neck, that day." Even whilst the rotten plague was in an uppercut-touristic rabbits-hits upon everybody's guts, but, but, but yes? "Below the belt, is what I'm trying to say, Bert..."

Oh, sheet, ma-hite, how come you talk so much? Take a leave, if you please. Yes, go take a leaf out of your Bookman and read. Then close up this shop and come back." Because I want to ask you another question about that. Like, how was it when it was about Slim? Yes. The lonesome stranger over there, with him. The one who was oh so unprepared and mean. Yes, their enemy is who I'm talking about, Emily, seen? Yeah, man, the one whom they'd wanted to go and do some chemical adjustments on, yuh syi mi?

"Yes." Yes, to try to level out the imbalance that was meant for the ambulance. How come it was so easy getting through on your main squeeze, Lii?

Then up again to the come bat, with you. Come on, man, it's your turn to go and bat like a champion, of a truth. Bring your best bat and come score some runs for these people on the lot, my youth. So that they may be able to laugh and giggle and have a good time, playing along with the fiddle.

Boy, that burner-boy sure knows how to bat like mine. But didn't somebody make a big boo-boo out of this little bamboo sop of thine? Yes, of a truth, my youth, they did. I thank you for the quid.

6

Border Crash

Border crash it was, and the walls came tumbling down fast like the floods, on the high lifestyles impacted by lucky eyelashes. For those who would have managed to survive the myriads of Mark it crotches, sorry, I mean, crashes. Taking potshots at taming the wild bunch. Got the hunch? Anyway.

The boy was sent to live with them when he was about six years old, going on ten. It was for both their benefits, they'd said, and was made to fill out the other people's platforms with their free content and signed off on the whole boatload of dollars and cents, with an amen. He needed a place to stay more than anything else at the time. As for them, the eventual winner of the problem is similar to mine. They needed help around the house, and a little company too, I'd supposed. Along with another reason to manage better their efforts at getting away from the star-studded wine that they'd always dumped on folks like him and me, and soaked our clothes. The boy was sent up the social ladder by that man's father, who had recently become Sonny Boy's step, up the same sort of fatherly ladder. To enable them, and him too, at the same time, Hingh Sue, to get a free pass, come on through. Let's sit down and talk to you. The boy was a fat one; he ate a lot of anything and everything that he could cast his eyes upon, but was quite unlike that other little brat who still would not. Unlike Lucy Slim, a lot, he couldn't help himself out of getting big and fat. To them, he was Sheamus, but to you and the rest of us, he took the name size of his shirt, that which he wears as a "Shut" over there. He will hit upon greatness by tomorrow, or by the time it's all over and done in proper sorrow for me, or will he?

It was a strange day on the battlefield, anyway one chooses to look at it to reveal. They weren't having the sorts of victory dances that they were accustomed to practicing on the winners' chants, Sis. Come to think of it, nobody was having any. Not the rest of the king's men on the home end, Emmie, not them, not me, and my friend. Something rotten was in the evening air, picking at the cotton out there and weighing heavily on them.

"Where?"

"There, look where I'm pointing." But the show must go on towards the proper end. They didn't have long to wait for such, but no cause for an Amen. Tough luck was what turned up; it was nothing as they had ever seen before, the bitter cup. Their energy was draining fast, out the door. Rashes were popping up all over their ask... as... who's asking, for more? Yes, as always, you again, I'm sure. Asking for anything and everything more, anything but the eventual fate of both them and the other men that they were beating. "What's happening?" many among them were heard asking. The fighting was done by evening, but no one was claiming anything in the form of a victory to win. Very few were still able to claim anything. This was quickly noticed on most of them and on their behalf. They were gone, not only the warring faction, no, but the barber, the tailor, and the night watchman's tailgate keeper. Even the lady out walking the baby in a pram, go seek her out if you want, who knows, you just might...

Everywhere, people were dropping and dying, one after that man. On everybody's lips was the same unanswered question about why, Hingh. "Is this what they told us was coming down the piping? What then was the purpose of the protection that we were given? It didn't seem to be protecting anyone." By then, though, too many people were gone for them to be questioning anyone more. Those remaining were way too few and far between, and with too many issues to deal with all at once to tackle anything else but him.

Since he already has the power of life and death in his hand-me-over basket, he was able to hand me over the garden to the red power button cross switch, which he'd promptly taken over from the crazy ole ...hitch. Has his finger ring on it all the time. It was only a matter of time before the war chips popped out of the frying pan, flying, thyme, and there goes the bulk of the Kinglanders' civilization, dying. But Fatty can still remember the good old days, like...

...

Here we are alone again, in Kingsley's den. All for one and one for all was the way they crawled. It was the premises upon which they stood tall. They had pledged this to each other from the very open end of the beginning. For some of them, this was the right call. Well, for at least one of them. It was to serve him well in the end, or more like, nearer to the end of him, than them. Or did it?

It so happened that, when the time comes, yeah, that time. In a little while, it would be time to divide the looted spoils. Built upon this "all for one" mantra, they would have ventured out and prospered. Even if it was to be for a short while, they would have prospered and done so in fine style. But then, upon one glorious return home again, with all of the loot that they'd earned and won while hopping and popping out and around in a circular den. They sat them down, readying themselves to go to town. Jolly and young was the dividing night. "Got things here to divide and to share up, rightly," he said. But that was not going to happen this time, mi bred, because "Golden treasures make the eyes go blind at last." Or at least, some of the time, and this time, it was going to be one of those sparse "sometimes." Sitting all there in a rounded line, just like it's done every return-home time. The Kingsley king was to begin doing his thing, as always, the sharing starts and ends with him. He began a-counting on: This is mine, this is mine, this is yours. To the other man on the other side of him, he began to count the very same sin. "This is mine, this is mine, this is yours." Before one could sneak in a pacified word, came the chinks and swash from battle-tried swords. Thirsting for the blood of the Kingsley sort, out of him who had now transgressed the established art and would have dared to despise the ritual rites. "The dirt will bite you, Kingsley, upon this night." But, reprieve, reprieve. The king knew his sleeve. He knew him very well indeed, the face of the man in whose hand was the sword, drawn in anger at the neck near the head of his lord. It belonged to him who had once saved his life. Hence, he'd proven his worth, value, and might. "No bloodletting," said the king, "no more bloodletting, no, not this evening, not tonight." Before the night ended, all was done. They were to have hugged around, and the passion tossed down. "You're a good man," he said, "You deserve a better deal than you were being dealt. How about us calling it quits and being done?" Comes the rolling chuckles, off Kingsley's tongue. "It was merely fun, now, we're even, son." All for one and one for all was in his soul. This is how this current Kingsley rolls. He had a plan at the time when he'd knelt himself down, in the treasure ring around his throne, and beside the pile of looted things: silver, gold, diamond, and rings. Rubies were moody and could not sing, and yet all manner of other precious jewelry things.

"Nobody touches anything here until I'm done," he commanded those squares, and then some. Unlike how it was known to be done before those times, there. Like, when he would have gone in first and parted the pile with a clawed rod. Or any other such parting device that's hard-boiled and bad, and based sometimes upon how large a pile is. Or even on the sort of hardware spoils, kids. This time, however, he was playing the clever... He would have gone in first, yes, and would have carefully counted out the mess, or measured it out, handful after armful of looted treasure, and stout. Placed each in a heap by itself, each man's measure, all ready for his shelf. He'd warned them earlier that night about that; no man should venture in to take his portion before he's all over and done, as opposed to how it was done in the past, where, when he was done taking his portion. Each man would dig in and try to outdo the other to come up with the biggest bite out of what remains of the stolen apple pie. "Oh no, babe, don't cry." Two or more people were angered by this, angered at the king's bad manners (Hiss). Yes, Mister

Quick-silver temper, and the kid. (A table fist). The kid, though, unlike how it was for the "Quickly one-flow," the kid never did. Like, he never said a word or acted in any threatening way, nerd. He just remained put right there where he had lain himself square. Backed up against the board in a corner, bored, and wearing a stone-cold sword upon his armor cord, and an indignant stare through it and out of a gaze-ward fear. A cord that could cut a man through, like a blistering word of anger, but he was to be riding out his last night there atop his grave light. When all was said and done, he would have feared worse off than Mister Quickly-one. But not for very long, because the King would have walked around and continued doing the routine in front of each person, presently not too clean. Then did it again, until it was all done. Well, not quite done, I mean, there was some drama left yet to come, and it would have been coming towards the "done," and happening before we got up to the done. Yes, that, the part of it, as we've come to understand the spit-splitting word. As was to be revealed later on in the nest of the cockpit bird? It was all a test on the part of the king's jest, just to see where their heart wanted to be best. Probably, it would be found with him. Best thing. There's no better position for a man to be found in than on the right side of the king.

"How art thou, oh haughty Hartland from out of the Heartlands?" The king's right-hand man, that said Hartland one, almost got his right hand chopped off, or the left part of his best heart, or both. Or more like, have his ear bitten and written off, end quote. That was to come about when he tried to wit-talk some senseless nonsense into his friends' chalk, my king. Trying to bring him back to some semblance of real smarts and Kingsley reality, really — "And sameness, too?"

"Yes, Neily, it's true."

"Your Highness," he jested. "If you don't mind me saying..." he was heard spraying these corrective sayings. "I think that the boys — "Yes, yes? Yes, Hartland, I do mind, and speaking of 'mind,' that is what you ought to do, mind your own damned business, and leave me alone to get along with mine. Now, who else amongst the bunch of you... Which one of you might have a bright idea here? Let him speak now, or shut the trap up and let me get along with my business here." Looking around now, still. He was looking each man down on the hill. Looking them squarely in the eyes, brown, or eye colors yet unknown. But still, a response was not to be found. "Now, since no one has anything left to say, quit wasting my time here and obey. Let's get this done and be done." So said he, while clasping down a heavy, freshly washed, dirty hand on his dust-filled short-pants knee. Then, bending down again, he picked up another round; a haughty handful of the most valuable pieces from amongst those bulls, on the ground, clasp it firmly in a mean fist pulled in hard and round. Just like this, he then spat a hissing, biting snake-sign kiss.

"This is mine, it's all mine, all of it." Wielding the same frightful fist all over it, he spewed yet more kingly spit.

"It is, all… mine." Kingsley King's teeth were to be further ground. "I do with it whatever I please, and if it pleases me to keep it all to myself, that is what I will do, Paul Phelps. If it pleases me to give it all away to some poor old widow, somewhere out there by the bay, that's what I'll do, okay? If I say you all get the third part to split up among you, then a third part is what it's going to be. "Okay!" Now, tell me, who is the man amongst you to overrule me on that?"

The answer was late in getting to the "Come." Or maybe each man had to first go fix up his tongue. It never did; that answer remains; it never came. Must have been a prayer night hack, as picked up from one of the warmonger's tribal rites swats, perhaps. Because, like, because there never was such quietness in an occupied rooming mess before the king's vest, before. Not anywhere in the kingdom, nor… Not even in a city four square, sure. He was done with the talking; it was now time to finish walking and continue to get through what he'd started to do. Slowly, he stepped over and through the piles of shiny, glistening treasures and blue. As he went along doing what he was about to do, before he was rudely interrupted by the mal-aligned, maladjusted (the crew). Now, the dividing will go on stridently. Spread out there across the floor was the door to all that they had never had before. Kingsley wobbled his way between them, clay, walked back up to where he had been sitting, let's say, before. He then picked up his crooked divine dividing stick of the crooks. Then proceeded to pull heaps after heaps of the "this is yours" piles of loot toward him until... He was going to smile again because (ardent) he was all done. Yet, no man spoke a word off his tongue. Whatever "speaking" was left in any of them would have taken a stumble, tumbling, and fallen through the sword, down to the floor, humbled, along with each man's jawbone bundle. Well, so it would have seemed, to this long-toned bull. But, not for all of them, nah!

The kid got up and ran from the room. It was as if someone had lit up the spoon. Or more like, light up a firepan somewhere near that place where he sits and drools, all night long. Or, up until that point in the plan, when he got up and ran. They were to find him later that night, just on the outer peripheries of the meeting room light, riding away upon the pointed points of his sword of grey. "Not too bright," ...and bowing himself down over a pool of crimson blood. "Oh! Good gripe."

Mister Quickly-one wasn't too far behind him on the ride home, sickly. The only difference between him and his form of departure was that he would have taken a more familiar route, out. Lying squarely upon his feather bed in his own house, but... But he never did speak a single word to a living soul from the night of the drawn sword up until his departure, a mere two weeks later. "Oh, dear Lord." Remember, don't forsake her. You know, his partner?

Before we get there, though, to that point in the show, there's some more unfinished business to tend to. Kingsley, the king, was to take out the third part from among the glitzes. The part that everybody there was convinced was to be their part of the gifts, Sis. Well, he would have given them that impression when he first went out on the mission. His friend, though, that same Hartland bro from somewhere out on the Heartlands row, was sitting there as was the customary chair. Wearing a cheeky smile on his fashionable bile in the process of the "revealing" style, there. "Probably..." That was probably because that was the very thing that he'd wanted to say to the king while he was there doing the dividing sin. After all, even with the third share going to him on the call. Kingsley's third would have amounted to and be heard to be equivalent to the total of however many of those men were there in that rooming hall, there and then. Whilst each man's net take would have been piling up on his plate to be equivalent to his cut of the bakes, plus one. This matter was settled, good and done. Those who were good would have been settling home gooder, to be finding themselves much better able to deliver a kingly biscuit dipper. Whilst those who were found to be "not," would have been gone and done with, flat. Into a "thy kingdom come" slot, Mr. King, Kingsley King, and his sons. Now let's sing along to the Kingsley song and get this done: Kingsley, Kingsley, Kingsley King, and his sons.

"Note from the author." Just a note of thanks to you for choosing to read my book and for sticking with it thus far. You must have liked it a lot. At this point, I want to ask you, my reader, yes, you, my friends, to take a minute or two to post a review of the book on the sales pages at Amazon or any other such sales pages. Now, go out to the races. This small gesture is so very much appreciated. If you like it, don't keep it to yourself; be sure to share the love. Now, touch my glove and swear you'll tell someone. Thank you.

7

Sheamus' Story

He was a stranger, came into their small town as some sort of wandering one door "her" around those parts. He had just buried the children's mother and began to settle into his life properly after the dark. That was when life took a further downturn for somebody. Trouble was accustomed to coming and troubling everybody, and them, in those days. By way of the raiders, first and foremost, but now, here comes the plague falling on them in the dome house. With it, though, also came that lovely lady and her walking legs up the lane to save me, no, I mean, him. To save him. She would be bringing her little boy along with her into the caveman's den. Well, she was his mother, and he, the stranger man than me? He was to hop in and marry her off to become Sonny Boy's new daddy bad man, and full of talk. Then began to settle in properly with the new pillar and socks. He'd lost his wife of two decades, he'd said, to her, and him, yes, he was there sticking his nose into people's business, which suddenly concerned him. Along with my nosey peeping-in forehead, yes mi bred, not just his."

The story was to be heard going off like the occasional boom blasts that were coming at them from the boy's pops, to get the chatterboxes scampering off and running away from the site of the gossiping talks, or to... towards it. Like, to go about doing some more telling of their own and laughing off their tops, with you. In and around those parts of the stone ends. We'll try to fill you in on some more of the details as we go along the road. Walking ahead of them and their wholesale and retail business that they were trying to run for new clothes, bread, and bedding.

Both were recently widowed, well, she was, and he? He'd lost his wife of two decades, he'd said to me, but were they married? Not as the records weren't showing, and as the story was to go around those parts and carried further in, on the stone ends.

"Oh, hail, no!"

Yeah, they got hooked up like that, like, with a hail of a lot of ham her and a nail. "Oh!" By a newly installed mutual family friend, as you can tell.

"What's her name again?"

"Um! When I remember it, I'll fill you in on those old habits, like those sitting there in the dustbin waiting for the rabbits, getting ready to be dumped in on that, and this, you know, but..."

"But why?"

"Why should you be alone when there are so many single women out there looking for a home, though?" She was heard asking this of the bro. No need for that, not when there are so many single women out there looking for a home, I mean, a man. Look, look at them, those eavesdropping peeping-toms. They're laughing now because they know that it's true. But never mind them. Aren't you looking for a good man to take home, too, my dear? Lots of suitable women are out there looking for a good man to take back home to bed with ten door nests and care, and can't seem to be able to find one. She'd said these sorts of things too, at his shaking hand, and the staring eyewear, yes, Hingh Sue, was way too close to the knee strings, yes, just about to go down begging, on the bending... Somebody was looking deeper into the future and seeing some new things coming in and shining down on him. Yeah, even before he got around to saluting her. Just as much as you, Sir, as you'd been trying to do, from then on, and heading in. Well, I'd supposed so, because the tares were there too, guess where? Yes, man, there, dropping on his gaze from head to shoe. There was no denying it, he was torn to pieces beside her knees, Sis, quietly and quickly. Even though he couldn't seem to be able to tear his stare away from around there, from this part of the rather nice chick, ee. The place where she was speaking those wonderful words of his, yes, they are now. He'd managed to take a peek in and tore them wide open enough to look, though. Tore them wide open to look at it, and that was when he saw the axis long ago, sit, sit.

"Oh."

Although the smoke and the dust coming up out of the ashes and such blazing heart now set on fire, were threatening to stop him from reaching out and up any higher. "But he could not stop looking at who?"

"Me."

"No, you liar, you, not you at all, but her." She was staring right back at him, or somewhere closer to the head top than the chin, where she was leaning in, next. Must have seen something there that pulled her into him, because...

"A good man like you," she said, with such tenderness in her egg, I mean, leg, as she walked on up and in, close enough to be touching skins. "A nice man like you shouldn't have to be alone to grow older by yourself in a cold bed (old bones). I'm your good luck charm here in the cloth on the alarm clock, you know. You'll need something to keep you warm before the alarming clock goes off announcing the breaking of the new morn, and I? I know just the right person for you."

"So, um, what's... what's wrong with you? You seem 'right' enough to me."

That's where and when I got my first kiss from, yes, her, and that was that. Yes, the hook-up was now on the attack and walking through the board at the cookout shop.

"Oh my gosh! Why?"

"Yes, my dear. That's what a lot of others were asking at the time, too: 'why,' why not you, and I...? Well, so I hear."

They both were done with raising their own children's lump sum off me and you. All but this little Shae here, or two. One of those grown children was to feature prominently in the boy's life; this said, Sonny

Boy's life and times, too, as a matter of "Fat" fact, like those foxes that were plentiful at the time, and gnawing at the vines. "Want to hear more about that score to go and get the deal signed?"

"Yes, of course."

"Well, leave it at the door, somewhat a-jarred, as it was before the card, handed off to you as soon as you'd stepped in the bar with those tugs of yours. We'll come back later for the car, 'coward.'"

"Say that word softly, man, not so hard, I don't think it was meant for their ears, just ours."

The man had a son who was a highly rated and very well-placed champion in the king's service to command. He took to liking the boy, and eventually took him in, as a service to his father and for protecting the family line, the wrong thing. Fatty was more than happy to have made it into the big time slot, e, mi Pickney. Yes, my child. He was quick in bringing along his old friend from a long time gone down home, too. In the person of Dedimus from the old school, not you.

So, now those fat foxes are getting a bit fatter than that, and they're still gnawing at the vines on the lot over there. Yeah, man, those fat foxes are now theirs, not mine, like that one, for instance. The one who was most responsible for his meteoric climb up the royal line, a long way going the distance. He wasn't even "bloody" related to him at all, but he was more than happy to answer the call. He was rich and very well positioned to see things through quickly and to make things look as good as they do on the Sonny Boy pickney, and me, as they are, on her. His lady love came from somewhere around the throne above. The missed stress up and out was given to him by the helper man from higher up, with lots of love to stress him out, and over the stove. See? Yes. Okay, continue to look, because... She was very helpful in getting it all to happen, getting things fixed up properly, and popping the cocoa jars flown in free for somebody looking more or less like me, not him, and for the pleasure of pleasing herself too, at the time. Like, for the love of that same old fat sonny, Amos and me, because... Yes, I know, he was the man of the house, of course.

"And, and why?"

"Why, what?"

"Why did he do all that?"

"Because he must. Nothing is too good for Sheamus, especially when his wife would have already given it her thumbs-up. Of course, his buddy, best friend Dedimus, who was coming in not much later, on the bus, was to be an added benefactor of it all." Coming in to sort out the house, and to get things fixed up good and properly, and happening for somebody in the hall. Like, for Sonny himself, first and foremost, then Amos and me, of course, because he must. Would have always been there to cover for him whenever Shae would shirk on his work and go about screwing around. That was what he did, to him, and her, and me on the ground. As this and other such things were to have turned out and become a fact for the rest of them to see, and to talk about over tea, not us, but for folks such as him, and she, yes, the lovely lady he used to call mammy.

"Tell me, who told them about what had happened between him and the wife of that other uncle, of sorts?"

"I don't know enough about those facts from gossiping talks, okay?"

"But, but, how come you — "Okay, Mister Smart, as asked, listen up, because it was because... Such things were to be found happening every morning, and continuing all day long, darling, even up until evening. Chatterboxes were chatting about it every day. Such reports were popping out of everybody's mouths of clay, as their first cousins sang the chorus, okay? So, it wasn't hard to understand very clearly the reason for those." The lady love wasn't wasting any more time with me, so they began to work on it very quickly. Just after they'd managed to get him a job and a place to sit and stay in town with, yes, she, not me, weekly.

"Liar, you."

"What, what did you just say?"

"Never mind me, just a slip-talk from the zip code on which I sometimes park the jackass cart on which I go riding the roads around these parts, carry on, carry on."

"...Permanently, as a matter of fact." That place, as it turned out, wasn't round as you'd supposed, but flat. It was the last place Sonny Boy would have ever imagined chasing a sit down upon the hem of a frock... sorry, I meant to say, rock, on a rock without a frown on his ask king parts.

Crown Hill it was, below or above. Well, not quite that high up the cronies' town to get to see the Crown Hill Kiln where such crusts were minted and baked in until brown with tint in love, but... They were soon to become the king's chief fighting men in the region, alright, yes, no less sparkling and bright. But not hanging up his leggings that close to the crown itself anymore, to have been standing on the most royal grounds with stealth, as before. But the sonny boy's life was changed for the better, although it sometimes seemed to us as if it was turned upside down, mi breda, and then got turned back around again for the worst kind of "best," for mama and papa if nobody else, and ever after, as I'd guessed.

"Because of him, I suppose."

"Yeah, man, that's the truth." Go wipe your nose, because... "Yuck, look at you." He got himself so tightly woven into them and their ways of doing things that he would have quickly forgotten about his branch on the tree limb. Couldn't say for sure whether they had managed to live through the myriads of attacks or not, to make it out, to the we-win. Until he was to find himself running away from the rest of the big shots with his doggy pup and Dedimus hanging on his shoulder like a limb. Hopping along like a three-legged man, in the middle of two walking sticks for balance and a Scotch, like, sipping on each man's bottle of stolen scotch handed down to them from the mean one. He didn't have the heart to walk away with his doggy alone and leave his only friend from days long gone, without even a bone. Knowing that he would just lie there and die, mi dear, as all the rest of his friends and alibis had done. So, he picked him up along with his carrying sack to add to the two that he and his dog already had and hopped along the road ahead. "Looking for—"Hoof, Hoof, "oh, mi Bred, mi dead yet?" I mean, "Am I dead?"

That's what I heard the brother man say. Then bowed his head and... and...

Meanwhile, "I have no money, Honey," he said to her pretty little bonny rabbit's clad outstretched hand waving at his own salt and peppery graying hairy strands somewhere around his headband. Came in from somewhere nearer than where she was sitting there on the other side of him on the feather and straw bedpan, at first. She'd by then moved up a verse or two. "Well, you know her, no?"

"No, I don't."

"Well, I'll continue along on the hunt until you catch up with me and get us to overcome." What he had at the time, though, was a house.

"Oh, no."

"Yes, bro." A tiny house with a few doors hinged from the inside out west some more. To be wind-blocking everything that blows o'er the poor thing, and swinging his weights around like a baseball bat at it to swing the rotten opening back in, to let them outside of the Portsmouth, then back in again once or twice a month, yes. It was happening up there where the wee house was built on the hillside in Portsmouth, I'd supposed, and squinted. While the quilt hinted at tossing a fiber thread at my eye, and lied about what it thought that we did. As those nosey passers-by got the walking legs started off running ahead to go and lie with spies. Like, those roaming rover guys, while they were to be seen lying, yet some more. Or sitting down together and laughing off their arts at the little bredda mi bred, even the poor... "Yes?" Yes, my brother, that's what they did. He, like all and everybody else around those parts in the yards near the sea, was ordered to stay home by themselves to pause the cocoa pods of tea. But then, shortly afterward, the fatty boy Sheamus and his crony cubbies were called in to stand before the king and then sent out on duty to fight for the said king and his buddies to win. Fighting to ensure that everyone else's door was closed up but theirs, and his, and that they were all made to become shut-ins, from the outdoors, that is.

The order was sent down the ladder by somebody else from, you know, like, from another rung on the upper border. To get us to get up from a round of beer in these very parts, since the bar barred us, too. Had to close up shop on the half soul of your shoe, maker, and socks. Yes, go ahead and make her lose her tops to the bottoms, if you want, since you seemed to think that you can, even though everyone around these parts knows that you can't. But how could she have known that fact, and so quickly? They were asking this even of the little pickney, yes, my child. "Besides," I had to have lied when I gave her my reply. "By someone from not too far and very well-known around those parts of your town, too," I said, but. Well, as it was to have turned out, he was someone not too well-known about, mi bred, in truth, like...

Like what was his real job, and how he was going about paying his scouts and getting it done with them winning the gold. Such things were not known about him; that's why everybody was asking. Not even in and around some parts of his hometown, in person, that is. But he sure was up in arms about someone who has got something on him, like, a powerful noun for a name, whiz kid, and quite a few quid were to be blamed for this, that, and on all of his biz, Inez. Whatever he says, they all say, and it would become the staying sayings and the playing games of the new day. Just like what was said to have happened on that and such other occasions, Dame, don't forget, eh, his name, so...

A closed-in they became, along with all the rest of them, and trying to live out the plague-bugging game from then on. A crown-coated virus it was that had caused the alarm, one that, unlike us, comes with a royal name strand, on the bus.

"Oh, c'mon, that has got to be wrong," said this starved of a drunken man.

"No," I said, in my response, I'm not leading you on, not at all. A virus it was, one that came down to them from above. His name was even signed on the line below, inked with his stain; few in our realms would have known how to show. That was the very place that was to become the complaint-receiving and reports-reading center from then on. As was heard by every average Joe and the same sane Hingh, yes, Sir Sam." Yes, man, thank you for dropping in on us and listening in. The more people like you that we can get these facts to, in all truth, the better it will be for everybody to walk our booths, and follow all the way through, so yes. It was our pledge ore to have been able to show and tell you this, Sir.

It was sent down to the entire peopled population from above their home station. Thrown down on us through the fingering hands of a known statesman; yes, the fat one. But how could they have known about such one-door full outcomes that were to have fallen on their son?

"I know, I know," he said, in response to her effort at enabling him into it and to get us, as well as him, to agree, not to beg. "Never again should we become bigger beggars than Ned are... so that we should ever have to beg." She was doing this to remind him how such things go walking out on legs, and that it was free again, you know. Just the same as all the other stains that came before the pain.

"Which pain came before?"

"The same one that came earlier on, slapping on their but tons. Calling in on us to place the blame down, instead of up. Like, up there from whence, in fact, it came, when it came hammering on the backside of the brother man and every other one of these lames, like us. Don't start thinking that I'd forgotten about the sister, no mister, no mister, leave her right there. Because everybody was dragged into the mixture, fast and unfairly, yes. A gift from the king and his governing sisters, it was. She, who was at the time responsible for governing the tugs and the other guard's men, too, did the signing and slew their way down to everybody in the house, with him and you. In fact, it was so designed as to exchange ownership of the game from the bottom up for themselves, and for whoever else was to be found with them and her sitting on the shelf, amen. And coming in from other men too, to everybody with him on words, not their good works, say amen again."

"Amen again."

"Thank you, because it's true, very true."

"Yes," he said when he'd confessed to her diligent odd dress, "but we don't need it, never did, never will." Look, look at that fox, that's the same fat fox that was running off to the kill, there he goes again, going on towards the killing tracks, if you will. Look at that, and then at me, kid, if you please. Well, if you want, otherwise, go over there and sit with your aunt on her knees.

"But, but, why? Should I even do that, spy and go? No, I don't think so."

"Of course you should, not," not when I've got everything that I need... head right here in my own house. Even when so many holes are in the roof that high water is now dripping down from an eye and dropping to the stopping on my thigh, as if I'm about to cry and die. Sitting here on my tightly woven tie, made of rye to try and dye it, whilst I'm lying low in my own arms house thing, even when it comes to the ending in the evening. That will be something worth a haughty Amen. "Ding", comes the chime in. Neath, e? Yeah, man, but let's eat this, then continue along my free man's square, yes, sweet Sis.

"Damn right, you are."

...

The funk of last night's leftover mugging like a stale muffin was in those times, still sitting heavily on something best left behind. Like, on his bleeding breath of the dome thing, not mine. Or off, off the dumpling he'd fished out of the dustbin of abject poverty where he was, yes. That was the familiar companion on the ship, filled with bugs, for him and his entire family, at the old address, plan it well, mi tug.

So, in bed that night, he searched for delight. What he found was to come face to face with him in fright, in his dreams too, he was looking down on his longing eyes as they shone upon you. "Good night," he said and went off to sleep on his side of the bed. Woke up the following morning still yawning and found nothing but you and her lying upon him, I mean, the hem. Upon the hem of his nightgown garment, and faking the waking past the dew again, down the bottom arm ends. "If even when there should come the end 'ding' in the evening," he said. That will be something worth a haughty Amen, "Ding-ding," comes the chime in, again. Yeah, man, but. Let's eat this, then continue along my free man's square all week long and lick my sweet tooth up against the rest of my teeth. Like, right here. Like, even while I'm lying down on my bed and sucking my thumb."

"Yuck, you mean?"

"Yes, that's it, that was what I meant to say, Sis. I've always done it like this. Yes, my dear, hurray, now that you've gotten to know it, go away, just as you'd longed to hear me say."

"So that was when the decision was made to play rough and tough with the man dem. I mean, men, with those men."

"Yes, those same old folks were at it again, throwing muck at them, and at us, too, of course. You know them, those might "e-men" from the low end, I'm sure that you know them, yes?"

"Yes, I know them, I guess."

"Okay then, so, 'I guess that' you should also know that, once they get started on the war skid path out, they don't bother to go slow to the stop, shout yes."

"Yes."

So, that was when the command came down from the top man's hand, and fell to the brainiest companions of ours, looking on. When they're not out looking for *Pum-pum yam to fall pan dem plate fei dem fei nyam*, yes, the food was falling like gawling on their plates for them to eat, you know. But it came to pass that when it came at the last act, it got them to stay closed in and shut down to Rastafar-I. Say this word loud and get louder, guys, yes, or was it up? I can't seem to remember a lot these days, my guy. But such was to remain on them, all day long, amen. Into the nighttime too, on what was said at the time to be their piece of the clay to walk their shoes. Or more like, to make potted brews and red pea soup, as some were beginning to notice this truth. That, as it turned out, was to be the same kind of tough luck cup of red peas and scrap meat soup that I was talking about. As given to the youths to burn out the gas on the rough rock bough.

"But, but why?"

Her concerned eyes upset the wise old guys when she started out saying this.

"It's, it's, it's — "Yeah. I know, hits after amazingly great hits, no?"

"No, not that, but it's because, she said, when she'd managed to digest the task out of its ask and reply. "Because…" Go-getters were (by then) going in better and full-fledged to go in and gut her by nine or ten. To come over and see her at the line-in, to go line dancing with them, and yes, us too, yes. All of us, he said, to those over there by the sheds where Ned was hiding out under the bed, with you. But the parson's edge of a pastor never looked under the bed; that's why he didn't see Brother Ned, in truth. But that was how he would have heard about it and passed it along to the rest of his crew in the knit outfit. This is their last-ditch effort at the final attack on our bread and butter. But as for her, as for him and her. They were more than half sure of what the king's ton of tugs wanted. They wanted to kill off the whole pack of willed off not e-dreads, to rawtid you know and gut our oats.

"But, but, why?"

"It's, it's because," he said, when he'd managed it enough to man up in age and digest the wait e nests out of it and asked her why, again.

"Why do you want to know these things, though?"

"Because…"

"Oh, well then, I'll tell you. They were trying, I'd supposed," he continued with it after wiping his nose, again, they were trying to get out of it and to man up on the proper responses. "Somehow," he said, in the answer, ring sled back at her and them fast and full-fledged.

"Somehow, we've allowed others to act and abuse the ax (or nots) to convince ourselves that we're not, like…"

"Like what, overly self-conscious?"

"Yes, and far too relaxed, shuts. But they could not seem to see that we didn't need such a thing as that. Same as how they did not notice the facts, like, when they'd convinced all the rest, well, everyone else but us, isn't that as it is, and was?"

"Yes, yes, I guess."

But we are, just as said, and somehow, maybe it's because of such things as that, that's probably why they couldn't see, yes?

"Yes, yes, I guess."

"You'll probably need to go and address those many guesses at your business address, Sis, and respond in kind with your response to your odd ads, that is at rest resting there on your newly arrived guests list next, because..." Well, perhaps it's just me by now; I digress. I'm probably the only one left wearing a self-made odd dress, even as it seems to appear to upset some folks over there by the way I wear these dresses around my waist, Ted's knee, here. Yes, I'm talking about me and not you, Miss Ad-here.

"Oh, yes, sir, what is it?" came the response from the good lady who would have heard and wanted to contest and go complain next door.

"Never mind, my dear lady, I spoke out of line already."

"Yes, you did," she confesses to this, then turns away and leaves.

Well, perhaps not, but who's going to make her any wiser about those facts of yours? I don't think so. Not me, though. No, I won't go back and ask her for such things as these, and those, such things I can do well with oats, a twig of rose, but... They'd convinced you and the rest of them, too, all of the average Joe-ish partying few, that they are still in control of all of their screws. Those that are sitting over there on the electric boogie chair, and who continually look down on the rest of them and us as if they knew the news, and then go off pretending to care, for these fools. Sorry, I meant to say, foods.

They'd convinced them that they need "Dead", their forms of cure ring-seeded aids, since they were the best there ever were, as agents on the page. Whilst pouring Paperman's pens in them, on amens, inking them in books at the moment. Then send them out to pass it along to the rest of their sisters and brothers, men, as agents of the government, meant to save another one.

"It's to rebound us from the plague uproar," they said.

"Well, I'm sure, yes, it is, isn't it?"

"Yes."

"Oh man, poor us, again, but, but..."

"Whatever happened to our son?" This bigger ask was coming from behind him, near the talking parts of the woman.

"I don't know," he said, "I, I'm beginning to wonder about that one. I can't say for sure about any of these things nowadays, but, c'mon. Let's run along."

Such freedom from the plague that came from them in the first place of the ten pits was just the beginning of the practice. If you didn't know these things, you might as well quit. One way or another, it was traced back to the same brother.

"But what for?" Again, I ask Har, I mean, her. Yes, he'd asked her, not mean ole me. "Where are they now, those cured folks from the outside of these closed-up doors?" "Stop, listen, did you hear that?"

"No?"

"Well, I suppose that... No, never mind. Enough of those, they're of less importance to me than a twig of rose."

"I suppose so."

"Yes. But they can try as hard as they may, they're not going to drug me away, nor shake me trembling out of my clothing today, no. Not on any other daily show starts her upper kitty cat either. But I'll tell you where they are as a teaser," bar, sweet, eh? Yeah, man, like a sham, those cured-as-cargo folks are already gone or coaxed. Gone to the graveyard, I'm sure, every last one of them and more.

"But of course, what else did you expect?"

"Okay, what can I say? Why, though?" He continued to try to know.

"Why would I bother to want that, my guy? Should I even do that spy and go?"

"I don't think so."

"Neither do I, not when I've got everything that I need right here on my free man's square wheat bread."

"And it's sweet, right?"

"Yeah man, sweet like a sham, and a lot of such things too, that we want to nyam, so that we can go and get it ready to eat while going along. Want a piece? I've got it on low heat. Seasoned and ready to roast a pum-pum yam to go with the duckling stew I'm on with meat and wanting to nyam. Even with the wheat in my cod fish teeth to go and get dinner for the children's pickney dem as the beginners, and me, no?"

"No."

In those days, you see. There was increasing crown-coated noise flowing down the hillside for free and rolling down to settle in at the root of the big tree. Even throughout the people's conversation from far and wide, yes, wider than she — "Who, you mean, the plus-size lady across from me?"

"Yes, she who is... who's she, anyway, do you know her?"

"You mean, she, that one right over there, I don't think so, but, big har up nuh, I mean, her."

"No man, she done large already, I mean, she's already on the larger-than-life size."

"Mi knoah, yeah man. That's how I like my ladies sometimes, though."

"About as big as who, again?"

"She same one.

"Yes, that one sitting over there amongst those who came to sit in the shades and talk along about the not e-dreads, to me, even. Or just to hide out there from somebody, in the shed, too afraid that someone will agree."

"To show her up the tree?"

"Yes, mi pickney, my dear child?" Boyd, go, go inside and stop running around before I wax your backside with what's left of the wrath of the hide. Enough, man, please. Allow me to carry Ann in pieces on my shoulder above the sleeves. Or shoulder her in comfort, above my knees. Yes indeed, you may look at her, "Isn't she sweet?"

"Yes, sir, pops, she is."

Yes, I already knew that before I'd asked, you may look at her as much as you want, yes, of course you may. "But don't even think a second thought that you're going to see it, let alone taste the meat that we're about to eat. I know that was meant as a rhetorical showbiz feed. So, let's continue to go to the sheets."

"Okay."

No, not you, I know you would have liked to, but we were just about to eat before you came dropping things off your teeth. So, let's continue to tin you in a canteen, and then go. But first, may I ask, "Where were we in the conversation for the talk show to take on the task, at home?"

"Right here, isn't this the same old shoppers' fair where the gnome — "Yes, I agree, but we were running towards Ran, and the rest of the thieves in the clan too." Yes, man. Such conversations were running for way too long… so long that it ran headlong into the other brother's reasoning plans, as was heard coming in from other conversations going on then, down to the boogie land. Like, they were seen going down there to go and continue doing what they were doing.

"Like what?"

Like that, like, they were boogying the hail out of the clown, like so, "Come on, join us," they said, "and let's go, like, let's go down there and boogie down all day long." Yes, of course, they were boogie Hingh on down, and landing plumb amongst the sums of the local people pop you lay shun, or none. Hardly any were left by then, but. Those who were there, talking the talk, King, were talking about how they, the everyday-Joey types of people, okay? Who's asking anyway? Anyway. They were all talking about the same thing that day, about how they had been used and abused by everyone, and the news. Then cast out as refused, something on which they could hardly even bother to look back and muse. But as they were beginning to see the time and patience striking the clock, that's how and when they found out that they were now bouncing back, and they were hoping too, that it would also mean that they were finally getting out of the user's ironclad grip-lock to mingle. Yes, man, bouncing back from plastic boggish types of wasted scraps, like shingles. Finally, boo, out of the truck too. On the much-needed, aahs! and oohs! "By a lot," they said. By a whole lot at that, mi bred. By their efforts, at last, that's good, "Isn't that true, my boss, Mister Wood?"

"Of course, of course, it is."

On such other things too, as what was the strength of their metal from birth, back-a-rock. "Or was it all David's fault?"

"Mi nuh knoah yaw man, I don't know whose fault it was at all, but."

"Mi pop-off truck, look yah; yuck."

"What is it?"

More hard luck. "Go on, go on," said the big boss man, go on and sky laugh, if you want, because, as for these select few who claimed to have known a thing or two. Another pot of stock to go and add to the bubbling Ben-Johnson-day stew. Because — "What's that?"

"What, the Ben Johnson Day stew?"

"Yes, what is it?"

"Listen up and listen up well, good, and quick. It's more or less like this, like a sort of condition where everything is gone. Usually, this comes around on a Thursday morning, or just before your payday comes, when there's hardly anything left in the pantry cupboards but crumbs, to cook up a proper meal for the coward. But come, come along, because the family over there is ours, and they must be fed, no matter how you feel about the bread, nor if you have happened to have eaten anything yet. So, you put a pot on the fire and bring it to a boil. Then add whatever your hands come across, such as pickings and spoils. Whatever other leftover scraps your fingers can bring come to the pot, boiling. Then add seasonings and salt to taste out the fault and stir. Usually, that meal tends to be the tastiest ever. But be careful not to let the children's eyes fall upon the process mi breda, no brother dear, or else."

"Yuck, what is this and... and that?" That may be all that you'll get them to taste out of the pot, upon the pointed end of the stirring fork. Otherwise, though, they are likely to be asking for a lot, Moe, like, more of the same, which in itself can pose other problems on the front door, since you've not secured the recipe for this one as yet, as you would have done before, but...

...

It's crunch time now, said the tick to the cow, but the cow thought that the word was lunch, somehow. So, she went out to get her dinner plate and ate. Playing a catchy little rhythm on her beats with the chap's sticks. Ended up giving up her hide to leather their seat at the backsides of the deserts and mincing some folks' preferred pieces of the meat besides the dead earth.

"Really?"

"Yeah, man, so they said at the time, too, 'This is really sweet,' yes, whilst licking each of their fingers up against their teeth, my brother, Woo. And watching her head shaking with pledge her while she was sitting comfy within her rocking chair under her settled-feet legs too, but — "Or was it, wasn't it above?"

Anyway, that was it. No, not for the tick, but for the cow. The cow cod soup man on the corner couldn't resist the will to corn her. So he too got caught up in the loop down the corner, like this. Saying his little bits, like...

"Time now to take the farmers' hands to the plowing program," said the super soup man to that other one. "Mi blow wow," he exclaimed, "What's going to happen now to them?"

"No, no way," was what I heard someone else say, on that very day when they said what they had to say to Ned. Everybody there was having their little piece of what they were saying. Well, it was also when the cruel and heartless brutes brought their schemes into hard play, like Foo Hing's suit, made with ease, to soothe them and their pleading overlay. Salute me, please, yes, and work those lazy legs below the knees, Hingh, like these are. Yeah, man. Thank you for the ten Q.

Yeah, man, those commands were to be heard coming along like quicksand. Coming in from those who were there, combing their hair, and pretending that they were the smartest ones anywhere, to see, okay?

Well, so they say, and then they started to move the gear shift into a real progress sieve-like leaky relay. Fairing as well as they could for themselves at carrying the water away, for themselves and them only, and the food too, while doing so. While leaving behind all the rest there to stay in the mad nests and pined away, I mean, find a way, like, if they can. They could, you know, so, here I am, wearing felts on the wood, even in my hands, there's one there on your right hand too, good evening.

Let's get mediocre and done, said another one from among the other Ore mango, same as I'd done. Or perhaps we could continue the walk through these nonsense talks for a couple more cents of sorts to put into the pocket loop for the rest of the gnomes' combs to lick up a stalk, and spew. Come back, come back, there's a lot of room behind you, man, "come, come, come."

That was the sound as it was heard coming down the chute. That meant the trucks were rolling in and backing into the booth.

"But really?"

Yeah, sit, man, sit. Sit down quickly and take notice of this, Leigh.

Don't forget: This story is told from a Carib-Jamericanadian perspective, in a richly blended language mix of nonsense talk, double entendre, sensational spelling, poetry, and Jamaican patois inserted wherever it was found fitting. Yes, wordplay is the order of the day around here.

8

Go West, My Son

They ruled the bloody bleeding place with a tin man's bleeping heart face behind a biting teeth brace. Bloody-red water-pumping song and dance fill the place, dripping on and off the wet sword right after each case of them saying their grace, over your coffin even, and coughing. Yeah, man, saints they are, and were, always washed clean, starched from their scenes and stained white with an upstanding name such as hers, standing on the premises off to one side at the gated door again, as a gap in the teeth space speaks the absurd word, to them. Or some other such choice musical chords, sweet to the taste, amen. Yes, yes, Mi lawd, Oh, my Lord. "Busting in the — "No. Not busting, but basking."

"Or was, was… wasn't it asking?"

Meanwhile, someone was out of the house and walking the tiles south. His name is Robbie Sly, or Robert Sylvester, when going out. Everywhere he went, he was running into wants, and out of spoils and demented bread, but butter was a bit harder to come fatter, in any semblance of comfort for her, no, mi bred, not all of them were his business-fixing style, so he thought to himself, I'll quit and just smile because…

Look, he's lying face down on the ground now, trying his darndest best to try and hang on to the last "blow-out" of his breathing breath in his chest under his brow, because he'd forgotten to take up "suppn" to help him out along the way out west of the south end. But with "nuttn" but nothing left under his pants button today. Not much strength is left in the right side of his vest to get him upset enough to continue along the road west and away from us. But he's just about to get lucky, with a little help from a packed nut e-buddy by way of a helping hand from a duppy sort of personality.

"Who's he?"

"Follow along, and you'll see." The days of fasting since the last bit of food he'd gotten (ten) when he'd gotten his first count are adding up to over twenty-three, and now, he's looking out for his honey again, not me. That was what had saved him last time, from starving his name off the KD's Times headlines. Smoked honey it was, with a bit more than a few of the bee bugs baked in on his glove. He would have added way too much smoke to the storehouse of tyrants flying all about him. Trying to protect himself from the sharp end of their stinging. But then, it was to be proven all good for feeding him, in the end, but now!

"Am I dreaming or is it real?" Miles wasn't sure what to feel, but he liked the way it felt. He had to go a bit slow, though, and savor the flavor. It was a taste he'd never, like... experienced before.

"Or was it a case of his own taste buds steering him away from the familiar door?"

"How... Anyhow, a hungry man is a glutonous nyam, so..."

Look, the stranger is sitting across from him on a fit Fig firewood sort of grounded tree limb, hanging like me, down to the ground, and looking at him. Trying to figure him out before going too much further in, I think. Well, so thought the Miles fellow from within. But "where are you off to?" The stranger opened up the conversational talk book in a soft-shoe type of tentative motion. He didn't respond, not verbally, to show him the home front, home, Noble Leigh. Just a slowly shifting right hand showed off the show-off western direction, ish. The stranger reached into his side sack for a drink of water, like this (or not, it could have been something else, another) and offered him one. "Have this," he said. Miles gulped it down in about a dozen swallows and said, "Thank you," when he was done. He handed the container back to its rightful owner's bottle holder, pillowed his head back down on the assembly of both arms, and bled his eyes quickly shut-in, just a bit older, as he went back to sleep, beside him, there. Still looking at the bundled-up heap wrapped up beside him, beware. Look, they're walking together on a westbound trail now, and probably rehearsing the many questions in their heads that each man would have liked to get answered somehow. But as of yet, no such spoken word has managed to come forth, or even once upon a half of the eighth. "Who are you, and where are you going?" Miles mildly opened up the floodgates and showered him when he was a little more awake than his brother Slim might have been.

"Don't go about asking questions you don't want answers to and might quickly grow to hate," he said, when he finally spoke at all, then continued ahead.

Look, back over on the other side of town, somebody was fixing up to settle down. Miles and Lucy Slim weren't really twins, as many at the time said; Lucy was just about a year older than him. But just as they were beginning to understand some things about the world that they were living in, the rotten plague started blowing in. Soon afterward, they began growing accustomed to losing many of their families and friends to the rotten old cowards. The mother lady would have had a falling out with them and the baby when she fell to some dirty old warrior's blade... ee. And father? He would have made some amends. Got okayed for early retirement pay, so he could take care of the only thing he had left worth living, loving, and paying anything for on the home front: his two boys of sorts. Although he was supposed to have been retired, of course, he was to be found working on call as if he couldn't get tired at all, nor say no. The roaming brigades were out actively cleaning people like them, out of the land, dead glades. The more the people complained, the more governors who were made to govern her's lied to them, saying it was nothing that they couldn't amend. Yet the more the posse grew, and even more they carried on with the culling tricks, killing them softly with their love songs on vinyl disks, like that one, and this. But now, this is quite a new level for someone's boredom. Miles would have skipped the house on the day of the dirty jokes of a fight, and gone out towards the south-southwest that night, to hide. Slim would later follow him, deciding to go walking, but…

"But, the order, how did it come about?" "*Mi nuh knoah*, but listen to this guy, he might know."

"The order," he said, "was sent down by somebody from around our town." Someone not too well known around those parts of your hometown, but… Well, as it turned out, he was someone not too well known around some parts of his own hometown, either in person. But he was sent in by someone, like, let's say, Kingsley, perhaps? I'm not certain, but he sure has a powerful noun for a name, whiz kid, and quite a few Quids were to be blamed on his biz, e kneeze, yes, my pops. Whatever he says, they say, and it will become the kind of saying game of the day. Just like what would have happened on that other occasion, Dame, don't forget, eh, his name. Because Kingsley, it was, yes, the same.

"Go-getters are now going in full-fledged to gut him and her as… something, or another, and us too, yes, all of us," and the brothers, as he was heard saying to those over there and you. This is their last-ditch effort for the final attack on our bread and butter cup. Wanted to kill off the whole pack of willed-off not e-dreads and gut our oats. Yeah, man, wordplay is the order of D-day here, too. So, look at what we've got 4 you, two days, you don't say. I mean it, don't say it. Just list ten up and obey the profits you'd gain by way of the correct predictions of the prophets in D cups, because… This is a hit, song number won for you. 10 Queue.

"Team Players," I heard someone holler. Team players were the games of the day — oh, you've all been played now, my friends, like so. Losing out on the winning dice throw. Of course, you're a winner, but you know. Sometimes the monkey wrench from the King's ton singer's gold end bench comes hollering. Getting up to their old habits… sheets of swinging her on a binge on her dinner cup, cupped to clabber her ring. While coupling the tablecloth and gone are all your lucky charms, corn Hingh. Gone to the new beginners' farms wing. Such a shame, though, the good times had run their course, for the good livers only, of course. Things were getting from bad to worse as they were beginning to see such things coming in by way of the empty purse. The stuffy chest panting rancid air they received but no longer wanted or needed here was even worse for wares than these. They were heard increasingly complaining and cursing the clerks at the Days Inn. Those who were shirking work there at the clubhouse evenings, and even worse than that thieving… thing, was another one, two, three times out, are you in?"

"Yes."

"Well, I'm leaving for the best. But first, let's finish the reading of the verse at this address, unless…"

"Unless what?"

"Whatever," like, like, it's like so. Here we go; they were, at the time, busily complaining about the wines and the time as the signs were showing off at the posh gathering places of mine. No, don't laugh, because I ain't lying. Those who were near and dear to the Stevens' news knew. "Nurse" was what they'd named him, phew!

"Ooh! Who, what? Who did it, and what was the reason for that name, though?"

"How would I know when nobody told me so?" I guess somebody was upset, because yes. The jet setters, like all the rest, were getting upset at the time and staying sweathier than wet, somewhere under the collar gear of mine, right there.

"Where?"

"Look where I'm pointing, it's there, near the upper neck tier where I'm anointing… look nuh."

"Where? I still can't see anything there."

"There, look, man, somewhere under the cloth of some sort of chest gear that…" "Oh, I see."

"Finally, soon I'll be free." Meanwhile, every day, Joey types of fellow… shipping people slightly. Slipped one-handed onto the slowly weeping knives of the knights, like me, and were always just on the verge of a breakthrough from the sellers' plight. As seen through dry yeye pickney dem, those children who are there even now, rubbing their hands across their sleepy eyes and picking a fight with my children and my eye to blow-wow, along with you and yours too, my friend, remember how?"

"No, I don't, but could it be so?"

"Well, it's for you to find out, and me to know. One way or the other, though, he's still my brother, so that's why I've got to be here even now, trying to find the right way to say and do the things I've got to do properly to blow wow. To, you know, like, to get us all to go through and side-step the noose, and that includes him too, no? It's like, they were getting closer to being the sellers of cell phones to call her."

"Really?"

"Yes, they were. Yuh feel me?"

"Yes, but, but did they get through to them at all, though?"

"Of course, they did, because somebody would have told me that they'd wanted to call her before — "Where, where was she at the time, down home?"

"Well, perhaps, I'm not altogether home now and sitting on the rats' packed throne there to be sure of that fact. But somebody wanted to give one of those things to her to give to you on the swap super. Which never came through as the said seller fellow would have preferred it to do, Sir. Because as soon as he reaches out his anxious fingers to grab a supporting role on such things as the dice lick flickers upon his dinner, 'blibbling,' came the ringing sin ting, or something."

"What was it, the phone?"

"No, not that sort, alone. But something else that was made more at home with the shelf, more or less like that nasty wart itself, a piece of work of some sort, it was... It was the fork dropping out of his finger-gripping grasp. "Ring!" Oh, mi blow cloth, I mean, my kerchief. There it goes again. I wonder why it's so smart. Why is it so hell-bent on falling when..."

"When what, what's going on with you up top? Are you going crazy, or not? You're not wearing your stinking thinking cap, tin man. C'mon."

"You know, you may be right, but then again, it's not when, but from. The thing was falling from the other thing holding him back on, and in his hand was the strap, um."

"Looking for what?"

"Ways, I guess?"

"Yes, it's got to be that."

"Yes." Looking for ways and means for far too long, because somebody was always itching to go off on putting on the whips. That was when the darned thing just slipped out of his grasping grips, just like that shilling over there, and this. Some new crisis or another dice-lick just happened to pop up out of the blue Lagoon, dead abyss. Just like a dagger ring blabber-mouthed chick's bladder, again, to lick dung the brother's lickerish ton of tongues, good and properly, amen. Just like this one side dead pain, such a shame, even. Which was what slapped the harshest of setback king spell upon you and him to...

"To what, to go and sell to the rest of them in the packet crew?"

"No. Well, perhaps. Could have been intended for that, or some other kind of bad luck e-pot, but... Wanted to send it off to the next Bidened bidding newcomer coming into the coin slot, overcoming a late come... her beginner spot. Coming in to unpack, you know, instead of the "ring" thing you and he'd wanted him to bring, or to the rest of them to send it in. Those who (as it turned out) could scarcely even find a pocketing dime to talk about. Or even to go out and spend buying the thyme, shout, yes."

"Hallelujah!"

"Well, I guess, I'll give that much to y'all." The people wanted answers, so that was what they got from her. Whether or not it was a workable one, Sir, it was, in fact, a Hamster. "Look at it, there, isn't it cute?"

"I swear! Yes,"

"Yes, yes, it is, my yute man pickney dear." But to be fair. It wasn't clear: To many, it seemed feasible, like what they had promised to give him and you, despite the spike in the wheels, too. The one that is much too tight for your walking shoe, so. The plan was then set in come...

Motion, for them to go out and overcome B Leigh Ocean. Come on and sing us some songs of the pee on no man. Like, like, to get them to overcome their unyielding devotion to one, trying to get some. It was so designed for all the world's people, pop, Hugh Layshun, and growth hormones, to come together on oat (or none) and then go back out. To go work, king towards a common feathery goal-laden golden feathered plan, yes, yes, mi bredda brother man. Some were to be paid to get the lay and packed cram to perform this one act. Others had to pay them for the falsely alarming clock at the outstation. "What?" That one was preferred, oh, over any other one door ring command, so — "Reasonable enough, no?"

"No."

"Well, pack up your things and go on, continue walking slowly, because — "I know, I know, no need to show me up and out, I know that direction, so carry on with your talk, king show."

"Okay, I will." The leaders and elders of each nation stood tough. "Rough enough?" Yes, so they thought. Standing up strong on the easiest seller selling the plans in the form of a shovel of shifting sand, well, perhaps. Quickly shifting from the rough to land, 'Ding' on your handling and harming your arm, Hingh. Just like that mandolin and this one, darling."

"What, the shining shilling?"

"Yes, slick, slightly unsightly givers appeared to be willing to give it to her, so. They formed together in alliances with the weather, and those others they'd called to get the piston," yes, mi Breda. Got together with everyone so that they could get their handles on. Like, like this man over here and that one, those who thought that they were brothers, having all things in common, but that one was badda, I mean, worse than the other brother, that's why they'd bothered. That's why they went with them and you to go hitch a ride on us and get on through the border, in comfort.

"But of course, as was the usual, the most."

"Yes, the political class, unlike the rest of us (the lost), wasn't going through the iron cast, not on the bus with us towards this time of loss. No, not with her always asking the king too many questions about the ask, nor were they ever going to be found left out of the acting ax man with his one act to perform. Not even those sad asses, as these two men over here with their two axes to compare and send to you, clear off the arm. So, they too went and signed a packed queue, just like this, to whack, guess who?"

"E-ewe!"

"I know, I know, 'me too.' That was what I said when at first I heard it coming from you, mi Breda." Regularly, they were to meet up in a tiny, far-away hot hut on the back of a truck, to organize and plan the re-construct...shun. The other sadder fellow, not knowing enough to have known any better, or even that one.

"What, the we — "Yes, the weather." That was why he was always coming up the back side wetter than wet and running together, to get her... Running off his mouth to make others laugh hahahahaa for nuttn but nothing, well, for a while. While gathering the straw for his dying as a child, chatting off his mouthful of talks to make others laugh with them, and going wild. For a while, things went well enough, yes, my child.

"Now. Nuh mek mi haffi cuss, enough of that style ah yard mi cum fram fuss. Stop it before you're overly spoiled and..."

"Okay. What can I say, Mom?"

But there was another plan hidden somewhere in the pan tea ponder.

"Hear that? The brother man just kept talking, over and under me."

"...Known by one and allowed via some chatterboxes' suss to the rest of his clan, and such." But now, the clan is down to one because of the mashallah that was brought on. The rest of the goners from that corner are all gone off to somewhere or another, now, in the minds of those few left in command over there, wow!" Look, it's all signed, sealed, and delivered, somehow. Well, so they thought. But, it wasn't like that, a blow-wow, there was a crack in the sack box. Because they weren't that smart to have known the facts that there were many others left locked up somewhere under the sand ore, somewhere out there in a far corner of the Kingsland, or… I, I think they are, you know, like… Those who were calmer than this one door ring one here, and who're still lurking somewhere out there, at least one of them was cool, calm, and collected. Or… no, leave it right there where the rest is, beware. Because look, there they are. The two of them came together with the rest of the men to make up the work-shirking pair of walking shoes in the car. If nothing else on which to muse and giggle with "har," I mean, her.

"No, not so. Please, separate them and tell the truth-oh."

"Ugh, well, listen up as we now tell the rest to the youths in the waste in deeds, no?" "Yes."

There were too many of them, like those groups of coots among the youths. Group number one was from among the morons. Group member two has one of their own, walking out in front of you, on both sides of your arms. Somebody would have known the new sounding gear of hews, coming on stream without the proper Mic crow chip fuse as used from a long time down the home spheres to get the hang of it, and hanging on, yes. There, even. Somebody knew that these moronic few could be made liable and become somewhat reliable. "Such 'someone' had the manpower to make it happen," they said, and didn't she? "Yes." So, they were made able-bodied. Able to understand the fabled daddy, like. They quickly learned how to take command from the other men's Superman, coming to the weak weekly on "tell E-vision." But as time went on, someone came home, and the rest are now getting themselves known. Getting ready to be made known, too, are the others over there with Hugh, wearing his lone shoe. So now, since he knew that the real power base was really in command, it wasn't long before they too caught on. That was the real, reasoned-out plan, for however long. It was so designed to let them go through the wrong rung by rung, but they were to live on. Among a few of the other men, and this one. *"Mango see dung."*

That's what I heard someone say as I was about to walk away and go home. Or something sounding a lot like that sound, but...

Those were never to be among the goners in the van, farmers. This they, or somebody else one day, like, from among themselves or even someone else from far away, had decided upon, okay? Yes, in the minds of a select few of the ones in the van-former this time. Yes, yes, the bull bucking ram forming faulty kinds of minds had also signed in. But for the most part, those sorts were of no threat to them from the start, so that is why I'm in. I was there amongst them from the beginning, so they could just as easily have gone out and done me in, you know. But they did not, so that is where I'm at. The remaining few, too, were no threat to them when they were starting life anew, like how things would have turned out with you. Hence, the plan to save for them and us, the bounce back day when...

The bulk of those people were drugged and laid away, starting with little children; okay? Children who were stolen away from the field of play, while their parents worried and pined away. "Bring back our children home," they say. But, how did they come to fall so hard upon such bad luck chords? With the made-up thing from the doctor's cup, Hingh?

"Oh lord! Could they sing?"

"Perhaps, I don't know this as a fact, so don't go about quoting me on that. But now, take a sup out of that, drink, drink. Drink it up, Shrink."

Contrary to the way the real winners would have planned and reasoned out things in getting to win the Stan Leigh Cup. This was designed for them to wait out the switching-over phase-out time to get up and out. Yes, the switch over time, you know."

"No doubt, Hingh, now go."

...Which the good deed doers of those days, smoother than we were when... But they were there planning it better and implementing it for everyone and whoever else... Yes, the coming phase should be here in the coming days; it will soon come running into the sun to meet upon the coming better ways. This was made (supposedly so) possible when the planner's plan was to come down on some in a whispered shout, and a clenched fist pump "ping" at the air, without...

"What, without what?"

"Yes, that, look outside and listen, haven't you heard it yet?" It's still sounding off just as it was heard boasting with talks there above his mouth that year.

"Yes?"

"Yes, yes, mi Breda dear, like you'd guessed on a pat upon the romped-up backside of the desert as I'd supposed and said this to the scout out there and lied," just like you already know, I never do. Besides, I was busily ramping about with the kittens in the garden outside the house. That was when the son came out and scared away the mouse. So, I'm sure you know that it wasn't me who fist him good and proper, Leigh. But the chest, too, was bashed in..."

"By him, I'd supposed, yes?"

"Yes, not me." It was somebody else who'd punched him good and proper. Punching at the chest too was his papa, yes, he was, the "show-off" that he was, and whispering it out, "Yes! Phew," was what they did next. "Woo, this is good," he said. The wolf whistle came through from the brotherhood next, Ned. Then, the next thing to be heard from them was this G-string bungee cord, "come on through. Come on through, oh my Lord," they said, as it was heard coming from the headship of his brothers in the hood of his kindred in the yard. The next move from the house was to go out and medicate all of them, those "Nonesuch" the most. Or everyone of those with you over there, as I'd supposed. Did it with medicines that they were never able to understand the coded dose, ever. Even after those who were amongst the creators of the medicated plague for safer safety, for many were to be found stuffed away under the other sandy clay, Sir. With the rest of the planners in the plan. Say "Sure."

"Sure."

Thanks, now, move along for more, up in ranks, because, unlike you, those over there were the naysayers, not you. Those who weren't going to get the biggest bang for their "realest" players. Those no-never-coming-back ones there, toeing the way to get gone, clear. Some with their eyes openly eying the flashers on the wagon, beware. Of drunk driving, if nothing else, because... Still going are those flashers, in the on position proper, and blinking their way along in the refrigerated corpse-carrying van, Papa. But there was another plan, remember? Now, all of the planners of those other plans, as it stands, are goners, except this oner and his doggone lover — "How did it get so far pushed over on them?"

"We'll tell you somewhere nearer than you, to the end, if something isn't to be amended dead, or alive."

One piece of the puzzle is missing from the board-up nozzle within the game over yonder shoulder ring. The key, of course, the one that was left somewhere still stuck away with the beholder, not me, I'm short, down to your shoulder. Nor with you and yours, until you're older, perhaps. He still doesn't know where to go to find the beastly keyed-up forks of gold. The only one that is designed to... to, you know. To open up the chamber beneath the sea, of sorts, so I'm told, yes, it's there under heat. That was where he wanted so much to beat, to be fair, because... Somebody had passed on the key to someone else just before closing their eyeing and dying on the day of the big kill-off. Yes, they'd packed their most prized possessions in a tank U can and tossed it into the sea with them because. Someone from among them must have thought it through and figured out a way to get them cured on your asked, favors. The sea was where they D side... dead was best, for sure. Because that's just as much a perfect restart happening spot as nearer to the husk of dust, where all the rest of the calmer kinds of stuff are stuffed away now. Stiff as this, look nuh, look nuh, and still fast asleep to blow wow.

"But, but, how did they do it?"

"That's not fair, don't ask me to go through the ship just to get you into it, go over there, and ask them."

"I know, I know, they already gave me an answer to that one, but it's not clear."

"Well, beware," he still believes that he can complete the feat without it, like eating, yes, without the key. That's why I agreed to bring them with meat, so to speak. So that, no matter how hard he may look, he still will not get to see it, yes, the cook. You already know that he likes to be with that and this. But, somehow, only one person has the key. I'm certain it's he, no, don't tell him it's me, nor she, yes, that would be "her." That same one who is over there pointing back at me, trying to lie her way out of the certain tea. She's the girl who's got a date with Leigh. So he will soon be able to unlock it, yes, the locket, without the key in your pocket, or will he? Yes, yes, that's it, Leigh is quite a lock, it... picker of pockets, go do your practice; perhaps you, too, will grasp it. Like, the pick for the keyed-up lock of his, that Dickson, dick of a son. It will remain as recommended; "Dead" as it is. Unless he can find a good old locksmith or the master key that is locked in it. That's the only thing that is going to enable the lively comeback kick, but... "Sausage, where's the sausage? *Mi rawtid*! You really expect me to eat it like that, and this? With not even so much as a little cat supper on top of it? Man, how could you?" Anyway, let's carry on through it that way. As I was saying, and still want Ted to say.

I agree, she can still see, and now she wants to go over there to the washroom to go and take a p...p at deep peeping in the lavatory. Yes, man, to try and see if she can reconnect me with her lost certain tea of ten thousand teeth that she'd taken with biscuits this morning over tea.

"Really?"

"Yes, oh yes, that's correct, and that is why Mister Robby Sly, no more 'guess,' unless it's on eyeglasses for your headrest. Or perhaps the other cap for your odd dress, like, that one can't do. Unless you're still Stone drunk and slower than I'd already pronounced her on your... as is, yes. Why would I even lie, though? Pay attention, manly guy, come on, let's go. Don't be shy, because..." As you already know, that person was then tucked away with the rest of them under the sea. She's the only one who can go get the reviver fixer-upper kit with it. Yes, with the key from somewhere or another for me, just to fit the proper fee. Even if it must come from somebody, like your brother, probably, not me, nor she, but if needs be. The same long-lost key for the locket in the sea, down under the deep bottom-ish, go get it for meat... I mean me. So that I'll be able-bodied enough to make good on the promise to revive her and fix her upper tricks good and proper, for me, and all of us, on this. But so far, tough luck, my star.

The aircraft had dropped them off out there in a deserted place near the park.

"Where?"

"There, on the sharp end of the fork." Well, in truth, it was of no further use to the dog and them up there in the booth of a cockpit where they were and scared the thin lining sheet out of their boots, you know them, no? That Dedimus and Sheamus were a pair of friendly pop e-dog shows in the gamehouse, and would have continued until the very end, no? Yes, man, except? They were all together there and flying high through the air, like a bird of prey her, I hear. "High up in the air and vying for..."

"Well, something. The aircraft flying show, you know, had to let it all go and drop them on the wrong end of the domino, after it ran out of fuel and was on a nosedive down, and in. Hastening along on the way to go and take a plunge into thriving at skydiving through the air ring and into the canyon's columns and high rising. Yes, there. Dedimus came away from there the worse for wear and never got back firmly on his feet again to walk the squares. The parachute, though, was cute, so, like, so to speak. As well as the bitch of a stiff stick he was walking with. It too was slick enough to fit into that slot, and this. It was made to suit such mishaps as that, and so, somebody had to react. "Go, quick, get me that sack," he said to the cat. She was quicker than the tractor getting into the Wicker React her.

"Which cat was that?"

"Ugh, well. No, it wasn't that sort really, but I'm glad you'd asked, Neily. Shows that your attention is on the top chart, knocking those four Knight Ted beetle bugs off the slot to take up the next first number one spot, but no. It wasn't so. It was the same Sheamus' unashamed but very well-trained doggy bitch of a pup, that same one over there with her spotted coat running from under the ear and up, now sitting on the tarmac, shut up. She was made able, and quickly learned how to chat up a regurgitating talk king staple. Well, not quite, she would have known how to do this from way back then."

"From... from when?"

"Then, yeah, man, from way back as a matter of fact. She was quick enough to come back with the stuff in the backpack, Justin Thyme for that."

"For what?"

"Like, for them to have been able to skip the metal lick scraps with the said batch of luggage and get the little bitch of a doggy pup strapped to the backpack. She handed it off to the half-lame one, who then packed it tightly in and strapped it down tightly on top of the layman's back before it hit the rocky desert Ted floor; 'Braga-dap-dap dap,' and burst into a flaming fire bawling uproar just like that, and much, much more than before. Like, oh, man. It was such a massive, raging, flaming puff of smoke that I almost choked on the swallow flying down my throat. Big enough to have been seen from afar off and out, if any human's eyes were still able to spy and watch falling chips ditch the skies..."

"Uphill? Come on, don't lie."

"Ugh, yes, Will, nice try, but no, it wasn't yours to ignore, nor mine. They would have been surprised at what was to come, hitting hard at their side-eyes at the bottom that time. "Until?" Doggone doggy bitch was really cute and sniffed. Came over to the man with a salute, like this. "Hey," she said, "this should be a better option, okay, 'mi bred?'" The parachute was, at the time, stuffed in the pan of mine, no, not mine, but that doggy pup's of Sheamus, going from swinging to and from, swinging while hanging on to a pawed up jerky head for a hand (me down on the bus). Carrying the sack along, you know, towards home. Yes, she was the one doing it like so. Jerking her eager, up-uppity, purposeful face in the wrong, like so, my clown. To continue the song "...to, to get us from here to go there."

The puffed-up windy thing was there and hanging onto every word of theirs and hers, so it would have seemed, as it occurred. As she was heard swearing on the sayings about how it would have occurred to him when she said this to the Sheamus show and them. Look, somebody's now weeping a tear, like so. Weep! Yes. It's to you I now speak. Yeah, man, that's it. Yes, the parachute-puffed-up bitch of a brute not only could shoot but but, but... Did I tell you the truth? Did I tell you about that foot in her boot?

"No, you didn't, but I already know all about that pop e-show biz suit, so..."

"Okay, I'll tell you some more later when your... but, but until then, let me continue to explain." She'd learned how to dilute a speech for a whole week. But none of them were told anything about this, until the belated switch when she was forced out of it with Sheamus' head spinning around him quickly, to lock faces up with the talking bits of canine chips Lii. Then, upon a gasping backflip, men and bitch skipped the ditch on a swing with strings, before the canyon floor came up to meet them.

"Still in?"

"No, that's the last thing they would have wanted; that was why they had to skip the darn thing, Mass Kidd." Yeah, man, that's what was about to happen, but the dog would have saved them by heroic acts from Mount Haven, yes, there. They were, soon afterward, after the dog's talk was showing that her gods had heard her words that came hitting up against their earring chords. That was when the chat stopped just as quickly and quietly as if it had never occurred or happened at all. They were then seen footing it quickly, to the already opened door for the ditch, Leigh, and now, pinch me, like this. "Whoa! man, that hurts." Yes, it was so.

"Oh, sheet! no."

"No? Go ahead and say so if you want to... But as said before, and as was heard coming to my ear in the doorway of the fish store, and running off with you a little bit more, on soft shoe, it was so. "No risk or?" "No." Now, look, on their way they went on to go, doggy and them. Toeing a deserted track to go meet up with them."

"Who? To go and meet up with who?"

"With whom? With the jungle tribe, oh, yes, that's who."

"You mean...?"

"Yes, that's who I'm talking to, not you. Those he knew were living there before. 'Hopefully,' he'd said a day or two before. Hopefully, they are still there, and more poorly prepared than before." Sure, that would be the preferred outcome to score. "But, preserved to survive and still to be found alive, for a while yet, at least. Fair and cure, too, even as fair as they were before last..."

"What?"

"Who just said, 'What?'"

"I did, before last what?"

"Last that, as in, year. Like, these past tough luck years, as a matter of fact, when last they were to meet me up there on the warpath, at the corner down the avenue."

"Where?"

"Down there where I'll be patiently waiting for you, otherwise, up, like. Up there, I suppose?"

"In Heaven?"

"Yes, there, you've got that one square on the nose, my dear friend, for once, you're forgiven." That would have been his thinking, though. Yes, he knew about them from somewhere, about the first time when those tribal warriors were to be tricked and shortchanged out of their fox terriers' hunting games. The trophies they'd claimed, winning the names, too, were also taken away from them and given to you, no? But then again, short is what they have been ever since, even as short as those pygmies over there in the sinks. Get your water and drink, Skink, then leave from around the precinct. Yes, please, thank you.

9

He Raised Me

"He used to be my right-hand person," he said, "we did the heavy lifting together, you know what I mean, the hard stuff. I lifted him high enough to become number one, just by doing what we were, like, spinning away at the wheels on the right-hand side. Working things out with the highly sophisticated mind, and stout... Ours were the ultra-abled brands, you know, no doubt. He was numbered among the mightiest in the land, for a time. Too short a time, though it might have been, but now... ugh!"

He paused and swallowed hard, while shifting his sack-eyed looking gaze around to the Essence-ward. At the dog, you know. He was trying to explain it all away to the dog like so, I'd say. Like, telling her why things went the way they went to sway the ski board that day, why he had to push so hard at the last-minute sword to send his old friends away, bored. Not much was said about the "how" part of the pushing sort, though. Like, how he'd managed to get it done, no.

"Oh well," he said, while rubbing away rigorously at the dog's stretched-out head, still lying where it was; center-staged between lying down front pawed legs, pillows they were for her weary head. "We'll find a way, I'm sure," he finished the small talk and closed the door, banging up, upon doggy's shot at reverting it and reverting to the sleep-faking snore shut up. ".."

"Or was it, like, wasn't it, of the holey tracks that were to be left from the boring card?"

"No, but then again, what the heck. Let's reconnect."

He'd squeezed out this spoken joke as a whispered grungy pushup, heaving upward on both, well, on the left hand mostly, note, not that much on the right one, Boasey. The right-handed stick on the other side of the kick was pulling him further upward to stand upright with it. Yeah, man, that trusted writing pad of his. That said, the helpmate companion of a right-handed stick was really hip. It then (gradually) straightened him out good and proper to go and stand up to his permanent hunch-backed standing position, and prop her up... you know. Like, as it would be said when one is desirous of saying it properly. Catch the drift on this side of me? Yeah, that's it, just like that, Leigh, and this.

"Damn right," he said, nearer to the end of him, when he was a wee bit older than she and parting off to bed. The dog lifted her head and looked up at him with dread, then put it back down again on the pillow far away from his bed. That final push did much more damage than Sheamus had planned for Sam Midge, you know. Well, the push to secure for the man his victories as planned, not the one up from the grounded seat to upright knees where he now stands, on tall toes. That's why Shae was left with no other way than to give up his pay to go away, dragging Dedimus, his friend, around with him on Sam's one hopping wooden leg below his kid's knee. Since there hardly seemed to be anything else going on around those parts of the peer by then, *mi pickney*, oh yes, yes, my child. Oh, my lord, forgive me for being this wild. Yes, yes, I agree, I'm a bit spoiled, but... They destroyed everything in so doing, including the food storage bins. The dog didn't respond much to him at all, just rolled the lid off one half-opened eyeball and cast a grudging glance at him, hard. Doggy would much rather get some sweet shut-eye sleep again. Lying comfy on the barb in the yard, amen. Since there hardly seemed to be anything else going on around these parts of late, oh, my Lord, wait... Nothing other than for a seemingly purposeless walk, king, and then stop, Hingh. Just as fast things are known to happen (or slow), like dragging the feet, heels, and toes. They were going nowhere in particular, though, as seen through the eyes of the puppy dog show. Nowhere other than to go meet up with the caravan (of love), yes, and so, we were to be seen stopping now, and then, you know them. Trying to follow a path away from the open gate in the known direction towards the home end, as it states.

"That's all we ever get to see and do around here of late, my friend," said the dog to herself and them.

"But that's about it for them and you, no?"

"Yes." Essence, the proper and proud dog has got her fill of that sort of discorded pop e-show nearer than the elder head to the elbow, and is now running on little more than an empty polish to a shining pot of sort head out chows. Downright deflated and flat, is she. Hanging around here on these empty and recently parched-out barren spots of flies and fleas. She would do well with a bone or two. A real doggy bone for him and you. Like, not those kinds that are lying around under swarms of flies and their buzzing sounds, but, like, those she was accustomed to having back home on which to nibble and chew. One with a dash of marrow somewhere in the narrow, yes, there. As some kind of score somewhere within the board for them to eat up and share. Or just for her alone at this point, who the heck cares? "Just put it where the beloved juicy marrow used to be stored in sorrow," she'd said. "Whether borrowed from the wings of a sparrow or scored before there should come tomorrow, mi bred." Yes, put it there, even if it weighs a ton. Not as dry and tasteless a bone, though, as the one she had been nibbling away on of late shows, while the last vestiges of her strength slowly seep off the plate, and out of her den. That's why the dog didn't want to respond to his talking front end anymore. Nor to carry on with it any further, through the wide-open door. The dry bone, though, was on a walking plan for her plated shoulder ring-less hand me down to the toe, as if wanting to hand me down to the toe-toe, yeah man, that one. "That's what kept her talking on?" "Well, one of them was doing the talk, King. As for the other half-skinned thing, like…"

"Who, you mean, her?"

"Yes, not him, not Dedimus, the king, nor that shameless lump of a no-walking mess as it occurred, but her. She wasn't. She'd yawned at that thing and shut down on him. But that was what got us talking the first time, Hingh, remember? She wasn't planning on carrying on any further with Norm, I mean, none, not with any of them, another step toward the forwarding ship harbor landing span, you know."

"No, I don't, but…"

"Yes, I understand, I'll tell you the rest, though."

They had earned a welcoming drink of dirty, disgusting something Sin Ting from the sink at this latest running away from a watery stream of not so clear as Chrystal brawta. Coming to them in the form of thirst-quenching water, and then waiting out their remaining fistful of faith without another. Waited so long there that they ended up losing a brother. Well, they were waiting and hoping that he would feel a bit better, but — "Wait, is that the gate?"

"No, it's not, but it's not what we're talking about this time, fake ape, get back to the track."

"No, you can't force me to do anything I don't feel like doing?"

"No, not yet, Sue Hingh, but… Let's get back to the subject on the firing lineup, Jack Kette, that you're in then, because…" She was anticipating another, among such others, like a bit more loyalty from this other one-door ring brother first, for instance, wink-wink, at the drink bumps, and like, what dates next. Yes, to go along with the fruit cake on the plates, you know, yes. Like, she wanted something sweet for her sweetest tooth to eat. While waiting to see what perils, for goodness' sake, Aunt Beryl, or bad nest, you know, if you prefer, but don't none of them got it get yet, because… She was wondering about that, and this, like, what perils would come after this date, but so far, so good. None of such pending disasters, as could.

They had lingered a bit too long, Gord, sitting there and thereafter on the gourd, and ever since, oh *mi lawd*. As seen through doggy's opinionated eyes, questioning, "What for, for formatting? What are we waiting for here, what? For a wad of steak to fall from the sky upstate and onto our dirty plate, perhaps?" Sorry, she meant to say, place, upon our dirty plate, placed here on this grounded spot.

They didn't plan to wipe out the whole worldly fam in truth, as old scouts would sometimes do it to the youths. But there was a fluke thrown into the pan, coot, and out came the salute, from guess who? Then came the saboteurs' boot, kicking off the sabotage of the scouted youths of the truth. Just for the record, booting out the rusty tooth from the secured place where it was written in the book and placing it in a glue gun. Well, if you must know the truth, why not come? I guess you're going to want to hear more about that wild pack of bad as your... Those who were numbered amongst those who were sent out to look at you, first, and found out that you were cursed. Now, from amongst some other ones come these two, of course. Started out coming in amongst their friends, who were just the same as us and them. Those who didn't make it to the end, sitting comfy on the stone ends, went to work whipping up the cure from the curse until they ended up with the end; worse."

"Where, in the back of the hearse?"

"But of course, what else did you expect from their works?" All except the remaining pained few went the way of the curse. Or at the blades of others who, like them, were just doing their work, but this much, they never knew. Well, there may yet be others of those young fighting brothers left out there somewhere, that's the hope for the Sheamus and friend pair. See them walking there? Look, they're the very ones who were, a moment ago, seen sitting right over there with him on the starvation square, beside the deadling, still lying there. But that's where they are going now, footing it bare.

"Wow! You mean, to the square, like, to starve—"No, no, not to starvation square again, they've already been there..."

"Where then, in heaven?"

"Yes, say, amen."

"Amen."

Yeah, man, that's the game, rolling on. Essence was wondering about that, and much more, but as for Sheamus, he knew he must move along on foot. No point in sitting around on this barren patch of land, dead nook, with the now, clearly dead Dedimus, and mourning over the mound. That's not going to spell "Good" for anyone. Nor should they linger any longer, Gord, sit, sit, sit down. Thank you, man, now. "Since there's still breath left in the nostrils, what the heck, Syl, pay attention." He would have been there thinking things like this to himself and his self-will, yes, my friend's son. As she kept on listening to him and his talking and asking such disheveled questions as last things, coming to him then, and now, to us; as if they were bubbling Questy Onion Rings, rolling off her head's frontal siding. Mi blow wow! "Am I in...?" she asked, again, "am I alive? I am still alive, right?"

"Yes," this was what I thought I heard when she said it to the blue side of his head, and confessed, my girl. Based on the evidence-based hair in my high-risk iris, "I guess we are." Well, as seen from this side of confronting my eyes near the head, where I continue to chase her friend's chicks around the bed to go ask her for a fist to beg, but... "Perhaps the killers have lost the will."

"Which one?" Asked someone, "Yuh mean the...?" Pointing.

"Yes, that one, the will to kill William Bill. Boy, come on."

"Look," he said after the pausing paws got much too long for her claws resting on the bed. The pause he'd caused them, you know, was long. But he was willingly waiting on the dog too, because he knew it was hard on her walking foot in his shoe. "We'd better get moving along, girl," he said further on, "so, come along. Come along." He said this while waving his arm at the way up ahead, yes, as if it was a Rasta-man tam-tam to go along with the kette drums to beg... he was beating on. "One thing is for sure, though..." He picked up again his talk king song slowly, like so. "Whichever way the guessing should go, this right here is not the type of guy fellow square..."

"No?"

"No, I'm not one of those, not the kind who is about to go helping the swine killers out any time soon. I'm not going to help them any more than you, scout fellow stout and fine... Not like you were when singing the blues over the guitar with wine, doubt?"

Look, look at you, stop gazing around, man, and pay attention. Now, look back at me, look near to my mouth, and see if you won't agree with this one golden tooth in my plated mouth full of teeth I'm wasting on... you. If I'm going to die and fly away in the diamond to the sky. He has got to shake me down with everything he's got on first try, or with whatever else he may be able to spy within him, and I? As for me. I'm going to dye it while living, you see, in such situations, stations, and giving a given key. Or I'll fight as hard as hell to one-up his sword to sell, even to quell the hell out of his tiny cell as the last thing before he hears the final bell ring: Bang.

"Hey, man, go easy on the eardrums, oh man." (Rubbing his palm now over his eardrum).

So, "Come along, child," he said again to the dog's half-opened eyes aching with pain, now multiplied a thousand-fold by the loss of their old friend Dedimus, whom he didn't bother to lift a shovelfull of dust to try and cover up. "After all," he'd said, "he's just another corpse lying around near the waterfall on his dirty bed." After weighing down his handful of remaining precious crown possession bulls on a strenuous upward pull, and after adding the kingpins he'd pulled out of them on him, hard, he — "Oh, lord. You mean he, he pulled those chains and other such precious things out of the people?"

"No, you Idi Hut, go, out of the drawers near the bang gut, to beat you." The gold chains on his neck, too, were another thing he had to do, and then... When he was done doing those things to me and you, lonesome hen, he smoothly swiped his right writing hand over them, yes, those same sparkling shiny arm string Hingh sin ting things that are now hanging over the shirt dirty and blue like him, and you singing the blues, with stain. Then leaning in and heaving himself, hitched and hanged up against it, he — "What, against what?"

"Against his piece of walking sticky prop lick king stick that he's about to strike someone like you with. Look at it, it's still there, isn't it?"

"Yeah, I can sheet, I mean, seit. I can see it."

"Good, it's right there on his shoulders where he'd hung the wrong end of it, the fold-up hammock you know, witch it, I mean, watch it, watch it, mind you step on it. Yes, that's it, the coal fire that is about to burn out the brier under your feet like an old tire to light up and heat..." Right there nearer to that spit in the white-collar slit was where he'd hung it, still as white as sheet. Though it's not as sweet anymore, certainly, not as that piece of cake, "oh sheet wait, gimmie a piece."

"No, aren't you on a diet?"

"No, not on a diet anymore, I've got to grab a slice or two of this before..."

"Before what?"

"Before you gulp it all down by yourself without even offering me some." Now, though, let's get back to the sum, with a drink of water... Gulp. It's surely not as white as it was before, you, Miss Shirley Core. Surely, not as white-ish as the metal zippering slip, "Oh sheet, what's this?" he said. "How long have you been hanging out there and looking ahead?"

He'd asked this wide-eyed and gazing downward with dried-up dreadlocks up in his eyes. This would have happened while he was gazing downward to spit, as often as I. That was when he saw it, open. Both of us at the same time inclined TikTok tied-in, near-the-clock ties end, like a token. It was as loud with the ticks as if in time with the rhythm. Mick clicked the clock, king ticks of the clock with the rhymes. Then add a squirt of lemon or lime, and hand it off to meat, me at the corner where... That was when he saw it. The flying fish it was, the one hanging from the swing there near the little bug of a zip her upholder of hers.

"Oh, no, wasn't it his?"

"One of those things, Mr. Holding, please, hold him tightly squeezed, because he saw it and panicked, so, don't blame him too much, guard dammit, no. Well, let's get back on track with the horses, yes, it was he who did that, not me, I'm the kid with the cat." I must have forgotten about that quickly, due to, um, the familiarity of it, do you know what I mean? "Yes." Yes, the fact that his three-finger jack of a right-handed grip was not yet grabbing a supporting role model upon it, but. The stick was favored over and above it, yes, the savior's wish, for you. Right up until this slip up of the eyelid, or two, because that's what I did, I mean, he. He grabbed it first and moved on to take hold of it, to carry on with the baggage of that and this. That alone was to be it, the thing that has been dragging him around of late, Keithy Mingh. Hungry to a stinking sick, and light weight like him at whom I'm pointing the stick, and Fitz, who's always fixing away at something. Hiss.

"The sun is really hot today, like, like, parchingly hot, I'd say." He said what he wanted to say to the dog, now walking away, yay. Right, you are, doggy pup, look at him there walk king by the wrong side of his right left thigh, Hingh, up. Oh my. Look, look at them.

"I can see that you're tired." That was what I heard before I was fired. But let's go back and listen to the lie-ads. "Look, they both turned and waved a sulking goodbye to the abandoned lay-by." Oh yes, that's why Mister Robby Sly Stone, who was drunk and slower than I. Come. Why would I even lie? Pay attention, manly guy, come on, come on, look. The dog's long, panting, wagging, water-dripping tongue is now bouncing him from a swinging position to a swung, upon a haunting blue-grass musical refrain from the little country band. Yeah man, listen on, again, and go on, go sing along to the same. Well, if you want to remain a person with a famous name. But look at them; the dog is hoofing on, on ends, as they too are trying to do a sing-along with friends like you, look.

One foot in front of the other now, they're walking along the ledge again, somehow. Togetherness for them of late has become a strained walking pace; that's why he was trying so hard to maintain speaking terms with the dog, in haste. He was kind of careful like that when it came to his doggy pup. The one he'd picked up at the scene of the sneak attack from way back, but. "It's kind of late already as it is now," he said and bowed his head. "They're all gone to bed to blow wow." Yes, all of them, even him, the lifeless friend at whom he was pointing. But he lied again, or at least, he was mistaken, because... As you already know, my friendly side-eyed guide is such a shame. Some were still there and busy on the square, slowly making themselves a bit busier on the way to go, nowhere. "Including him."

"That one over there peeping in on the square?"

"Yes, and many others at the far end of the path west, yes, beware. Out there, where they are headed now, and still walking like cows, slowly. Not so fast as to be parting with him, though, Leigh." No, not a chance of them parting with him that fast as with the thing at which he was pointing, like so, "I never thought..." Stop. He paused again and swallowed hard, while gazing off into the distant nook, *mi lawd*, yes, my lord. Looking off toward that, "Look at that... that was quick," he said. Way back in the distance is where the hissing sounds come from. Flying in on our hearing from the swarm of flies that are there and busily bouncing off and on. Flying the traps on the attack, my star studied the gear of a son, from back-a-yard. Busily buzzing, loud hissing, and hard, yes, yes, my cousin, Howard, can you not hear them? "I never thought..." stop again. He was trying hard to make conversation with the dog, walking slowly with him around the yard. That doggy pup is really hard, like, no joking. Like, a hard nut to crack at the pack of cards on winning a token, but he's also very smart, and that's what's wrong with the wretched small talk. Anything else would be your fault.

"No, oh no."

"Oh yes, don't even bother to argue with me and the rest on that talk king show, of chest. Cause I know the fox who keeps the records, and she's the best."

"The landscape up ahead is bare and void of the people in the yard square," I'd said and lit my cigar on his hides too (beware) or three of my eyes on the weevil before the bed wood comes bringing in the evil, as it was said then. The one behind us, too, eyed managed to say, when I said what I'd wanted to say, it was the wide-open and broad view. As far as in my fogged-up brainbox of such things, he knew. I mean, I... I knew. Those who used to walk there up until yesteryear, as seen in a doggy's kind of days, my dear, were all gone over to shack up with you on your terms up page, and soberly sorting out your homing rage and the clever. Or on whatever else at the time, he thought was good behavior. But now, look, "Oh! My savior." Essence's shoe caught up with Sheamus's foot, who...

"Who? Whose foot? What, huh, what, who are you talking to?"

"You mean, you mean, you just wander off in your thoughts and leave me here a loan, talking to myself without a sound? Come on, man, sit down and behave yourself, cool it down, as long as you're wearing kelp or whatever else. As I was saying to myself." Wink, wink. The shoe quickly caught up with Sheamus's foot, who was...

"Whose foot are you talking about, mi cous?"

"Why not ask him, that guy standing across from you and listening?"

"Okay, is it Sheamus'?"

"Yes, yes, that's his foot, the same one I was... was talking about." It belongs to him. He who knew himself what he must eventually do to help you out. Probably better judgment would have prevailed for him than you, and my head top would have felt it too, even then, such things I knew. She'd lingered as long as she needed to be in the nearer direction towards the Windsor landing span than you, "yuh syi mi?"

"Yes, man, I can still see you, carry on, carry on."

While counting on his counting fingers, three, hoping that better luck would bring her to me. Wanted to tally that thing up within her, you know, on him, even, but never on me. Or he could have been thinking that her better luck would rally up and backspur the fork out of it, yeah, I'm talking forth my myriads of chats about that essence of a doggy pup thing there, and this, he, yes, him, I swear. She'd lingered as long as she could, yes, Gord, my good hard friend from the schoolyard back door near the Holm wood. Trying to convince herself that he would, as said, and as you already knew what I'm about to say to you, and Ned, like, that he would go on and get ahead, of a head, or two. Trying to convince herself that he would go on and do the right thing all the way through. But all the evidence was suggesting that her once good, friendly boo, her master and best beastly buddy companion disaster..." "True. Can't deny that my yute."

Was he going to walk past her, and in the continuing direction faster than you, as was said in laughter? Walking on and away from her, still lying there on the cold ground, dead, spread that has lately become her bed at night? Rock Stone was her pillar, too, despite you. As everyone had guessed on the rites, and then left the left one there to bite... After casting a spell on you, with the ice. The cold brute of a trite that he is. The one that she leans on for child support, from, guess who? "No, such things I was never known to do, depending on which of those 'such things' you may choose to squeeze a husk off and get through the noose. Or at which of those ears on either side of the face you may direct your talking to."

"No surprise, coming from you, I guess," someone walking grudgingly beside him said, under his breath. Surely, he wasn't going to leave her there undressed, like, like... The dog turned around to look over the distance at... Then carried on carrying on with the question. "Would he? Is he going to? Like, leave me here with nothing left to eat or wear, and not even so much as to turn and look back over the left wing, and stare?" She was heard asking, or more like seen. She was seen asking these last things by way of those bubbling sin ting something, look, those bubbles that are still raising hell, and rising beside the outer face side of him, even now. "Is he going to? Would he do that to yuh? A piece of wood to work on the book." Yes, that was the asking without an answer, we got like sew so food feh goh cook mi man soup. Wow! What a mess, now, look for yourself and see. Go check out the facts for me. She was throwing her wonderful one-door ring-inquiring looks at him, the one at whom I'm pointing, she was looking at me too while asking, and them, anyone else that she could see, except him. She wasn't even looking at him anymore. That's why I had to tell her the rest of the score, and what to do next, as the right thing before... since she seemed to think I knew squat about such things.

"And more?"

"Yes." Well then, I'd guessed I had to continue faking those talks in Kingston of things as if answering her and him. When it comes to doggy's strained inquiry, as she will soon be passing by the quarry and asking me the same questions again, like. "Why me, why, why? Whoever spun and done in a friend like that... thing? Who is the person, and why is he in such a hurry to do his buddy a whacking? Did he hate me that much, Martin?" So wondered the wonderful wandering doggy pup, at her good luck now unprospered, on such. Now, though, she doesn't seem to want to wander along any longer than I am, I mean, anymore. Just use that door as an escape route out on the shore. Because she doesn't seem to want to wonder about that or go on wandering around with the bore. Not even sure about what you're saying anymore. Surely, not any longer than she was before me. Like, like, no longer to go along with her walking than she has to, like, walk alone with him. Yeah man, that thing of a tin man one there at whom she's directing her stare while shaking her shook up, uppity head spin. That one is preferred over any other, but him. So I would have heard it said of my brother when I heard them saying things about each other, for the first time. Like, when I'd first come and listened in and got to hear the brother's doggone lover kneeling, begging, and pleading. Surely, she was not going to be going along as she had been doing alongside that man there and him, or even this one over here who'd skipped out on the suffering. Suffice it to say.

"I'm scared." Essence's eyelids shut down to rawtid, so very hard on her window chord that it squeezed out a tearful squirt of the sheet on the orchids, I mean, eye tear like pee. Her mind by this belated time was all set on the road back home behind, but... Want to see more than what's on that sign? Well, "Look, look up at that 'Big Jill' of Seymore, isn't that a bit more?"

"Yes, yes, it is."

"Okay then, look at this through the back door and then place a bet to guess on the other quiz. See that one, too?"

"Yes, I see. What's happening to, to?"

"Look, man, look. Slowly, the gap is closing between them…"

"And me?"

"I'm sure that's what you're going to say, that you see, but no. Just between the dog and him," so that Sheamus was able to reach out and touch something as he was reaching out to rub the dog's head against the dumb thing, right there beside the nose, endgame. The game slot of snot that used to be there is now not. It's just about frozen somewhere off to, to, you know what.

"Yeah, man, frozen solid like these dried planting seeds of yours, no?"

"Yes." But he likes to be rubbed and squeezed. They both like it when he rubs a squeeze out of these. Like, like when he'd manage to lie about how old he was and squeeze his way through the doors and into that rub-a-dub jam session that was going on at the club. So, there he goes, rubbing out a rub-a-dub injection somewhere near the neck column, reassuringly so, I'd suppose, and thought spent the facts in a row, no? "No." Yes, yes, she said, and agreed to pay these debts, all the way to her deathbed. She seemed a bit revived now and going straight back to her thrifty ways of old, as she pulled her once low-hanging head astride a wobbling leg and said what she'd wanted to say to the beautiful one, and the bold, yes, there. Besides the man's weary-legged tare, it's now bouncing along in strides with the man's near rest part of the knee cloth on a keg with TikTok tides. Yes, he's wise; that of Sheamus', right there near his right left hand, dead swinging swing swung pair of the boastful risky watch on pride, pay attention, man. Watch, so that you won't run into anyone's crotch and crash while we're watching the wristwatch wide, well, only one of them is proud by this time and loud, but… He was seen showing off his wristwatch wider than the broadband fiber that was hanging there beside our… Yes, under his shoulder and screaming everything within him to report what time of day it was, prepare. But no one seemed to be listening, except the firebugs, look, there. At the same time, and in the daytime, it was glistening in the sun and up against the clouds. Otherwise, one may say, it was wide and unfair to the other brother's eyes over here, and his ears. He seemed as if he was just about willing and ready to break up the pair. Well, so it seemed to us over here.

"Although a bit surprised?"

"So I hear."

"I mean, I mean — "Yes, I already know how very mean you are, but give me my money before you hop back into the car, because..." The wristwatch was right there swinging forward and then backing up to go swing his wrist back again, and awkwardly, along, widely bare. Unfair to that one left lying alone by himself right there, who should have been making up the regular half of a pair. After which she, the doggy, not me, matched strides with her friend from over the yard end on the other campus side, dead-end tarmac, again, I swear. Somewhat like they used to do before the rancid rain came through to tear. Yes, my dear. Happened just before that strain of a saturating stream came showering down on you and them, "isn't that true, my friend?"

"No, it's not."

"No, you mean...?" Well, there they go anyhow, just as they used to do in the times of old, you know, the pain kind of... well, so I'm told. There they go, walking on like so. Look at them going, going to toe the way down to see a brand-new host on The Daily Show, in the east wing.

"If only we could fall upon a new source of energy, call though. That would be a whale of a lighter day on the great toe." Essence, yes, it was the dog who was thinking so. Look at those words like fuzzy bubbles rising from somewhere near her guzzler pothead engine beside the hearing aid and helping her spread it up and outward to gaze. Wider than my old schoolyard buddy's gap-toothed smile, from a long time gone to part our ways down the aisles. Onward and away he went from the early days while passing by me and all the rest of his friends' thick-headed, weary-legged tare to get there and see...

There they are again, heading off towards the car, to get started on the way to his Headley show afar."

"Where did he go? Where did he go?"

"I don't know, but?" Thought I just heard someone saying so in a whispered inquiry. "Well, perhaps they're trying to know by asking me. Did somebody tell him?"

"No, how could we when nobody around here knows?"

"But, but..." "Did you hear that?"

"What?"

"Didn't someone just ask the same question again?" Perhaps it is coming from afar, like, somewhere over there near the bend, out there over the lightning, thunder, and rain with the rainbow." "Yes, perhaps. Or from over in the other town square, no?"

"No, pops."

"Hoof!" She squeezed out a lazy bark like this: "hoof!" As if to say, there, look. At the same time, gazing off yet more into the distant nook, as before. Somewhere over there, yes, yet more. Way up ahead of the wide-open, plain glassy door. There's something out there, Essence is more than half sure, so. Beware of her.

10

Finding a Way Out

While the war lord's itchy fingers were busily rubbing up against the window on surfaces near the peripheries of the red power switch in Windsor...

"What, you mean, the real seat of power?"

"Yeah, man," that place where the beautiful windows are, was equipped with the full whack of an attack on the hind side of your thick head cup in the stir ring where she'd cried, "yuck! And... "When, you mean, when she'd cried for the cop, and then go and lied her face off?"

"Yeah, man. That was really the center, you already know this, I'm damn sure." Sheamus, though, as he knew he must, was busily plotting a comeback. Well, he was strategizing and planning how to quit the darn thing while it's hot, to get moving on in good time, to get out of there and be gone clean. Out of the house is what I mean, you know. Yes, while getting the biggest bang for his bucket list of spam sorts, coming to him off the programmed, scripted pea soup pots. "You do know what that is like, perhaps, mi pops, right?"

"Right."

"Like, the man wanted me to go and get the biggest part of his palm onto the bars of golden yarn, first."

"Oh, c'mon, you're tripping, man." *Curse!*

"No, I'm not, I'm just sharing the nay kid fox, but, yes, yeah man, I'm coming along with you as we walk on and chat." So, you might want to know, he would have won even more than that one.

"Which... which one?"

"Look nuh look nuh man. Mass Eddie was a wonderful man, and full of wonder in his charm, but, but, look, look at that one hanging there on regions of his calm swallowing tram line, yes, that's what we're basing these talk king on this time.

"Or is it off?"

"Like, off mine, yes? Perhaps, but... what's that, what's wrong? Cough, cough. Cough again, man, do it fast while I'm hitting your awesome back pain away, and from anywhere near this column of a framing stick of yours, okay?" Yeah, that's fine, you're all good to go now. Because it works every time in clearing the choked-up tram line away, anyway. On or off, you're going to be okay, because it's always good enough to knock the back part of your ask for a talking calf when you're choked up from talking too much while swallowing. Or from not chewing fast enough before you go about hollering.

"Enough of that, let's move on with the task of getting you masked. Yes, put it on before you even move a foot off the path," but for sure, look, such things are running now, out the door even. Running on the inside of somebody's neck down in there where lies more lies and going across town to get gone down the aisles for yet more wives, and even further, yes. Like, where he was injured, what the heck. While he was carrying along with them and their carryings-on, as if it was the norm, he was (at the same time) keeping a watchful eye on these things and sighing. As well as on other precious stony companions of the high ends, (clever little thing you, I'm crying), and all of your belongings too. Things he wanted to hang on him and bring along with them, to get them brought home, back to you. Yes, man, before heading out on the town some more, alone. Sheamus would have seen that sort of scene before, yes, he was sure. Because he was there at the first fight night, tallying up the scores. But now, look, that's him there, walking the road and slowing, but still, he has got to keep on moving."

"Where's he going?"

"How about dancing and singing, perhaps it's for that thing, Hingh, no? Or maybe...? No, it wasn't that so, forget about it lately. Oh, wait,

Leigh. Perhaps I should tell you about this, yeah! It's that important to the script, so here goes. Perhaps it was to go out shopping for...?"

"What, for what?"

"For that, like, food to take home to the pots."

"Like, for bones, He could use a loan, you know?"

"Yes, that's it, I B leave it was to the I V leagues for bones."

"Yeah, man, it was for that. Yes, Mr. Jones, you just hit the ball home with the bat. The dog has got to eat, you know."

There they are, going, the dog and he, slowly, trying to go and find what's left of those other far-away friends with no name known to them. He just says, "Hey there, my friend," whenever he runs into them, but still. He wanted to even up the score with Essence, his friend on tour, that's why the walking shoes are now hanging behind his..."

"What, his back door?"

"Yes, cute! Cute, I'm sure, but no. It's swinging from his crooked stick on his poor shoulder, back heavily laden to a sick... On the bent crooked end of it." Yes, at the end of his walking stick is where he likes to carry it. "Look." Out into the hopeful village they go. Look at them, they're headed there now, searching for — "Hoof, hoof." "Mi blow-wow! What, what just happened?"

"Listen up now, no problem, just yardie sin thing aggen." Again, I heard her pain, "Oh, by the way! Did I tell you about how it happened that day? Like, did I tell you how he'd managed to lose his toe? I mean, finger, his proud finger from above the toe, I think I might have told you, though, no?"

"No, you did not."

"Well, listen up here, we're going to tell you the facts." So proud was he of his favorite finger ring key that he never misses out on a chance at showing it off his hand-me-down arms strung on the armchair in Windsor Park near the lawn to me, where — "Where is that?"

"Out where he used to walk..."

"Yes? Tell me more."

"Yes, just around the back there, is where he would sometimes walk and stare." He's always known to be pointing his nosy hnows nothing into other people's business affairs, and such things. But in another reality show, he didn't know, so he didn't stop when he should have done so. He followed the wrong car in the funeral procession swap war and defied the cop star, yes, Mister Mistar. The one who was at war with them from the rising of the morning, even. That cop was warning him to stop and turn his act around the back. But he did not, because he'd considered himself the real super boss, there. By the time he found out what the cop was on his axe talking about, and that he was going in the wrong direction, south, of here. He was more than two hours' drive out, and far away from the vicinity of the very place in the city where he needed to be (beat it), like... like urgently. As usual, he got into his old habit of talking a bit too often for his new gal, and for the pleasure of pleasing off his own good God-given boo pal. Then went on to slide further into quicksand, defaulting the salt thing handed off to him by the woe man doing him like, like so by showing off his proud fork king, yes, my star king man, that thing. Shoving such things on him and showing his proud fingers off to him. Arguing yet some more, my pal Martin, while shoving things in the other guy's front door window curtain, sorry, I'm certain that what I meant to say was face. Shoving things in the guy's front face glass window case all morning long, in this case. To his own misplaced finger ring that should have been hanging on his arm, but no. It was getting into the business of departing from him and his framing case. Just in case you didn't see the foot race, look. Take a peek through this tiny space in the recording book, see? Somebody was there parading the nook, then took to chasing the unwilling nests off him and me on the way to the foot race with the record books. But luckily for him, only the shortness of a finger did he end up parting with.

"Or was it losing the sheet out of heat, like, out of the fork king thing he wanted to use for eating?"

"Oh, c'mon, stop laughing and pay attention, Martin, what's wrong with you, man? Damn, she's probably right, you know." Anyway, one of those two reasons was blamed for his grieving, okay? Because that dude was a harder nutmeg than one Wood had thought, much harder, even, than the one in the keg, that's way too good and much too hard for him to go cracking out.

"Oh, shegg, ditch that leg on oat."

"No, no joke, I don't want to have to come back here and hear these kinds of tasks, cold beer being toast. Because that's exactly what we used to call that thing; you should note Hingh."

"I already know these things like, you'd wanted to say 'shell' when that word popped the hail out of the keg, right?"

"Yes, since you seem to prefer the road of resistance less than light, but..." Let's continue with the road ahead, heated up like hot buttered bread, and bright. To continue on our way to go over there and spread the feathers on the bed. That boy, though, sighs and says, Oh! Yes, he was the one who sighed and said so now, go, yes, man! Go.

"But, why, why must I go now?"

"Because I said so, just like your mama never knows how to say it to you at the front, doe. While standing in the doorway and yelling at the stowaway, and further, Moe." Because he was sick as sleet, to say the least. So, to cure his raging fit of fear, the boy reverted to using his teeth, out there, bit the proud, pointing, sticky finger-licking drumstick of a chick flick king thing that Shae was showing off at him quickly, really quickly that day. As was the regular habit, okay? Yes, whenever he's walking those roads to go and grab it, yes, the left hind leg of a rabbit, the down-home way. "You do know what I'm trying to say, don't you?"

"Yes, man, I know it's true."

"Thank you." Happened after he was done with this act of disjointing him, yes, him. Went about breaking it away from the rest of the pack, hit, eh, and sent Shae's bloody bleeding stump away that day. Wide-eyed and dismayed in surprise, I'd said. Taring away to go and practice with his hockey team on his one-handed driving routine. Making up some super quick time, Hingh, on the ride in the next direction home, ended sometime later that day. Hastened in to go stay and say "amen" to the caretaker at the inn, again. Whilst still bleeding-mad about the delay he would have caused, I mean, have. He'd stopped and delayed, you know, all on the sobs. That was how he was to lose contact with his proud finger, Jack, at that very bumpy spot, Bob. Yeah, that very day. While he was on his way to the burial of his pal, with whom he wasn't all that friendly at all. Just happened to fall upon it all when he fell hard upon the line of slow-moving cars and followed it way too far down the Carron Hall, before he'd realized what he was in for. As you'd wanted to hear me say when you'd called, I'll go right ahead and say it to you, my pal. That was when he realized what was up with the small-talking cop with the beautiful noise, and what he was in for.

"Stop!" Was the one-word directive to him from the slow-moving cop, yes, he was that sort. That cadet guide was a little too tall to even walk a bit wide at all. But a slow-moving escort sort was he, trying to play things smart and orderly. Happened when he'd wanted nothing more than to get himself home to the West Park zone, to eat. So, when Shae ran into him, it was because he wanted to get home somehow, to go have his so-called din...din. Then go into the zone to park and get smarter by just doing some work on the show, working up his knife and fork that weigh, the right way, first, that's how. Like, like, to go partake in the partying after dark eight, and later on too, to go partaking further in some more of the already pre-ordered broth in the basin and listening to whispering talks directed at the corseted jet setters' sorts, Jason. Those who were there setting up the platters near the pots, like always, were busily chatting about the man and his pops in the hallways. Then, if he was lucky, he would move along to go inside and work his knife and fork on the "Dutchy" in the oven that was already set to "wok" up a spark. He couldn't let it slip and slide past; he had to react and fake a comeback, nothing to write home about that. Just a simple math, he thought. The act of his showing off the better part of his favorite and best heart nearer than that to his hand, dead down handling arm in the homely form of his finger ring charm. Which was nearer and dared her

to his heated-up heartstrings in Windsor Park, King Lorne. Although...
"No!"

"Yes, yes, Ringo."

"What, it wasn't me who..." "Well, who said 'no' a while ago?"

"I did."

"Well, I'm sure that you know a lot more than I about how such things go out to sea, on the grid. So, yes, I agree. I'll just try to tell the rest of the story by cell to that guy who's standing by me. Well, my version of the story, anyway, oh. Sigh, yes..."

"Did you see that? That was fast, he sighed and rolled the eyelids in the middle of the reply, Nidz." Now, here's the long-awaited goodbye. "So long, Nosey guy." So, here we go, back to the car show where he was, showing off some things to the brothers with love. Showed his proud finger off to the man, and the rest of his friends tugging along in line on the Boulevard (come on). Windsor Park City Boulevard, just saying this for the straightening up of the record, those disks that they're discussing, Sis. Discard that from the records, Miss, please.

For the life of him, Sheamus could not begin to understand the real reasons. Why? He asked repeatedly. "Why... why?" Why, he asked again, on the cries and whiny talks coming easily from a bit below the eyes and falling on his knees. The same ones that were a while ago gazing down at a pair of hands like these, messing around with fixing his tied-up in knots tricks at fly fishing, the flea Hingh ticks that were hitched and hanged up on his zip her stick. Just like it would have happened to him once in the presence of this guy who's here now telling us of it. He still remembered what had happened with the zip, you know, so. "Why, why. Why was the guy so hostile and quick to defile a nice person's profile, unfazed by playing tricks, and besides? What sort of person does such a terrible thing to a king?" He was heard asking these things of the child, dividing the usual smile on this part of his head's front side to spin.

"Wasn't it the dogs?"

"Yes, go leash it on the cord, if you don't want it to spin around and bite you on the limb, hard. But then again." As you can probably tell by now, to a friend, and per his reasoning, Cow, on the ninth farm end. He thinks a lot of himself, hell, I mean, he does, no need to be guessing anymore, about the Cubs. But then came this little bug, her thing to have them hug her ring in front of him, doing the other show off of the evening, again.

Back to that and this, though, my friend. Back to where we were and transfixed on hearing the rest of the hits, and yes, the misses, too, to the end. Talking about other people's business, fix her rings, for her. Things such as this. Like, back to the same, yes, that man and his precious cargo game. But first, put this penny in your purse just because... We'll get back to this and the real cause for you to support with it later on your ask... (or off), but now, continuing with the trip is how. Yes, Sheamus' tricks, mi blow-wow! Look.

Those sorts of precious wares and tares that were (at the time) taring in half his toed feet walking bare. Well, nearly, they were everywhere around that neck of the hooded town square. Yeah, Leigh. In those days, that is and was. There were many, too many such bugs to have been hanging on one sane man's wreck about the neck crib, of course. Those who had gathered and brought them in were standing in line and waiting for something of which they knew nothing at the time. But as for him? He knew he would soon be out and about, taking a swim. Because he was modeling and straddling the corridors in very well-placed positions to have been able to see. So, he knew they would have been gone and done with very quickly, like, just following the lines lined up behind the chord for a lick at the straight and plumb-licking stick, Leigh. More or less like, in a wink of eager eyes at the plumb plum, pudding in the pit pipe, you know. Put it down, it's not your own. Yes, the one that you wouldn't have picked before it was right to go, and good enough to fit tight below, where it was grown.

"Don't you mean ripe?"

"Yeah, that's right, sorry," I'll say it the right way, just for you, okay? Like, pudding in the pit pipe, you know, that you wouldn't have picked before it was 'ripe,' and fit to go, I know you knew it before. Surely, much sooner than she and he had thought to think when they had gotten to the come, coming in a cummings truck on the run-dung and running from something."

"Like, bananas and corning pork, to go work a three-course with cornmeal dumplings, right?"

"Yes, I know what you mean; green boiled bananas and cornmeal dumplings, isn't that something?"

"Yeah, man. That's what I meant, pops; isn't that something, to get home on?"

"But of course, of course."

Look at his eyes, though, rolling all over the crops that are growing out there on the farmer's lots along the groves near the commons. Be it known that he knew it then and had been positioning himself to get through to them. To all of it as a matter of fact, Stem's cell. Like those other misfit crap of thieving rats, oh hell, and to the rest of the profits too, my friend, alive. Not to be found numbered as one of them amongst those of the goner's tide. Like, that one-eyed one-door ring one there, and this one over here. They were more than half as prepared; you do know who I'm messing with now, right, my dear?"

"Sure, sure."

There they go, basking in the memories of not too long ago, like when Dedimus was still walking among them (much too slow) and was heard saying things like these regularly. Like these, and this; that's unfair, came the reply, as in, if you please.

"Oh, please, give me a hand up," was the correct answer, "no"?

"No, I don't know," he announced this while continuing to slide along the inn slide, dunced by an ounce, hiss! Yes, unfair too, was that shoe, though it takes someone like you to figure this out so quickly and on queue."

"Like, like — "No, don't look there, that's not fair, and yes, we're going to look and listen to the other car tune over there."

"Right, right you are."

"E-ewe! I was headed out to cry," he said, but again he lied, beware, mi bred. I was the person who said such, to him, yes, this bit — sized of something, nearer to his head than the chin. While looking at you in disguise. All this was used as a queue to misinform the doggy companion from his rather peculiar insight, Ted queued-up intelligence norm. "Don't look there," was what I heard, coming in next. "Nor should you ever stare, unless you want them to hear." I'm vexed.

"Notice the use of the word 'them,' instead of 'her?'"

"Yes, I heard it too, but..."

"What for?" Asked the other man in the car. "We don't want to tip them off the bar," he said. In the meantime, the puppy show was there, blinking the alternating half-opened eyelids under the covering eye skins of beads like kids, and wondering what was going on with the disheveled talk of his. The wagon car they didn't ask for was, by this time, speeding ahead. But luckily for them, it has its bar, you know, right there near the bed, look, keep on staring through this nook. There they are, even now, still trying to misinform the dog who's still unharmed like you, somehow, "Yes?"

"Yes, I know, I can still see some of it on the rerunning of the records from down below." Meanwhile, the doggy pop e-show was there, sneaking a stare everywhere, I mean, now and then. Now and then, she would have rolled the eyelid open a bit wider than his again, sliding it off one end of the eyeball, casting an enquiring glance at the brother's ballpoint pen, and squeezing off the trigger to trigger a hit song for them. "So long," said this one. "Am I wrong?" Asked the other brother. They were chatting and going along still, together, trying to figure out the weather. "Fair enough," he replied at the one rebuffed, earlier on. The one, too, who was broad-sided, would have had something else to say when he said it to u as I did. "I'll see you there," so came the reply, if you please. But again, he lied. "Didn't he?"

"So I hear, I agree."

But he, too, had lied when he screwed that reply out of the hog, and you, too, who were on the wrong side of the bride's, bug her off her bag.

He'd planned on leaving, yes, but on his own two-footed terms, Mingh, well, I'd guessed that both of them did. He also wanted to get his hands on those things in the tram. Those that he was so overly strung out on, pops, man. You know, those kinds of lickerish sin Ting (or was... wasn't it a shiny sum things)? Anyways. Those he took a liking to, and with having them on him, well, probably like, he was lucky from the beginning, so it would have seemed in that inning. The duppies must have been forgiving, that's what I mean, because his fully filled-up palms were later seen closing in on them. "Like... like — "On such shiny, enticing things to eat, no?"

"No, not to eat but... (Or was it)? Oh, sheet, wait a minute. That looks sweet. May I have a piece? Thanks, such things are really sweet to go heat up with liquidized kinds of luncheon meat, perhaps, as I'd guess. Or some other kingly bits and pieces of sheets, no?"

"No, not so much the things he wanted to eat, but the ones to hang on his neck, shoulders, toes, and feet, those, yes?"

"Yes."

To go do it, like, to go slow will still be sweet, when they're all gone to sleep, of course, in their homely beds at the bottom of the sea, of sorts. "Look, they're crawling all over him now, and weighing him down to blow-wow."

They then went along the way to walk along the road, with more than a little help from a brother's hands in the gloves. While traveling, a way to go west as if going to wring-go while he swings low to the west end with it. When they're all gone to sleep, I guess the sheet... pass it over. It would be neat to have a sheet or blanket to cover one's darling's feet when she goes to sleep in Nova, wouldn't it be? Like, down there where they are now, way down deep below the shelf fish nest of gluttonous teeth to blow over yuh..." "Wait a minute, what's this? Is that...?"

"Yes, yes, it's the shellfish nest. Look, it's where they go to look at the eye-witness news, like, just like those others over there, and this to get used to, what the heck. It's just the same with those, too." Yes, those in the nests sitting there right by you are who I'm talking to. Like, he and his friend Keithy Mingh. They're all from the same type of note, Hingh nests, he's sleeping in. There he goes, pointing at them like kids lined up in rows, I know. Like the little children's *pickney dem* that he is. (Bids, more bids, please. Thank you). Well, it was not really at them that he was pointing, but he was pointing in the direction where they were left sleeping, on the ninth end in the huts, we think.

"But, but, who put them to sleep, and when did it begin to happen, like this?"

"He did, he knew they would soon be gone, you know, like, gone to bed down in a sweet sleep on the ground, dead woven in with a yarn, oh."

"Oh, no, you mean...?"

"Yes, he was just about to get gone, to do the walk over to the yard cover. To be there in the evening and doing his thing when he's bedding it down with Debbie 'Deb' on a wide-mouthed, breathy yawn, unsober. Or with whoever else might be so inclined to come over, with something warm, of course." While he was there, biding his time carefully ahead of the line of corn, you know, and licking it up against the post. Strategizing, as already said that morning, Ringo, when it was said to his top man arguing on like so, the most, with mine, even. He was readying himself to be able to slip-slide his way down the slippery glide of a grease pole one day. That was his planned-out strategy, okay? To get him to be gone clean out of the back door there, and I mean, get his things out and be done that way, and get out alive. With eyes wide open to stare inside or out. On a one-tooth speech to get to say; that's the key to thrive, my dear, on oat. Well, that time of year is now here; he's out, and with me, I swear, yes.

"Where, where's he?"

"Well, I agree, he's not really with me in such proximity, but he's with the doggy poppy show, if he, just like you, yes, if I may continue to guess. May I?"

"You can do whatever you like, wise guy."

"Okay, I'll try." If he and his gentle touch are anything, on which to go down by the sea and such. Such things would be good enough for him and us to swim in the darn thing. That could be something worth wanting, "couldn't it be?"

"I guess it could."

"Yes, I was just—"Hush the fu—"Okay, okay, no need to answer me that way. I'm just asking these things rhetorically, Bey, but B, listen up. The last time he'd reached out and touched something soft and warmly brushed. Like, briskly brushing up against his Bee-spoke's tux, still crisp and clean, and in good luck as it looks, it was himself on the arm. As much as with his good luck charm, and by the immediate alarm that was quick in coming on."

"But it's now gone, right?"

"Yes. The good luck part, darn." However, he was still very much alive and going along in the wrong lane, headlong towards the river, in the same direction as home.

"Yes, as was the mission, mi G gnome?"

"Well, perhaps. But he was going anyway, suffice it to say. To be getting gone away, flat, from over there on the rock, and still hoping to be found with your fat in the pocket of his what's it not..."

"Don't you mean, your 'wat-not?'"

"No, but your 'what's it not,' but to be found still sniffing the air when he gets there."

"Or not, right?"

"For that much, he wasn't well prepared; he was a little bit on the side that's scared, but... As soon as the odds were a little bit in his favor, look at me, Clair, and swear not to tell this to the savior. Rub your hands together and begin to savor what you're about to hear, because... He grabbed a hefty handful of colorful flavors..."

"Or two, wasn't it two?"

"Probably true. Yes, two hands fully filled and stretched out now, for more food. On wolf whistling behavior, just like you, wanting to have it all packed in and ready to go. Filled up to the brim with treasure as given to him by whom? Yes, from him, not Hugo nor you, as you'd claimed." It came to him from the savior's pair of sticky fingers above the shoe (such a shame). By any other name, look, they're walking there again, the two that remained, as we already knew they would remain together to the end. "Of either, or all of them," as per the agreement they'd signed in the beginning. So, there they go, slowly, so no?

"Yes."

"Yes," is the proper address, but he was being very careful as he is even now. Being careful not to be seen while toeing the way to blow wow, no?

"No, that's not the way it went, on the way to go."

"Okay, show me how to find the way then, since you seem to know a lot more than they, them."

"I know quite a lot about those fat foxes, so here's where that class is..." He ran as fast as you out of the back of the lock-her-up clan. Sorry, I meant to say the door. The locked door, there, that's where he was, and trying to go through, and that was what got him through to you. Or nearly as fast as he could ever hope to muster up a cloud of smoke and spew chewed tobacco like you. So, I swear, it's true.

"Yes, I hear you, but did it really happen that way, though?"

"Yes, it's true, he was gone. She went home to go and save her toe from the corn on her yellow foot, a form of spike-heel shoe that morning. Been running ever since. Well, not in the actual running spell to the sink, it's too stinky to be minced. He's walking now, as you can clearly see. Look, that mooing cow over there looks just like her to me, doesn't she? Look at her, toeing the way to go, but. Surely, as sure as what you'd do when you go to do the dodo, doodling."

"No, not me, I never do those types of things, you are accusing."

"No? I thought so, but, but?" He then ran as fast as you could out of there to go on and get through. Or nearly as fast as he could ever hope to muster up a spark to light up his smoke and chew more tobacco just like he often does with you, I swear, it's true. Just like that, he was gone. So, I think you should stop at the rest area spot and take a p-p, man, press pause, and go over to play. Just to see if you still can, mi P, okay? While walking there and passing them by along the shelf, with meat, me... Not she, nor he. Those who were running over anything and everything they came across along the way, in. Even over the corpses of many, who, not so long ago, were their props, and his. Like, properly, his friends and colleagues, his companions, pop e-show, as sent to me, from the kings. Good thing I'm wearing my invisible lens this evening, they're not able to see me, but I can see them, and I've given my consent that I can and will see them, so send them on in. But as for them, when they get in, tell them they should not look at me, not ever. Well, sometime in the future, perhaps. Or was it the vice-versa swap tar wine? "No, wait, don't send it just yet, my friend, Li Dent, on time." So said the one who helped me to pay the rent on and half a dime. He's the same someone who was heard saying it to them, "Don't send it yet," he said. "Since we're so close to the end, in effect. Instead, we might as well continue to descend," but until then, "I digress." That was what they said to me and all the rest before leaving us all in the west. Yes.

He would further drop and shed some of the load from under his head, and from touching up against his beard, dead clothes closing up the bedspread to prevent Ted from looking ahead.

"Or two, right?

"Yes, of those," as he knows very well how such things go. Heavy as Lead on his Toe-toes are those. So, he went ahead of the Ways and Means committee, committing more sins than she does, often with me. While I was leaning in to speed up things properly, same as she did, living off him, for me and my paps, Leigh, can you ceet?

"Yes, I can see it."

"Okay, continue to look at me because that was when he sped along the road towards Linstead. If you don't believe me, turn around and look back at the headship of his kindred that just slipped off the road near the sea. Up ahead of those things is where they are, trying to deceive me. Look, see that shiny spot glistening in the sunlit dusty wind way up ahead of us and coming back?"

"Yeah, that I can see in the lay-by and stay slack. What is it, my pops?"

"That's it, right there. That's one of his bling things that he'd dropped off there from last night's evening's way-fare."

"When?"

"Then, like, while on his way in to get here, that's where and when. I mean…"

"You mean, he was…?"

"Yes. He dropped them there. Reluctantly and grudgingly so, so I hear. But then again, who cares? Go pick it up, man, if you must want, like that one, for instance. Look. He won't mind it at all, Mr. Evans, even if he misses it on the paper trail that they wanted to fall back on and half balance because what the hail?" "Woof!" "He dropped them there on purpose." Pause. "Why," you'd asked, because…

"Yes, I know, it's because of us, right?"

"No, not at all, but because, and only because he must, he's Sheamus after all. His life depended on it, and such ordered protocols were in place. Protecting and preserving his life is first and foremost my pal; be advised if you can't be nice on this night."

"Oh, as usual."

"Sure. All else comes after, but." If he's as lucky as somebody had taught him to sucky on the sulk, when they taught him to read and write the wrong things he read, when he'd said those things to the kids on laughter in Kentucky on the south. Or even as it pertains to her preferred parts that were lying lame over there on his bed between his knees of sorts to cut me. And yes, her too, mi bred. "But of course." If he's as lucky as he had been thinking in recent times, as singed and plucky as a swine. Or even as he thinks he's getting to be, like, a little bit worse hoarse than hinged on Stokey ole me, and mine. Someday in the future, he might even get to come back from behind and go pick up his marching boots somewhat as shiny, from where they had dropped him loose and dying. While he was there trying to salute her good luck, which looked so fine. Or from where he had left them off, in the nooks behind.

He wanted nothing more than to be seen kickback on the money he's gotten from the kickback king scheme, and get to use it (if needed) in aiding him in picking up again these things. Or some other such things, amen, Mister McAnuff, sing. "Say amen, again."

"Amen, again."

"Good. Isn't it a good thing to be able to crack a joke or two as you walk by your hometown folks in the neighborhood shoe?"

"Yes, that's a nice feeling, I'll have to admit."

"Anyhow, let's keep on moving and see if we can ceet." Among them are these things he'd dropped off his name, no?

"No, oh no, not off his name, but from where he'd dropped it on them while on his way over to the spotted riding. Wanted to get them out from where he'd dropped them in hiding, back then. Some of these abandoned and almost shiny things by then, too, will be specially selected from amongst them for you, "okay?"

"Okay, I hear you. Sounds good too."

"Now, though, all that he's got left hanging there around his neck from the stack pile he'd grabbed on the way out west, and which he's now pulling out of the bag, no less in style than when he'd left with the grab, are his five gold chains of the Danley sort, again. The type that the neighborhood drug lords and Dan dadas used to wear as props on their necks and hand cords out there. A cache of diamond rings padded onto every refrigerated, sticky-fingered thing, and thumbs there, too. To go modeling and bring the blinking thing in, to show off to you and them. Even in his oversized walking boots, to which he sometimes bows and salutes and which are now rubbing up the pain against his great-toed toe..."

"Oh no! That can't be the truth."

"Oh yes, couldn't you guess? Why would he neglect those three-pocket vests? Would you? Bust-a-move on through." Oh yes, that's why, Mister Robby Sly, Stoned, drunk, and slower than I. Why would I even lie? Pay attention, manly guy, come on. Look at this one. His custom-made LA Lou is a drug lord's saggy type of shirt-suit is just as cute. The one he'd culturally appropriated to himself from the youths. The same across the town clans' sleuth at whom he used to pop pot shots and shoot... Well, not he, but his uniformed boys out there along the shelf. He took their suit while he was on the slide down the chute, trying to get himself out of the booth. It was intended as a disguise to help him slide past the eyes of any of his enemies whom he thought might still be left there inside, still alive, and telling me... Apart from the fact that he really liked that suit, guys."

"Want to tell us why?"

"Yes, no problem."

"Well, tell us some more about that part you poor, poor boy, and hurting, come on, let's talk about them."

"You mean, you really want to hear me talk about that?"

"Yes, yes, Mister Smart, as asked."

"Alright then, I will tell Hugh some more one of these days. But, in the meantime, let's continue to describe the will that's hidden under the sill that's still in the store ways of the house's doorways." That was wise, yes, yes, guys. But it's worn down to the bare husk now, the suit is what I'm talking about, cow. Yes, but he's still the hippest dude somehow. The hippest and flashiest manly thing your eyes have ever seen anywhere around these parts of the side wing, where... Whereas we... "Look at this, what place is this beside me?"

"The side wing of a parted cow fleeing ticks before the slaughterhouse's door, I thought that I'd weaned. That's where we are now. Look, look at those cows as they moo and chew the cud at intimidating the sows."

"Hogs, you mean, hogs, right?"

"Yeah, that's how. That's rather easy to fit somebody. He, especially so, Dally. Like, when it's hanging properly on his shoes, as chosen buds like booze. It's the easiest thing to come next to him when he's the only dude around these parts in the south, west of the hoods, still standing good, and as smart as tugs working for the clubs, well, so it seems to us. But he would have had a lot to do with that split in the slit horseshoe cup, cup to... You do know what I mean, I'm sure, like, what he's up to, don't you?"

"Seen."

"Yeah, man, Real Jamaican yardie sin ting something, so, keep on talking, king."

"...To have resulted in such canned sin ting as this one can of tin beans, yes, as this thing has been so far, seen?"

"Who, what, you mean, that's the salt Ting that was defaulting from Aunt Sue's cooking?"

"Yes, all of those."

"Are you telling the truth?"

"Of course."

"Well then, tell me what to do next, to get this thing to work?"

"*Mi nuh knoah, mi nuh really knoah, mi miss him that much, though*, like..."

"Yes, I missed him a lot too, but."

"I know, that was what I meant, not for you, though, Hugo, but for him." His cache of bling is as shiny as it's ever been. Look, they're hanging off his shoulder thin. "...Ringing!" Hey, "Go get the telephone, Kim." Somebody was heard saying this in her hearing with a voice a little bit raised over her fist, first thing, to yell the verse in. Before going back to raising hell once more.

"But of course, Hingh, I'm sure, and to view the baby lying there in the crib by you and him who was there snoring, no?"

"No."

"Yes. Not only theirs... their necks, but firstly so, true."

"True. I'm vexed, though."

"But-but, but why?"

"Because, listen, and listen up good, wise guy."

11

What About This Peace

Peace! Just asking this. What peace were they talking about, Sis? There was no peace for weeks in the house out east. Even in the very best of times, stout feet look fine. There was no peace for anybody to find when they were out searching the mine, trying to find what was designed to soothe the mind of the higher-up friends of mine coming from behind. To then go and fine-tune the little patch of thyme, each week, on primetime news, so to speak. A select few have some semblance of it in truth, yes, and all else that there were to get on looted cassettes. Since it was turning out to be the music that they liked best, for spoiling the youths, they have it. Yes, such and such at their fingertips, and tipping over a bit more into filling their pockets. But then comes this. Hey, you there, Miss, get the clipper and come, I'd like you to cut this tip down a bit for me. Yes, that's it. Now, spit on it and rub it with... rub your teeth over it on the spit to get it as smooth as this... Thank you, now, continuing with the singing of songs for our... "What? Want to hear more about the song?"

"Yeah, yes, man, tell us some more about that one."

"Okay, let's go up another rung, on Woolmer Town Mountain, if you're looking for advice. Because when we're done talking about those chicks who're living out their kicks dancing with spice, like this. Nice, eh?"

"Yeah, I guess."

"You bet, but..."

The peacekeepers were in a retreat hearse at the time. Planning and strategizing as to what to ride in first to get there on time. To use it as a riding whipping stick to beat hers, not mine. They would have gone in and done their hip-hop rap job of maintaining the peace tag. More or less like putting your tray of eggs in a weak bag, then going in and wetting it at the bottomless pit frog. So that with the least bit of jerky chicken bouncing back from the weak end, of some sort. The girls' eggs, you know what? Yes, they would fall out of the crack and get cracked. Like, like when one is heard saying something like, "Crackers with that?" The answer that followed would likely be, "Yes, yes, please, this is a nice cheese." But they had a bit of such. A little piece of the upper echelon and the elitists' touch; at least, they had a bit of it for a week, the thing they called peace. But some others were heard calling it a piece of sheet, only to find that they too, were really from amongst the goner kinds of misfits who... Well, not now-now, but then, as it occurred back then. They were soon to be facing up to the end and were quick to get targeted again themselves. The very next time they'd happened to hop off those ends around the bend. They were lucky to run into some of those duppies again. You know them, the younger minds of the daytime, and then, as it turned out. Those were there at the time, busily planning a comeback from behind the bus back of mine, and that was when...

Sheamus was lucky to have been counted amongst them, as the very best and first of manly men. "The more those select few got, though — "What, the more they wanted to spend on the crappy pop e-show?"

"You know them more than I do."

"No, I don't."

"Yes, of course, you do. Weren't you the ones who'd shone for them their shoes?"

"Amen, but, but, don't tell them, have me excused. I guess we could leave out the rest of it until, like...?"

Until not much was left anywhere for the rest of the pair of go-getters to go out and get theirs. Nor for the scared stiff out of their knit widths types of bringers to come, bringing the feathery wings to feather their neatly, nestling hens' eggs here. "Those hens were sitting on the eggs where?"

"There, I guess."

"Yes, but now. Beware of new faces coming in as guests, because just like it has always been with new clear, and the war horse. That was when the elites of the day started looking elsewhere and pointing the other man's stare clear in the air, towards ours. As usual, looking for ways to balance out the lopsided scaled-up chair again, on the new gal, friend?"

"Well, yes, I like my girl too, because she's so sweet, oh — "No, no more of this from you, because..."

"I know, I know, it seems as if you want me to go away from your horse, but..."

They will do those sorts of things yet again on you, my pal, and yet more so, too, school gal, girl. Trying to balance things more in their favor was to be the blamer.

"Oh savior, such a shame, no?"

"Yes, I was just about to say it was the same ore..." Or, if there remain other warm red watery veins sort of stain belonging to them, and yet unclaimed by the deadly pain by then. They must go out and find them in that other place, wherever they are and staying, in hiding, and get them to make it into the fast lane, riding. To get those places and the people who may still be there to become a part of their savior's game-playing fame. Like, in a new planet airy plain, again, and thriving.

The jet setters were setting up their jets to take off and then come back riding on the right white horse, or the wrong one, who's no companion to you, I'd suppose, because... Wanting to get their guests to hit the restart address, "by any means necessary," yes, that's what they'd said to me, with no contest. But that was just the practice galloping run that was quickly repossessed by some, as I'd guessed. They thought it would prepare them to get their many manly men working on the tasks to get those other men excited, and moving again to come, at last, as I did. That was when the roads led them to a survival town with no name, nestled somewhere out there amongst the hornets' rain as it was known to them then. Where the fittest of the fittest, and the quickest of the quick, go to get whatever there may be for them to get a fighting fit of... When trouble comes hanging around that wretched neck of his woodland niche (Ugh). And starts to settle in on their doorstep with the little doggy bitch, I mean, a little kid, good. Yes, that too, if you're more than a little bit removed from amongst the unlucky few, Mr. Wood. "Not only their doorstep, though, but firstly so, true?"

"True."

"All the others were to follow through, and then came you, nope?"

"No, this is no joke."

"I know, you're always going to lie about the odd dress, but things didn't turn out as they'd hoped I'd guessed. So, they had to fight back, and in fighting, they had to fight with all that they had, for the right to the living of life with a glad nest, I mean, gladness. Their lives, their way, and theirs only, okay?"

"Yes."

Up until the few from that part tick killer crew came down to two, as seen through Sheamus' eyes, he was at the time, looking through. Now he's off to go and take a bow to blow wow. Guess what is about to happen now? Just wait and see. You will, that's for sure, going to kill some off the wheel, because...

There they are, going, the dog and he's slowing, trying to go find what's left of them. Yes, those whom you already know are other friends of mine, but... In his minced-up mindset, as he sees things getting vetted on prime time, he's trying to forget. But look at him again, his ways are not mine. He wanted to even up the score with Essence, his friend on tour, you know. That's why the walking shoes are now hanging from his poor shoulder at the back door. His back, too, was heavily laden with the stick, and you, once more. There, where things are hitched grudgingly and bearing with the hang-up kinds of things hugging me and his pops. As he has always done, he's hanging them on the bent crooked end of it like props, yes, on the end of his walking stick is the rest of his clicking, crackling kinds of tits, I mean, tips; the tip of his walking stick was heard clicking on the sand. Out into the hopeful village, they're going along, look, they're headed there now, searching for... "Hoof, hoof." "Mi blow wow. But, but."

"But what?"

How did good-going sorts of living things ever get this good long-distance line away from proper and good living, anyway?

"Chickens were coming home to roost, her I'd say."

"Yes, the comfort zone had come falling and tumbling down the hall in one day. It would have finally fallen off their miserable, sorry, I meant to say, the miserly crown foot on the clay near the doorway, but then again, no way."

Cutting through the clutter, some were able to see a divided gutter. The fingers of the younger ones (or however many more than that one) were sliding up and down the pulse of pan-um world affairs and powerful gears. The real players were playing the Bears (unfairly so, I hear). Just as it was known to be done over there, all the time. But the new age sun had finally begun to shine on the younger men behind... us. They were readying themselves to strive for better and to come over, alone. Coming up on fair at last, you know, and sober tooth to bite at bones. "That was the way to go all around the Kingsland world and take it over for the youth, as it was known, no?"

"I suppose so, but..."

What they found there was alarming to the ear, to say the least, in talks so clear (or not). So, the old men quietly went to work chopping away at the dirt. At the same time, the young ones were doing their share of not snoozing and crying for their worth. But they were moving in on removing those dirty old ways of theirs, and the dirty nest itself of dirty old men's feet on the potters' clays. As well as those dirty old men of those dirty days themselves, at their last worth, when and wherever they could. "May I just spit it out and say it as I would, yes?"

"Yes, go on and get your head checked, like I knew you would."

There was a war waged against many, including the young and friendly, a silent war it was. Waged from the headrest of the tugs, to come tumbling down upon the young man's head on the bed of thorns. Youths would have borne the brunt of it for ages. As the phrase was and still is, the old were accustomed to winning the cages. So, that was just what they did at the first fist of rage, Idris. Yeah, of the kids, those over there who were the sort of naive who never learned how to keep their secrets. Go shouting it all about the platforms other haters provided for them so to do shits. So that they, old men I'd say, wouldn't even need to continue to pay dearly to spy on you, them, or they. Just needed to sit down, wait, look for a round of booze, or eight. Listen to what you're there telling him that you're about to do, and live high on, guess who? Yes, you, or low. So came they in, to learn how to rely on the youth's kinds of easily accessed insights, for the tightening up of their upper screw in the pants that's way too tight, for their bag of blight... before they go. But as for those younger men and their friends, they started building their niche for living. Like, bitcoins, bit notes, and bit slips, among other such things as this one that I'm giving, it's, it's... To exchange value, pay for servicing their sheets, and get things shipped over by you. Like wine and cheese with biscuits. Old men were to soon get wind of this; nothing has been the same sane ever since, my kids. How did things get so quickly out the doors and into the hearing of the old soldiers, though? By the legs of those very same younger men, it would be a great bet to go and play domino. Decided to side in with the old men for a cold spend, at the hands of those same old men. Men who were there trying to cement themselves into that old way, of theirs, of course, and in all the spaces in the doorways, on chairs of sorts. The silent war was born at last, and many were going to die and be gone to Rastafar-I, later on. Loudly, if that needs to be the command as decided upon by gray-haired old men, and soon to be coming in proudly, towards me. From the farm, even, where he was hanging out and still unharmed, that very evening. Along with the whole bunch of them, including him. That same one who is still walking along there, can you see him? Beware. While the old guards were over there keeping the ward over everything here, by doing whatever they have always been doing, hard and unfairly. The young ones were congregating somewhere beyond the dumb ones, and behind the scope of old men's images in Asian hair ring aids to get it combed once, see?

"Yes, I see."

"Well, finally, somebody is getting to see the vision, like me. Soon I'll be free. Good nets gray shuts me." They were even getting into bed with the lead ones among the freed ones. That was the key thing to get at the knee strings in the weed run of the kingdom, right? Yeah, man, and you've got a lot of eyes to see these things, Evans Homes, my bright —

"No, it wasn't me."

"No, just him, I agree, I can surely see him, look, he's over there looking back at the knee-jerking swing, on me."

"Well, look at me some more, and guess the reason for this low score."

"Why?"

"Because..." Well, as said before, you and I are from among the more horns, so go on, continue to sing your swaying song, because... Quite unlike you and me, those others over there across the pond can still see. They weren't going to sit around stoning the winds, twisting the nights away, and platting sand, like me. They were busily working on another plan, just the same as the young "man dem." Those whom some people sometimes call "men," but not all of them. Well, not the same as in, kind of plan, but they've always been planning how to stay in command. Yes, those older ones, that's what they do, all the time, until the young men heard the alarm and asked me why, the whine. Even though I lied to them in my kickback king reply, they knew right away the reasons why. So that's when they started getting their better moves on. Out of that, the fraternity was born. "Quack Plapp," it dropped, popping the hail out of the birthing sack, you know what? "Yeah man, just like that..."

"Yeah! Like that webbed-feet duck quack hopping along to go unpack, and to make space for a cache of duckling chicks to chase away from the hatch, yes, chasing those chicks of his far away from frock king the gray shuts land dead hatched up plan of his king man, mi dread Mildred, right?"

"Right."

Yes. It's what we're talking about, the kid boy of Hinghs' ton of towns tonight, yes, or no?

"Yes, I guess so."

Yes, that's the correct address, because his wristband took a swim on the wind towards the pond, to go waving them along. The one that is always on his right hand that is… look, look at it going, going, now gone. Swinging in the other direction is he and him, yes, and she too. Yes, he's dancing with Sue Hingh, but what a booboo. She can't even bust a good move.

The coming together of the young and brilliant minds of the new daytime was able to save a bit of the earth on the clay pine. Sheamus and Essence would have heard of them (in essence) and stayed fine. He wants Ted to have a stumbling fit upon them if nothing else, I mean, Ted wanted.

"To go out and see the spies walking the lines along the shelves?"

Yes, guys, like, they wanted to go tumbling down to a complete stop upon even a remnant of them in the town known to them to be closer to the pit of descent they'd sent and sold down home. Yes, going off to sell it on them again, and the poor old gnome. Like, on the young geniuses and their friends, as seen through the eyes of the men of wealth in their defense.

"Oh, sheet. Did it happen like this?"

"Yes, it happened to you, the same as all the rest of them in the crew, if you cared to know the truth about such things. Even before they could get a chance to say, 'yes' and touch skins, they were drafted in the pen with them." So, they pretended to agree with them, I'd guessed, working things out in both their interest with the pen in High Gate, a mistake, because… Wink, wink.

The young men went out and started another war that the old men would have known about even before they'd picked up their guitar. As it turned out, that war would have been more grievous by far than those before. The old men were to have zoomed in and gagged him. To come away knowing exactly what time of day it was and is. Then slid a slide into where the other of his friends were hiding, intent on deciding at what hour he was to be going out and striking the kids, buff.

"*Mi gut.* That was really rough, no?"

"Yes, man, yes, he's rough like that one, just like the desktop man when it comes to him hitting the domino, on them, or anyone else, yes." But we still want Ted to know more, so tell us. What was the clock humming to say to the bore in Porus? By the time the young and naive minds were to fine-tune the prophet TikTok sign. They were lying dead and dying at the hands of those lying old men, kinds of — "You've got to be lying."

"No, not even trying." The hammer was always quick to come out. Without a doubt, they weren't about to go changing that goat in the boathouse. Many did not know what was happening, nor what was going on in their hearing at the latter end, until they took it one step too far down the hill-figured ladder bar. Rung by rung, or some other such thing else that was made to run. *Climbing dung fig-goh siddung pan har* and to have a seat at his feet, beside her, numb. The young had to try to fight back and push the car home on an uphill drill, to the kill, or down. Any way one chooses to look at it, it was as if they were losing the snitch to the throne. But they were aided and enabled by the gods somehow, Mable, and of self-will to blow wow, that bewitched, in a black gown — "Yeah yuh, got to be you again."

"Yes, yes, Aunt Dorr, I hear you," even her, yes, her help was secured too, my friend. That was for sure, a true word.

"Or nerd?"

Well, so it seems to some among us to occur. "Or, maybe, perhaps they were walking over dead bodies everywhere in dreamland on the lines up there," some blabbermouths ran off spreading that meme, un-clear.

The after-effects were strong, those of the experiment that went wrong and quickly got out of hand. "Very few were to escape the on-slaught of that one; people who were dropping at the gated vehicle like that man who — "Hey, what's wrong with him?"

"With whom, him?"

"Yes."

"You mean, you just noticed him? Well, it's like. Like, he's just like a fish in all of this. That's how he's always been seen by the brutish lit-tle..."

"What, Jacket?"

"Yeah, or something closely resembling it. Just like sheepskin and shellfish from the sky sort, like this, you know. Always sorting out fly-baited clam for the cooking pots of Hart, Garth's funk kills music, as I've heard them saying oft time-ish; get to learn how to use it." It started rather slowly, to make things appear as normal as they possibly could. They have all of those same old players playing roles as ever, and carried those things along on deception, swaying the scrolls to sever Wood — "Or was it, wasn't it to save her?"

"Sounds quite alike, doesn't it, neighbor?"

"Perhaps."

Anyway, let's continue along on our good behavior to the last talks of the day, thumbs up, okay?"

"Okay."

Yes, as I was saying, lies were found amongst the supplies, as usual, guys. For example, hey, you there, my pal, just called to say hi to you and the little gal, that's all, but. No, wait a minute, since we're already here on the ball and stuffed fully in it. Let me take this opportunity to say one thing more to y'all that's clear — "On dim with?"

"Yes, sit, sit." It's like this kid. "Hey, kiddo, how is your Grampa, I mean, your old grandfather, how's he?"

"He's good, he's doing quite well, okay?"

"Tell him I just called to say hi. That's all, but "Oh my! Don't call yet, no, be sure to tell him this too." Like, might as well say bye to the bayou, because... "Who's that standing by you?"

"Mi nuh knoah, I don't know him."

Anyway, let's see if we can "tin" you with what we were about to say before we went low. You wouldn't expect the king and him to be doing that thing, "would you?"

"What thing?"

"Like, like that, and this, like. You wouldn't expect the king, priest, and well-trained warrior chiefs to go out and bury dead bodies like these, and do so on bramble burning him with smoking fire sticks with ease, would you?"

"Oh, please, no."

"No, no chance, kids, go. Here. Sneeze and wipe your nose with these, now. Go, you might as well go, because — "I know, I know, I was already about to go away from you and your as Ma, attack."

Go right on if you want. But, remember this, when the king and they are among the last of those manly men kinds of living things to be left there still standing. Or when he's to be found there standing up amongst the last of them, as the plan was. Others would have already done all the burials, yes?

"Yes, I guess."

"No more guesses and tests, it was so Alfred, it was so already as said, yes." Like, like I've said. They would have had all their dirty work done for them at the first reverse in of the Shaggy-man's hearse, thing, and up until then. Before those who did the cover ring, too, were found covered up and buried by someone in the purse. Someone from somewhere around the licking downs of the mercy these bends on the roads, you know, no?

"No, I didn't."

"Yuh mean, like, like, you didn't know about those rather nice automobiles?"

"No, I did not know about those in the ordeals, but the bends on the roads coming from the hills, those I knew all about, and — "Yeah, I know. From amongst the last of those manly men, if the fighting should continue that long towards the end, but who, which man would have been among the few?"

"*Mi nuh knoah*, I mean, I don't know, sorry."

"Don't worry, man, I know what you're trying to say already, a yaad mi cum fram Freddy, so, yes."

Those dead bodies, though, would have been buried, okay? Like so...

"Yes, I know. Buried by the motherly personality, nature calls, interest, and coming through to show you how to get undressed, just to show you who has got the biggest part of you still, yes?"

"Yes. Like, your heart, isn't that true, Will, will, where did William run off to, do you know?"

"No, I don't, but..."

So they called him, you know, Will. Like, "Hey, Will, will you let me?" whenever they want to go. Or come, like, when coming into some nice plum-plum pudding, or somebody else wooding, I mean, wouldn't... wouldn't they?"

"Yeah, they would, anybody could, Mister Wood, but..."

"Oh! Yeah, I agree. Anybody would have been okay to do it for them at this stage, even me."

"But, but who, who came from among them to get saved?"

"Ask Drew, he might know their names." This time, however, the two sides knew how to belie the true sign.

"Clever."

Yeah. So, that was what they did all in their prime, like, lied their way to the desired results of thine, while climbing up the leather-covered ladder all the time with you.

"Hey, leave me out of your argued, demented mess."

"Yes, you're right, I guess I messed up the odd dress, this doesn't apply to you, I guess, but..." The only problem was, and still is, as seen happening with today's bugs, like these; those saggy baggy pants wearing the tugs, at their knees, and the spy-filled frills too, of yours, is this: One side never knew that the other side knew. At least, not as much as side two would have learned from you, on the hide, like. Hush Puppies dog shoe type of biz. Guess which, and who that is?" Nudge, nudge. Now, spit and move.

"Freeze, what is this?" He heard this as he was about to pick up his knees and kick off running, as he would have done a long time ago, in sheets of browning, while running away from the thieves, and gunning for his latest victories. Or was it the peas that caused it? Like, the hot p-p pea soup he was about to feel running down his suit to hit the flop on top of his sock at the knees, first. Then continued down to the latter ends of his shoe heels, worse, but, but...?

"No, it wasn't so."

"Well, whatever you say, I'll go, okay?" Because, based on what I thought I saw, his jaw had popped the lock and dropped, right there where everything had rolled to a stop. Compare this with that. Now, relax, because it's been resting there ever since. "Ready for a drink?"

"Not yet," he winked and puckered the mouth at the foot, "what's that smell?" Um, what the hell, that thing sure stinks, like Mass Toots...

The tree stump world was heard saying to the drunk girl, in the early days of the pandemic plague jump, which was raiding a skip at the lump, at the time of diamonds and pearls; staying home is good, staying home is good. I'm sure she didn't realize the depth and gravity of what she was saying to the hood at the time, and even at the timely inclined booth of thine, filled up to the brim with wine. Did she ever know or understand the depth and gravity of anything, though? Anyway, "No." She'd whispered that part slowly. How do I know this much about the sweet house stick n go, Leigh? Had you asked? Well, that was and still is the very same person who went on to spill the bill and say a lot of other things about his asked, favor mi gran... Like, quite uncertainly, I think, okay. Among the stack pile of nothingness, she was allowed to get unearthed. Including calling it all a hoax, Sin Ting. Or something like dirt, when it warranted her well-positioned action, Hingh, so I'd suppose kids, and cursed at him. Now, wink, nope? Nothing would be as much as she did. But staying home is probably the only feasible answer left to us and them, down-home, Sir Kidd. I'm damn sure. Surely, there's nothing wrong with saying so, like, perhaps it's absolutely... Or like, like, it's probably so, I'm damn sure that it's probably absolutely so. All those words go together cutely, towards the truthy door beside me, yes. Surely and probably absolutely fits in the same open-ended statement for certain tea, "right?"

"Right."

So surely, probably that's the one we're going to be doing time, and time again, one shoe in (or out), amen. We'll be running back up on irregularities as such, regularly. We've been doing it ever since you, I mean, they, them. Ever since the throne was scored by them and crashed. Then almost got torched by the same sane Sam again to cross the Ross, rose, roses, whatever. No lack of such, but, but, but nobody is calling on them but, but, buttoning the buttons on us, the everyday joey sorts of earth dust, like, to do this and that and just... "So that when they ultimately and outrightly fail the people's trust, they can have us to blame as spikes lead on nails, with sharp ends up in hails, of bullet shots, perhaps. Hummers hammering us down, too, with the indoor mailman's ax. While staying at our gates and steering the cart at us, and nailing us to the edge of the pail too, to put... to, to, to do — "To do what, have you lost your tongue on that?"

"No, but what I meant to say is." To do us all a favor in return for doing too many dodos on nothing whatsoever. Even the pale washing ton pot of post-dated stale, dumplings and noodles to savor, on the up-scale. Couldn't get them to do good whatsoever. But... "Why would we do such a thing, though, what for?" The man wanted to know, so he asked, "har," I mean, he'd asked this of her, again, off the bar chord, re-frain. "Why would I want out of this little piece of my peace, for what business is it settled into the seats? Why would I want to go back into their messy boat fees? Sorry, I meant to say, to sit on the seat beside those pieces of hellish biscuits and cheese treats, as it is when wrapped up in feces, Sis. Like this, even."

"Oh, please, don't do that, she threw the request back at him fast. Don't show me things like that while I'm having my breakfast."

"You mean, you don't want some to tug along in your fist fast, and round too?"

"I'm good, you may as well keep it all to yourself, and Wood who..."

"Okay, what can I say? Why," though? He continued to try to know.

"Why would I bother to want that guy, Shadow? Should I even do that, spy and go? No, I don't think so." Not when I've got everything I need right here in my... oh my, eye water is now dripping down from an eye and dropping onto my thigh as if I'm about to cry. Sitting on tightly woven rye to try and die and go to sleep lying in my own one-bedroom house when the end comes. That will be something worth a haughty amen sort of amending, so comes the chime in "ding". Yeah, man. Let's continue, though, like so, "on my free man's square where I can grow —
"Grow what, Cho-Cho?"

"Yeah man, sweet like a sham, and a lot of such things too, to nyam, so that we can get to eat something with it while going along. Want a piece? I've got it on low heat, seasoned, and ready to roast a pum-pum yam to go with the duckling stew I'm on with meat and ready to nyam. Even with the wheat in my cod fish teeth to go and get dinner for the children's pickney dem as the beginners, and meat too."

"You mean, that's it, that's why...?"

"Yes, my guy, furthermore, why would I want to go back into that, or any of those miserable mess trucks he's got, full of roses? None of those out on the road is good enough to carry the many holes in my nose through the pile of stacked strands it often grows, Sis. How about you?" I had to have asked this and spew, you know, like...

"Yuck", was what she threw back at my ax at the toes below the gut, to grow. So that was how and when...

On the other side of town, though, the Lucky Slim one had just met up with a woman and became her friend to settle down, but then comes... After marrying her and fathering a pair of twins, girls like sand, to match the chances and desires of every one of those bad men, things. Bad things just started to go wrong. Direction down from somewhere around the throne ends, that's when the decision was made to play rough and tough with the man dem, yes hi-yah, those same old folks again, and us too, but of course. You know them, those our might e-men from the lower end, wink-wink, you know them. They're strong and mighty, always up to the task, same as I was at the last act when I was wrestling with D Al Mighty and whooped his ask back, for favors.

"Yes?"

"Yes, mi bredda, I knew them from back home, but..."

"Okay then, I get it."

So, you should also know that, once they get started, they don't bother to go slowly to the Arcade, bus stop near the star grid. So, that was when the decision was made, way back as a matter of fact — "Like school aid to go on the raids raving?"

"Yes, my companion." (Too darn craven).

"When really?"

"From way back then, Neily. Like, it was like this." They, like any and everybody else around those parts on the belt, had been sitting and watching food fighting them for empty shelves when it happened, I mean, while waiting for it to happen. At the right seasons for it to get going and coming too. Off the merchant's shelf, and into being viewed, while he was humming. "This is the right time," so they said, as we've been watching you watching them, and thought you'd said. "Curb your desires, tame the lust, and live simpler, like us. One option to ponder — "Under the compost?"

"Well, perhaps, mi cous, but that was what we did to come first, be-cause..." I'd say it that way too, if eye wore you. Just a bit more twisted and screwed hops. Like those who'd said, "Staying home is not bad at all, staying home is not bad." According to my story log, that's what this country and its people did to Dad. Yes, *if mi mad*? Well, no, Hingh kid, I'm not mad, but... My bad.

That other tiny country, though? Holy hyperbole, oh. Yes, wordplay is the order of the day around here. Yeah, man, a Jamaica yaad mi cum from, sorry, I meant to say, I'm Jamaican-born and bred, okay?

12

Fire Sale on Falsehoods Beams

"Oh, sweet Lord," she cried, "look at this, and then discard." She was shaking hard, because... The comfort had just fallen off them and their out-of-tune bungee cord. "Plapp!" it dropped, just like that brat on a rock from the safe side of their doorstep. It then rolled down the road to the other parking lot called the Car Pound, yes. So, tell me, Mister Brown, what's going to Hop...? No, not like that. Not in the same sense as how you'd hopped in my car nonstop, nor even in Lot's, but...

As for him, that same Lot Tory man, thing. He's got a lot to worry about this evening, no? Yes, he's got to go and put out a little fire now, as it is. He was told to add a little more salt to the pot for his wife, as his new business, because he was busy at home picking and cooking up the rice and peas. While she was over there chipping away at cooking up a nice shake of honey and malts at the same time, with ease. She was making up the bed too and fluffing the pillow at her brother's heated bedspread on his home ends, oops, where he would soon come to rest his weary head, right where the leg should have been. Now, Lot is left with doing the cooking, all by himself. So, not that sort, no. Not as it pertains to that Lot, oh no. But it's with the other rowdy bunch of scarred brats that we're called into the chat room, do the math, soon. You'll see them heading there.

"Where, where are they going?"

"Look, somewhere or another." So, like I said before, what's going to happen now to her brother?

"I don't know, but..."

"The high life had fallen from the sky like — "I beg your pardon, like what, bated flies?"

"Yes, it took the dive guys, just like that." The machines that were there in the past acted unfairly and meanly. Performing the task of transporting the rich and the smart from amongst the famous class I'm in (leave me with this). To wherever in the world they wanted to go, as they must, and yes, fast kid, reach out and touch. Or even to come from on a fast drive and talking about autocars, first and foremost, you know. Bids, place your bids. That's it, my kids, that's good, because...

Those, too, were taken down to the ground, "grinding ground dead," just like the travel industry person had said when they'd fed a bit too much copper and lead to someone's swollen head at the regulators' shed. Or was it? Might have been at the federally led executives' gated door instead, no?

"*Mi nuh knoah, mi bred,* but carry on with the jokes, you're there very well spoken of."

The walls also came up tall out of the plains on the border tarmac, in the same ways and means, coming to tea, as he on the ax. Same as how it came falling on them from down the lane, where they'd like to hide her out again. Like, just like they did to the carver of destruction on the corner post stand, where Rudy Bang-Bang was when he'd promised a piece of land-Don, down to them. "Come along," he said, but... When the time came to deliver the bread, Wayne. It wasn't forthcoming with them. Not in ways as it was promised to them on the multitude of talks from a wife's house on the home ends. While sweetening the deal with armored cars that she would have gone and fallen too far for, as they were greedily going in for the once-in-a-lifetime deal on the meal. Just a thing to stop the illegal immigrants from coming, and from bringing the criminal and cheap labor ring girlie gal class in with them, those dumb things. More or less like waxed-up dumplings that say "Phoenix" whenever you bite in. But there was yet another reason for the freezing, as some seers were seeing the seasons as they bit him, and it wasn't very pleasing to his eye to risk kneading. Not the least, as to say, "Illegal weed smoking must go away."

"Yes, I can see it."

"It was coming down on her, though, no?"

"Yes, I guess so."

"Yes, like, that other nation and her man in command, was... want to hear more about that one under his arm?"

"Yeah, yeah, man, keep talking on."

Under his steady and sure hands, even the busybodies were reined in and taught a darned good lesson about your daddies and moms, or two, mi bredren. Like, how to become aware of the beware ring ding songs of theirs and untruths, and like, like, how to get a grip within, and mind their own darned business, fix her Hingh affairs, my youth. Yeah, man, she's been asking for it for a very long time, over there. As long as the swinging sin Ting, something you have there, between the palms of the right and left hands, of the armchair. Belonging to those living on (or off the commons, sometimes) like his and hers. But as it occurs...

It was the fall of 3019, and the world was humming along to the tune of many beating drums (anointing). Basking in prosperity and shrugging off Sternreich's hard warning of the prophecy, that of the day's daily dawning, daily good morning shows, too, were to be heard coming through.

"On the... You mean, on the radio show?"

"There, I won't even bother to go," as the wise men and socio I-tallest tick influencers of the times then, were asked to remind dead them, and us, what we needed to do to cum fuss, sorry, I meant to say, come first. They, yes, they, those of the everyday joey kind of way, though, were somewhere around languishing on some scrap heaps of shoes to wear at home, covering a tall toe, and there also. Yes, it was the best of times for many, the 99%ers of earlier daytime years (I'm damn sure) had begun to get a foothold in the big boom of the daily shares, bought and sold. Some striking it rich in the stock markets, cash, or gold. Others in online business marketing, to top racket them up to heaven, my dear, and whatever other multiple streams of income Hingh fix or wealth propeller scheme Mingh habits they could imagine into being quick, quicker, clear, and clever as this... Yes. For them to join up with the 1%ers, they were riling up the anger managers' agents against, mere days earlier. There has never been another generation of misfits or entrepreneurial apprenticeships laden with so many multimillionaires among them. Enough rich tweens were coming in amongst those in their upper thirties to have the words "How the hell did you come up with all that dough, though?" Falling liberally out of the popped open mouth of many twice or three times their age-oh.

Suddenly, the Kingsland world grew much smaller for dozens ee, for far too many of them even, and they spared themselves nothing in the ovens to your envy, Hingh Stephen. The travel industry (like all else around the Third Land's country) was very lucky. Glistening in luxury and zooming the jet engines to get the happy-go-lucky jet-setting world travelers, poodle puppy Hingh carriers wherever they wanted to go in an hourglass tour. Fast or slow, anyway, anywhere they want to, they're going to go.

Meanwhile, the prophets, magicians, and soothsayers of those days and after this one were sending out the warning prayers to quell disaster. On laughter, though it might have been, mister man, still, and softer. The message they sent was for them to (just chill). "True." "Yes," telling them and her to stay her will, as it occurred. "The earth," they said, "is at her limit's plight one way or the other." Yeah, so I heard them saying at the time to the brother, Mi bred, but still. Others said to us that night. "That could never be right; something has got to give if we're to continue to live." Many high and mighty of the daytime, likely, would have rebutted the warnings slightly. Calling it a hoax, fake news, and the rest of the arts on which to muse. Storming in, all evening rapping up the views, but of course. On eye-witness news, even. Until, yeah. Up until there arose a whisper in a small corn her mister, yeah, right there in a small corner of a faraway land, like this Terre, warmer than cold winds in this icy corn or some thin of the bassists' sinister ring. A sign saying that some troubling occurrence had begun to hit them on the abhorrent backside of their fore-ends, yes, man, of their overly busy hands, then hers, again. Back and forth like children, they were passing around the blame. "Something with the potential to affect us on all ends, sir," I heard her say when she said it to him and her, then walked away. Then, that effect came affecting us as quickly as it did the call to the term, must... Just like an early morning wake-up call from the boss, and up. "Can someone bring me my coffee cup, please?" said the beast, sorry, I meant to say, the boss. "Bring in my coffee, please," he said, "ten Q." So, he did, just as he'd often do.

Though many of us Kinglanders took it lightly at the time, the entire world was soon told to shut down behind her g-line, girls, yeah, there it is, look... The line is wrapping around that building and following behind her. You know, like, there was to come the stern warning to them that says, close the door, and go inside your house for more, or go on, take a sneak peek in hers if you can't find yours. Yeah, man, the door is what we're talking about on these classic chords and scores."

"How convenient and pure!"

"Well, if you like," it continued. "You may close (or open) the lid on your fly-fishing kit door behind her and go in and hide all four from behind the point-blank firing line of yours. But, whatever you do (or don't do, do). Go into your house, Blue, and close those doors behind you. Stay there until you get further words from; remind me, who?"

"Us, of course, who else did you expect but us?"

"Meaning, them, and who again?"

"No, stop pointing at me, that's not true, it was neither me nor you. You should never be blamed for such things as they'd claimed, but..."

They gave out the commands, and we did what was wrong; we obeyed the quiz. But they all knew that they couldn't keep the Kingsland world locked up for too long a gig, as if we're kids, and twirling the finger ring seed at his..., no.

"Because?"

"Because of whatever interested whoever, with whatever each side was to come falling upon them with, with cleverness. Well, everyone except this one." One man and his lone country did what no other could or would have done to her clan. "C?"

"Yes, of course I can still see."

While the rest of the world was busily searching for goods, needed cure to their ills, too, as they should. Casting their nets out to fetch the magic pills, the daily food, and paying the lightweight electricity bills, all good. At the same time, they were searching out the magician's brains for the next miracle to fix her upper kitty frame of mine, to correct the ills for them, but. This one country, though, closed the door on everybody, Huntley?

"Oh!"

"Yes, and tossed away the keyed-up Bentley."

"No!"

"Yes." The borders that were bumpy and everything else that could be closed some more, Leigh. Came closing in on me, and even after everything that could be closed upon the executive order, was closed up on him properly, my brother. Yes, that sort was the cart that came from the call coming in from the front leader's quarter. Even falling to the bounce back, calling upon the mouths of its inhabitants galore, those who would soon be taking the other people's cure, yeah. Their chatty-chatty mouths were closed out, too. Then came the busy-bodies, and you. The reactors were reacting, and their canceled cultural remedies were impacting. Then came the repercussions, the acting out and upon, and the measured results about which they were busily chatting while throwing insulted coupons for several years later on down the road, without stopping to look at the sign that was announcing a signed-up sinking sandy, sulking sun, on their watering holes. Necessity, they say, is the mother of all invention right away, so... They had pushed this tiny country into a tight lid can, like me, look, man, can you see it? Or was it a basket, looking like this one-door ring sieve? Come, look, and see. Now, tell me, do you agree? Then tell me, which one is he? Okay, I'll continue to say what I see. While they were left there where they were, like, eyes wide open but "still can't see," more or less like fish on the markets, meant for meat, no?

"Well, um, you should know, so that's why?"

"Yes, I know, that's why. They'd cornered them decades earlier, forcing them to rely on their own ingenuity, innovation, inventiveness, my companion, and even greater on than that can, of worms." They did that gloriously, Sam, on their terms. To say that they were prepared and ready to go it alone again this year was an understatement from oxymorons to spend and go share the comments, if nothing else, my dear friend lists.

This time, however, they weren't pushed to smith her in. No Doreen, no, never were they pushed, is what I mean. They went willingly together. Well, the leader class went, and the people followed them in the dent, as was the intent, uncontented though they might have been going along with those tithings in the beginning, to the fullest length. Because they must always respond to what the elders across the economic power border would have hollered out and cursed, one another. Look, look at what they have become now; a country and people quite unlike any other in the post-plague world of cows, somehow carrying the calves and dragging the vehicle at the hind half. Well, the only other people, perhaps, based on the way things are beginning to look at last. While this was going on, though, the other groups were having some... like, some sort of a toe-toe in a field day on the farmland dead grounds. Things couldn't have been more perfect for them if they had planned it for Mr. Brown when... Come to think of it, Gwen, they probably did. Many are arguing that they did. How else could things have turned out that way for them and the Guinea pig? Isn't that what they were lobbying and arguing for, for decades on end, in the quiz? Yes, look at the records, my friends' pickney's... They would not listen to the warning and did not take it seriously enough to heart when they stormed him. But then the ice started melting, and they went in. That was when...

13

Sacrificial Lambs

Under the uncertain hands of the governmental plan. The words of the wise men came hitting up against their eardrums nearer than the headrest stand that stood on the stand at the backside of the pavement bumps, "Am I wrong?"

"Yes, but carry on, put it on your shoulder and move along before I have to lash you again with the weapon." This same old whipping stick that I'm now leaning on for support, you know it can already, so move along towards the outer court, tell us some more, Freddie."

"Okay, 'Seek peace,' he said to his fellow on the deathbed out east, nursing an ailment neither of them was able to prevent, not even the dread natty dreadlock that — "Not even the natty dreadlock? — "Yeah, man, that's who I'm blaming this talk king on."

"You mean, he couldn't prevent it either?"

"No, siree, couldn't stop the other dreads from wearing their locks on their heads above their knees. Although he couldn't remember where he'd put the key when it could no longer tune his guitar in the proper G car, I mean, chord, sorry. It was hard, but it was also said in the hearing of the one serving up the medicated cement in the yard, to me. So, Dreddy was he, the person with the key."

"Oh Lord, did you ceet?"

"Yes, I saw and heard it all." That's what the maid meant to be saying, too, when she said it with such certainty when she called. Wanted them all to get the message of the messed-up age in their mouths to call you out, you know, but they weren't listening at all. Neither were you, who was at the time, having a ball driving someone's new Volvo up the wall, good and stout. But how were they to be so sure whether it came through to tear their earring door off the queue near the cow stall, to hang it on the wall way out?"

"How would I know that? I think it's time for me to disappear fast from you and your acts."

Go on, go. Go and seek peace with the man of war, my brother dear, no less than her, beware. Not war, ever. Unless you're looking for more, but way too much of that scar already at your door, and so far, it's unsteady. Even if it's your enemy who is planting that seed of an idea within your car, take it from her, or him. It means the same thing. It means that he wants peace, at his feet, or a piece of something, if even to prevent a little piece of the sheet from covering your cold feet under the clay sheets of dumplings. At least, it could mean he wants a little reprieve with you, too, Steve. More time to be a little less mean than I am, I mean, he. Less mean than he has been with you so far. Or more, "more 'mean' is what I mean this time." He's first a fighter, though, as you already know, that I know. Don't ever forget to remember that early morning show. Never forget that pillar there on the back seat of his car either, my dear, now, go, go off somewhere and breed her, I mean, as a breeder...

"No."

"No, did you just say so, like, no?"

"No, how can I go? Not while you're here, dealing out this beautiful talk show, I can't just leave it like that and go, no, I won't, so. Go on, go on, keep on talking up a storm."

"Okay, my new mom, I'll carry on..." Gone was the one going down to see the band on the stand at the indie go-go show. That, though, I know that you already know the news, so just for emphasis, we're bordering on bothering to tell you this again, oh, and wrapping up the views. He knows all that there is to know about wars, and he knows how to win them too, even against the stars, the gods, fathers, and yes, nature calls coming on through.

"Through the border?"

"Yes, who told you how to say so?" (Too out of order). How much more so will he win against you, oh? Peace and honor are what he's after, Mama. These are the tools forward from here, Grandma Foster. How is your little grandson? What's his name again?

"Who, you mean, Bascom? He's growing up quite nicely and is handsome, too."

"Nice," however, he is not why we're here together tonight, carrying on, and telling the times and the weather to the knights, carrying the arms.

"You mean...?"

"Yes, that's right, that's what I mean." However often he comes, honor and respect him. Do it while you still can sin, for the good that comes to you from him, at the very least. At his hand, too, and his feet, that one there fiddling with your fingertips, like those, and these, if nothing else to put your finger on this thing, please. Thank you, I really appreciate it. There's nothing else that's quite as pleasing to me, Sis as... Not as you were this evening at the easing trick ads, even in the midst of all the bad cards that he sent over to you, and salt to sell the hell out of it on you all.

"Oh lord, what? Is that the truth?"

"Yes, you'd better believe it is, my youth."

"That must be why I'm always so blue."

"Yes, it's all because of that."

"What, the salt?"

"Yes, of course, it's true."

"Oh, man, what did I do to deserve this from you and at your hands?"

"Nuttn, nothing at all, it's just the easiest way forward to the fall, but..." Even while paying him back with the same salty sword that he'd used to sway you-ward, pay him, yes, if at all you can find his headrest, then go home and rest assured that you showed him no mercy than before, or else, he'll come back and do it to you again like the whack attack, but Ken. Know that and this, my friend. He still has the power to do that much damage to you and Sam Midge, much more than can fit into your crown-spotted dog sled carriage. Or even on that hourglass time clock of his... after eating the sausage on spilling sort of hot cornmeal porridge. Even to kill, and yes, he will, if you let him. Don't let him, even more so than you not letting him in to pass through the door unnoticed by the king, don't give him any more reasons than those two to continue to sin, no more than before you, you were able to hear. While killing you and the poor thing over there, oh, look at them, my dear; that one over there is laughing. Like him, he's always laughing with him as if he wants to be liked by liking him, even in the way he goes about killing. He then leaves and goes, after he's done with doing you in, slowly. To then find that he's still able to leave and be gone away from there with a sword in his hand, swinging and aware at your sleeve, as before. No, don't let him. Be sure to finish off the job, jabbing that you'd started to perform stabbing on the robbing lad's skin. Or you'll be sorry to rawtid, man, a yard kid, no kidding. Come on. Don't forget to remember this one, it's the most valuable amongst the pack of cards in your right and left hands of the van. A mangy dog, they say, is better than September, right away, okay? "Yeah!" As was said in the song to remember, one day. "Remember her? The one who was said to be a dead lion to a stranger?"

"Yes, for sure, but — "But nothing, kill that lion, if you're anything at all like Will I am, you will?" Well, not just you, but he, him, he always does, yes, and he will, again if you let him. It's about him that we're here doing this talk, king sin ting, or something, right? He kills and destroys a man, woman, girl, and her boyfriend if she was lucky enough to have had one of those things when he came in, on them. Since such kinds were beginning to fly out (on air), plain and simple, and were dying over there. All because of the clauses of causes in the clothes that he'd forced upon you to wear, all of you, and us too, yes. So, those were getting scarce when they'd happened to barge in on them and you, "Yes?"

"Yes, I guess that's true. That was all because of his desire and not so much his need to feed the fires and the demons he breeds, right?"

"Said speed, mi lawd, yes, yes indeed, my Lord, you're really bright, 'You liar,' someone else, and I was heard whispering this beside her while we were turning aside her head to inquire what I'd said when investigating which bed has the most heat to inspire those same batches of thieves from way up higher east. But let's continue along with the prayer and speech." Then comes that, and this. He kills some more because of his fear of the poor and his insatiable appetite for more. His happy nest is as hippy hoppy, I guess, and as tight as baked-on braids on their headrests and yours tonight no less, no?

"No, for good nests' sake, man, I'm half "frayed" of being afraid that, that... Why are you playing these games with my aid, I mean, head, with my head hat at, at...?"

"It's because of things like these, mi bred, and those, yes, my dear brother. I want to warn you about these things because of our love for one another, I mean, each other. Like I've already said, it's because of his greed to score, and chiefly, his fear of me, and the poor, yes indeed. I'm very sure."

"But, but please, tell me. Why is that?"

"Did you just toss an ask out of your mask? Well, I'll tell you, it's because he thinks that if you and I ever get a leg up on high, like, on your top horse to go and save her right left-handed thigh from kicking you in your, ask me why, and I'll tell you no more lies when I'd say, his, his. Yes, it's in his cold old fire pits that we're throwing the ashes, you know what I mean, right?"

"Right, I see. Like, by getting somewhere nearer to it than I might be, right?"

"Yes, to have been able to see the splitting images of the glitter in his eyes and get to slap a box of nuts and bolts on his no-holds-barred wholes that you'd given me on the backside of their hides, or inside of the note thing nests of his blue lagoon holes, nothing less. To get you closer to seeing him fall and die, yes, Mildred, dead. When he'd thought that he was only going to be bedding down there for the night, licking her where it hurts the most, Ted, on the poor thing's happy, tighter on his loose pride. Like, licking up something against a thing called a pillar, or up against the posting on a notice board of such things to kill her. Or anything else the likes of such sins, go on, discard, but first and foremost, hush up, don't talk too much in this mission yard because... Closer even than a baby's backside as it cried and cursed him out the doors with a pail full of the worst thing to clear up those warts he was breeding. Or even have him take a ride on her high tide to get inside and die from a slip off the icy roadside while coming back from going right outside where he was going to meet them. He took a trip to go out and kick the hell out of the back of his friends' new concept leather chair, you know. That one near the back end of his office sphere, where he used to spend weekends, yes, there, with Hugo."

"Where?"

"Up there where he sits and stares at his eyes while he plans and strategizes, pretending that he's not hiding from folks he'd tried to get destroyed from far and wide as... If that's his latest advice to you and these guys, then he lied, again. Just by saying that you and I won't do to him back as he'd done to me, and you fuss. Yes, and the fast one too, first and foremost. That's the first thing a man will hang on him and his hanging cloth, for wiping your nose. While he's wrapped up and tied up with pulling those strings tight on your horse's saddling gears tonight, or even off his clothing, fear and bright."

"Yes, but is it right, and when will it begin?"

"Next year, in the evening. Yes, go on and cuss, and spit out fears, if you don't believe him. Well, if you want to curse and get vexed, but... The very man who could have, and probably should have been an example, and a king's kind of role modeling sample for all good and clean, not just mean and lean like a tram pulled lean (or straight). But wait, no. It's more like, better to be a teacher for good nest's sake, a sauced sage, too, to guide many of his kind away from their mistakes with me, and mimes, like you. Or even with your bad behavior — "Behave yourself, man, stop that.""

"Okay, I shall, from now on, my boss, e-pops." But if not enough, we may be able to help him hang it up. Just by teaching them how to reach her, on the very first date, as the preacher did when she was given the ape as the very best thing for her faith, and he was to reach her. Teach Hingh, at the time, you know, as those times would so Dick taste, sorry, I meant to say, tates, like, dictates, and yes, to the benefit of your kind of people too. Even us, them, and the other crew. Guiding the boo-boo balloons who are into all my rooms, out, and into getting better for themselves, no doubt, and us, too. Even on pledges and oats, porridge, of course. If not as good as you and your tube do when they're doing the roads. Like, pictures galore to show off in the hood and to the poor, whenever he meets up with the poor thing and you at the corn "her" store. I mean, at yours, of course, that's good. You bought it like food, no? Not just you, but the ones who once knew Mister Flowers Wood, too. But now, he builds roadblocks and all sorts of barriers nonstop, always erecting something before the man's bus stop, Hingh. Thursday morning musical throwback of kings, too, to serve as the road maps into how to go about having a good time dumping something in on you and them as in the old times, again. Not even as good as a corn-meal dumpling with pork and dollar swine, on the road in, but just to disrupt things. Like this rope thing is your hope of every attempt at progressing further on the tenth link up, yet more to the Top Pen town. While swinging by to go and swing the wide-open Bonny Gate around you and yours, toeing the way down. But if you want to carry Ann a little bit further along the road towards a sentence in St. Ann's, you might as well Preston through down to the Port where Maria used to court the girls, and yes, the boys too.

"But, but why, why would she do a thing like that against you?"

"Why did you ask that, my guy, boo? I'll tell you why, as if in a swap, you, listen up well. It's because... She wanted to recruit those youths into the army barracks and boots to teach them how to shoot and inspire some real people-loving cops' careers in truth. But that did not connect with a lot of neglect, because some of those youths had some things to say about that on their ask, and they did a lot of those sorts of 'say,' saying things like: Some say that in the army the pay isn't very fine. They paid us fifty dollars and took back forty-nine, in taxes and clawbacks that weren't mine. So, they did not go. Furthermore, since you'd asked about the rest of the axes that someone had chopped off the oak doors near his axe, Sis, I'll tell you. It's because..."

"Because of what, again, tell me? Because I'd like to know."

"Okay, here we go. It's because the man has some very valuable stuff there sitting in the hut spheres, nearer than his rear, to the chair. Like, gold end stuff, and a staff. Crisp and clear as his as — "What, you mean...?"

"Yes, his Asthma attack.

At the time of the attack, it was as clear as his assumed accessories in his hand, cuffs, links to wear on his calf, stank and bare like Rastafar-I know, my star."

"But why do you always cut in with something stink right in the middle of shuffling a "sent tense" with the inks, like, while I'm putting forth my P's and Q's into my arguments? You shouldn't do those sorts of things without first getting my consent, okay?"

"Okay." How did such things get this far anyway, and when, you'd asked? I'll tell you then," it's like... He was just invited to the uptown fair, to go on and in the thoroughfare with the flower basket of the boss's knitted wit there, but. Tough luck, no such thing would come forth.

They were stuffed away, there. "Just as much as under his rocking rock band — 'Chair?'"

"Yes, that was the real hardware, you know, like. Things he and your other friends have gotten you to hand over to them, for nothing more than a swinging sum thing, to tin can you in, or something." Well, nothing new on this bluegrass Territory called Kingsland ore, eh?

Anywhere else under the sun, it would have caused a woolaballoo down your home, like, if they should ever do like they've done it to you and, um... The outcome would have been vastly different from yours.

But, over here, that's what you get, my dear. Nothing but tough luck and finger-licking forklifts to work out your shut, like, sweating your shirts off your gut punched in by a fist from us, yes, Siree.

After somebody was done with sucking the potted soft-boned stew to a glowing hue, guess what was to be found hopping in on you? Nothing new, might just have choked you on the way through. Just like a golden hen goose once did it to; yes, guess who? Lucky you. So you thought, but tough luck some more on your guts' bus as before. That's not how it was going to go, as it turned out, the door, no, Mi cous. But you don't want him to stop doing those sorts of ding-dong sin thing, though, so... He kills yet more, kills all those who get a vision of progressive things to screw on a door that was lying on the floor in the house. He then gets into the habit of getting further into your home spheres to go inside unannounced to do some more screwing around on the region's poorest road, the most. The one leading home, even. Even that one hinged on y... hang on, have to take this one, my guy?

Hello, yes, yes, yes. Okay, I guess. Okay, okay. Bye.

"Thanks, man, thank you for bearing with me and holding on. Just had to take that call from someone, but... but, but now, let's carry it on our shoulders the rest of the way to getting older. Now, where were we on the subject tree? Yes, some progressive things to do on his given land, dead screws much too close to me, and to proceed into enlightening others of his kind of light-skinned brothers, or dark as me and my mother's — "What man, tell me?"

"Yes, men, they are indeed. To bring them along with him into the waste in deeds, look at that girl whining again." Boy, that girl sure knows how to bust a waist, Ted, move that I'm in. But that's the enlightened end, my friends, as we're now beginning to see the end. Yes, coming first on or off, them, and friends, yes indeed, like... Like, when it comes to him getting to view us in two many of the ways and dead as nails. Come, take a look at these, and ask the cats' fleece-fleeing ticks with ease. Paws scratching and tongues licking dung some fur-coated biz knees as if it's nobody's business. The lime diseased TikTok tide, too, was gone, farther away from view. The one who was there a while ago, asking. 'Who is this?' and that meow cat of his? Yes, the one with the little pusses, still there scratching fleas away from "she," yes, her."

"Who me?"

"Yes, you."

"Couldn't be."

"Then who?"

"Enough of your off-subject booboo, let's get on with the real subject to take back to school with Hugh."

Tell me now. How then can you do it to me, and him too? How are you two going to sit there and poke a funny finger at fondling the screws on and off the other man's chair that is there on his... while kicking off the kind shoe that he wears, while sitting there on the bibs? Even as he's trying to put them on his son's feet to bear him up, chow man, command his... how could you do that one? Calling him all those derogatory names of thine and lying lame this time? Like, tooth, touting those very horns of yours that you strummed the strings on galore? "Truth." Even at the very names that you once looked around you and your teenage flame, and were quick to find such at your door nook to frame, guess who? Yes, you did, you'd framed her and fenced her in. Yes, at some point in time or another, Miss Dor-In. Yes, Ingrid, ask his brother. You mean, you already did? Okay. What I meant to say is, "were." You were fenced and framed in, again and again. Plain was the same, as such was found written in your forefather's writing book up the line, lame (or down). That was how you first got to know such kinds of names to curse out the tough cows, though, look, but don't... hush, shee."

"But I, I want to, to..."

"Quiet, quiet, quietly now. Take a pause and wait it out, for me." Wow!

"Okay, they're gone, so we can continue the song. Where were we? Yes, there. See?" Names you now want to place on such kinds of other men as you now see them in this case, and you? Look, look at them over there looking back at you; a mistake, now. Can you see them? There they are, looking back at your car, they've risen over the scar and flying cow, my star. Because, to them, you and I were kind, that's the reason why I'm trying, that's how Souci would have happened to come to the shine. Go now, go feed the swine, the moo cow too, mi blow wow, "Moo." This is a good time to ask another riddle of mine, so I'll ask it with an ax, Sis, now. What if you'd done the same to the other man kinds of men blame, and his children after him? Those same open-ended games that you're now quick to call out those names as if a sin. Or just leave aim, like, leave him with his pocket full of beads, in? What if you'd bothered to leave him and his children's pickney dem alone to carry a lame lamb home? Even on his back heavily laden, shouldering on to go and roam the "rawtid" sun down. With his pain and their shameful programs just the same as it is now strapped to the kid's ramp on his son's Bam-Bam. Wouldn't he, yes, him again? Wouldn't he and his kind be better off for it than dying? Like dying to go praising your sheet? I mean, your name. Praising the sheet off your feet for your good name's sake today? While leaving you far less afraid, and less cruel at shunning your grave away? Just asking this, Dave, that way.

"O,-kay, or was... wasn't it my way?"

"I'm sure that's what Uncle Frankie would have liked us to say, but..."

Yes, my friends, just a bit more of the same; word play, every day.

14

My Way, or the Higher Ways

"What are you waiting for?" He was heard asking this of the green-lit-up red car. That same one there, lingering too long in — "Where?"

"There, at the traffic lights where you are, thus far in."

"You've got all the time that you may need in the Kingsland world to make a decision, my girl," so he said, "to decide on the tough luck cow..."

"Oh, wasn't it the coughed-up cold from his head?"

"No, not quite, mi bred." There you are, twiddling with pearls, not sure what for, but... Look at this, girls, he's coughing up things on the calf, the right one there wrapped up in his left half, again. That's a clean hand dead down sock that's now baked on his lapped-topped-up shirt sleeve, a piece of cloth he is hanging it on, like these. "That's not the right decision," he said, "and since it's optional whether you take a liking to the gal on the bed, that same one there on the schemed-up plot non-partial, I beg... We're all here waiting to see what decision you've got for me and the marshals. Well, if any, but... anyway. Since you haven't made the proper decision on the matter by now, and haven't decided to do as I'd said, a blow-wow. Like, since you've not done what my friends and I wanted you to do, Hingh, we've got to decide for you, Rin. Test me and see if I won't be coming to take your TV away, along with every other thing you won't be able to purchase with your pay; just do the right thing, okay? We want you to tell us your decision now. The right one, not the left hand, a blow wow. No, not as you and your friends have D side Head two do on the dodos over there, in the west end. That's the wrong direction to steer the next ram, and very unfair for you to do such wrongs to your brotherly companion, by going out mingling with them on the bandwagon, and jeopardizing their safe tea. All that after they would have done what is right for me by doing the writings in my record-keeping bins when they went out and protected themselves from people like you, for me. Unlike you, who will not do the 'write' thing and take the protection, so that you will be protected two, just as the next one, like… like those people would have done before you, who will be forced to do the injection. Now you and your friends want to come and deprive them of the protection that they had been protected with for so long. So, somebody has got to make up your mind for you; that's what we're going to do."

If things such as these should happen in the waste and deeds, those who do it would have been made to take a leaf out of their tree of life and leave very quickly. But luckily for us and the "likkle" pickney, just a little bit of this is happening in the Kingsland afar off, far away from us on the earthly dust of our rocks, but…

The top head pan wanted to show them who was in command and did so when he came down on them with a slam. More or less like the bull-bucking traffic cop with a bogus badge on, to put on top of what he was not given at the barracks to brag, Mom. That same one who polices the bad drivers' crew of cronies, by driving worse beside her than your address dome is, "because — "What, because he's the only one allowed to advise her as, as is…? "Yes, but of course, did so when he caught you driving back at him at 110 clicks going forward in the passing lane of his onward road like this, one hundred max and mix on the highway of wasted bits of blown-off loads." Yes, bits of hen's droppings were dropping off their chicks here, there, and everywhere before the cocks' crows, you know what, and then comes chicken and chips for the children's snacks that they don't want to share. Beware! On top of what they always wanted to wear against their parents' eyelids to stare, like, like those over there bopping fast flipping, "Hi Lydia," how are things going with buy law lashes, and then gone are they sliding bye-bye through the low-lying grids where the crotch is and gazing back at you and me, Edah. To get your children's school fees and lunch money too, pulling it strong-arming out of the pocket loop. But, not doing it "my way," as he sees things via his eye way. You know, like, while he was barreling past you, or even when he was coming back at your jean car dot watch that won't restart after it had stopped two lights back. No matter how hard you may wind it up and shake it. Its tik-toking will not wake up again (sick). But, to him, it must have been because he was ticking it up to clocking max out and passing the fast scout, too, on the wrong side of the box, trying to get out, backing you in, in the process, even.

Then cutting in before us, and you to come over and adore most of us all the way through. Breaking the hell out of his neck to go braking up to almost a complete stop too, two trucks back, and a bus, Ted lock-tooth toot, the horn Hingh, blaring at you, to teach us a lesson or two, no doubt. Want Ted to show you that, you can't drive that piece of trin-ket crap box like that, so go and learn the codes on how to drive the roads fast, or slow, better off. My way is the higher ways — "Away?"

"Yeah, man, probably."

Meanwhile, "Don't use my highway like that, child," was what I heard him say, "Okay?" Yeah, man, these are the facts, wild, eh!

After all, hell would have broken loose when the cord cores were twined tightly around Ken's boots. Yes, lacing 'em up good and proper on some new age truths as a matter... The neck, too, yes, just as loose as his, as... One end tied to his walking shoes and choking the "hail" of a hosting out of the socks and bespoke high-end suit. As you'd bow and salute his beautiful baby, "Too cute," you had said, "Too cute." Now you're smelling what's left there, telling us of the half-cooked goose that's coming down the shoots, at the youths' clubhouse evenings. Then comes the convergence of the sediment you all were needing, and now, look. The noose, again, but as it happened. He was the last man standing among them, yes, those crooks from Mount Haven, again.

Everywhere he turned his head to look (he thought) heaven's angels were hopping off, or were they hell's? — "But, but, wasn't he right?"

"Come, follow along, and see tonight."

Freedom of speech is yours, and your aunt's, and yes, mine too. As in, my aunt's pants, that's who. Well, so they say, but you're only as free as the cup of leftover teeth you'll get as your pay from your old grandpa when he comes back from the grave today, yuh ceet.

"Yeah, man, mi see it."

Okay, you're pretty neat, but back up now to eat, I mean, to it, same thing, and it's to be used only to say what I want you to say. Like, to meet "me" at the corner down your avenue, of course. Like, like, when coming in to speak the truth, whenever you speak to me. One way or the other, my way is proper, "Okay, mi Breda?"

"Yes."

Yes, even if it's not as you already know it is, like, not quite as okay as you think on the shiver ring sleeve. Now, beware of shaking hands with thieves, they're prone to deceive... But not so with me and my hand me downtrodden... something, things in which you never wanted to believe, the dumb thing, not him. Like, in the way you are always shivering on the delivery ring whenever you happen to run into him. "Isn't that something?"

"Yes, it is, but..."

'It's misinformation to say any such thing in contradiction to him," so they say. So, this man is a who's who in their program, a primetime newsman on television.

"Or was it, wasn't it called, tell leave vision?"

"Mi nuh knoah yah man, I don't know. It could even be a lie, like a tell lie vision, all night long, but..." Look up, he's having a chat with the big man, a hookup, you know him. The big-time expert who knows everything but nothing, and the next verse is sure to be coming in soon.

"But that is quite another lacking in the room, no?"

"Shush, hush up and listen." Listen to the latest crop of raisins coming off him and the rest of the dirty dirt-man singing a new song to them. "Yeah," they said, "That's a nice tune (deh) man, got a beat to eat, eh."

"Yeah," I'd said. But let's go on with the talk show replay of the day, will you, mi bred?

"Yeah, okay."

He knows all that there is to know about celebrity shows and concerts. Yes, He knows a pretty penny's worth about such, "I'm always first," so, if you'd ask me to tell him how to hush up and go buy a new shirt, uncrushed. Just like that one that my mom once gave me to go and give to Mass Shut. That's not what everyone else calls him, but because I'm just a tiny tot, as tall as him, I can't call him "Shut" like that, then go back to sit comfy on the porch, and sin. So, back now to the one who's sitting on the couch, asking around. He's who comes first in such hallowed things and the farrowed ground, no?

"No, go back over there and sit down."

"Yes, I suppose that's four D best."

The reporter is with him, chatting. The reporter threw a hotshot question straight at him and in his cap's direction. Coughing, cough, cough, look at that, he's wrapping up the time he won't be lying, I mean, talking, doing so by coughing, and sipping on his drinking glass, often. To prevent those who know that he knows nothing from laughing at him, in front of them, even. But the questions are still coming, in the form of an answer as was demanded by a monster, of a man. Look at him, must be big John, or something else that's long. The answer was demanded from him by this same someone, sir, on — "Look, stir, stir, stirring is occurring at the back of his head, you know. 'What the heck!'" You'd said, like, while you were there and stirring his coffee morning like it's the cure, for him, and Ned.

Back now, though, to big John, not Joe, as said. He was the one who wanted an answer to fit his all-season planter through the back door with the heat in his hand, Sir. So, he asked him at once to stir. Coming into them via the Tell E-phony door called FaceTime on Instagram, or some other such Tele program. "Yeah, sure," he said. But he seemed to see it as something for him to spin on a span, Hingh pan tea Leigh is who he's fix hate Ted on. Fixing things up real slick, you know, man. Or better said than this, Hugh-go, like when he's coming upon it for the first time and holding it in the palm of his fist, fine as if he's reading and scrutinizing it to see if it's mine. But the expert has the answer to give him this time. Sure, like everything else, he's fine, like, when it comes to him finding things, and more nothing when it comes to him. "Well," he said while slapping his palm in alarm upon his leg. "It's not enough time for us to say quite categorically yet, Gordy, the caller. But I'm absolutely sure that it's probably going to be more like — "Mi granny blow wow, what's this I see now?" was what I heard next, popping out of my mouth, end door, while standing there by somebody, almost floored. Sure, absolutely sure, and probably, in the same sense, tens of thousands cupped pots of hot tea? To say what he wants to say to meat, me. Quite categorically, like, what does he think that I must beat? Really?

Yet he's the man, and not me. He's the expert who's going to sell me on what ported bowl of sleet is best for me. I a-greet. Because the other guy who's trying to talk up a lie, to meat, and everybody else you'll agree, is peddling lies, Miss and Mister disinformation and conspiracy theory, such alibis all allied, on the shelf fish and conch tea. Don't listen to him, you see, or else...

Yes, I see, and what I saw was that and this. "There's no freedom at all, not of speech nor thought, none left here for me a far..." "No, don't do that." Comes the hush-up talk from my uncle of sorts.

"Alright, man, let's just move along." No open-mindedness of sorts anymore. "Am I in a dead nest?" I shot back at the poor... guy.

"I'm sure it's not that," was his reply.

"Yes, of course it is," so said I. Such wicked nest eggs are gone from us, gone out the back doors to shegg with bacon pretending that she can cuss, when all of us know more than that, that she can't. As for him and me, if you prefer me saying it like that guy, B. I know this as a certainty; he soon will be, like, not quite as free as he once used to be. Before you know it, as well as him and I, he won't be as free as he used to be, when seen... Definitely, won't be mean, I mean, like, be seen on TV any longer than you and me. Sit, sit, sit, and drink your cup of tea that I'm dishing out for free, and be sure to drink it while it's hot, like me. I bet you wish your boyfriend were... Because, to disagree with the programmers' scripted Pea soup pot, is the quickest and easiest way to make you have to move over and go out to play around the back. Gone away to sit near the doorways in a corner lot on the bus of Lot's you know, same as he was, when he was sitting there and watching fools fighting themselves over salt, again. While shedding tears like rain, as if it was his wife's fault to blame, as to why the pillar was so small and getting smaller every day by default. 'Why,' he'd asked, "was it because of me?"

"*Mi nuh knoah* at all, I really don't know, man."

But, no, not as a go-goner, was he. No, just a Warner, Bee, who had to flee. But you? You were just sitting comfy there and watching the corner, trying to see if you could still storm her, I mean, see her. If you still can see and hear things like me, my dear, just nod and wink the eye bag and say, "fair." In this current age of the free world sphere where we now live for the remainder of the girl's brown hair in a sifting sieve, and the time that they may, or may not give to you and me, to can tin you to live. Or, that which may even be left for us to forget and forgive. But always remember to think positive... Leigh, positively. "Or shut your mouth, and just believe," as it was said by the preacher who beat her last week, in our neck of the woods. Believing lies such as these, even. But how did fine things such as these swine sins ever get this fine on her sleeves' hind string hanging from a clothesline to hang on Hingh? Grab a short cup of tea and have a comfy little seat over here by me, please. By the time I'm done telling the lie I'm going to try with, they're going to be bypassing what everyone else is asking me if I'm selling my sheet, you'll see that I'm hip as a heap of... for sure. They simply got sick. Yes, man, that was quick, sick with what was coming on down the skid. Sick and tired of being slick and fired. So says the rest of them and the lie ads, then they acted and were fired upon by the lost kid.

"Which kid, Nanny's kid?"

"Yes. She was standing there with a gun in her hand when they were asking her a question. Like, 'Gunman,' they said, 'tell me "weh" yuh get the gun from.'"

"Well, there you go again, talking off-topic to them, but..."

"Yeah, man, that one was a baby sham." She was one of those who were among the actors who reacted afterward. After the real ax man came in and waxed Ann, to mock our words, yes, she same one. That gal, that gal Shelly-Ann in the crib wagon. It was her, Mildred, and Orchid. Come on, nuh badda skid a rathid. Mek she lie as much as she wants, chatting bout sey "it wasn't me; it wasn't me, nor the plant they'd used for his tea." *Mi knoah*, I mean, I. I know what the truth is, and we all agreed that it wasn't cute, it was she, Jamaican *yardie sin ting aggen*.

Medicated at gunpoint was how it got started. Like, gum ninth —

"And half-hearted, right?"

"Oink."

"She meant to say 'right.'"

"Yeah, whatever you say, Ms. Piggy, you're always okay and bright with me, anyway. We'll go back to the attack because it was not that, no. Not really at gunpoint, but more like, at point-blank range, prime time news ain't... I mean, isn't, sorry. Prime-time news isn't painted bright when pointed straight at us tonight. Wrapping up the notches in the accumulated views plus tight. Late-night live shows, too, good morning is coming soon, right?"

"Right."

Now, here comes the aahs and oohs. Hush Puppies boots and doggy types of shoes are soft. Got the big booboo's jaw slip just by doing the talks; they had to push it back into the slot. He was talking too much, Fox, about those un-truthing, toothing big shots. Big-time late-night talkers accepted the big dollars that were offered, yes, the big money was coming after, hinged on the saucer. Tallying it up together, as offered to him, by the pauper's bredda, even.

Bigger balances are sure to follow him after. "Good evening, Master." Now, look at him leaving. Jumped on the boat going down to the fish-sellers quarter with the thieving... yes, the hut dweller who burst out laughing at the next slaughter with lying, downtrodden thieves singing the blues beneath the sheets. "Mi gut?" Now look at these and hush up. These things are never to be talked about, okay? "Okay."

15

The Nanny

It was the time of the Grammy. Long gone was my wise old granny, so to speak, when saying such things to the mammy. So too was the telegram man of the week, gone off towards telling the other man what to eat; everything was gone. Went off the program when they came in and took your freedom. Leaving you with nothing but nearly free, and as "we-dumb" as they come to be. Your rights, too, went away to sell you on the wrong things to uncork the screw towards me, like that— "What, like what?"

He'd asked that very question, too, but no answer was to be found coming back through. As for you and your new questions coming in ones and twos to me? Here's the answer for you: Can you still see? It's like this: to hit a sparkling shine upon his shoe. But yes, some did manage to get through, some of the time, okay, boo?

"I guess, but that one is mine, so leave it at the proper address. Leave it where you are fine, I mean, find, like... or was it "found," where you found it, okay? Well, I guess, no pay?"

"Yeah, man. Guess on as much as you want. But look."

Here comes Nanny and her sister, from the Island's lesser. "Is something missing here?" Somebody was heard asking in my ear. "I don't care but..."

Her mother was to be numbered amongst the dying worm mongers. She was gone fishing for sin Ting in the summer seasons and trying to keep her family alive and thriving among ours, before dying not of the usual vice called hunger, as you already know... her. The reason. But like, like, as was the custom, airy tea ding-dung, bells ringing on Christmas evening to tell this one, bringing in the glad tidings with him, no, not one?

"No, oh no, this is not the time for that sort of Christmas song, but..."

"Yes, I know the rest." It was by their speedily released diseases that fixed her upper kit, knee, Hingh, coming from within. As such sin Ting things were used to come hitting on them and her, really quick, sir, with Best Buy butter dish her out and upper. Back end-ish to go in and end this, while trying to scout her miss stress, too stressed out under her clothes and odd dresses at her old address to... But how did she come to fall so hard upon it, sir? Listen up mi lawd, and listen quicker. Because it was hard, yes, my lord. Oh, my Lord, tell me...

"Yes," he said, "I will, but with some conditionalities, like that you'll keep it close to your knees." He agreed, so here we go.

They forced her back to work the ore way too quickly to jerk it with her. Diction, airy words like these are for bees, you know, as it occurs to our works. The pork and chickens you know how to love so very much, like, when it's oh so finger-licking on the touch, licked up against the mug or cup. Just like a drummer drumming with a stiff stick. Slick chick fried chicken, eh? "Yes." Much too early in the morning for that cure and this Shirley ore to go working the Johnny Copper brush on the floor, Re. Look, look at the big mug. Yes, you can listen while you sip on it, and hug.

As for her, and how it was said to have occurred, she gave birth to twins, a pair of girls; she didn't survive the ordeal of pearls, as it would have happened to have hopped in and appeared on her and hers. Like, coming from somewhere around the world-class curves, where the hurt comes from first. It then popped up and out through the curved floor under the two-sided door.

"Where, you mean, from out there where she was used to be seen sitting on the chair corner?"

"Yes, there, or nearby, where we'd warned her not to disarm our... Not that sort of childbirth curse on her efforts at becoming a mama, though. Not as it was said to be the norm of these things and the carry-ings-on, first, and foremost — "Oh! You mean...?"

"Yes, that is what I mean, so be very kind to me. Now, can you still see?"

"Yes, it happened before the curse could get a moment to cry for thirst, no?"

"No. It wasn't the cutting knife that caused them to act at all. But that of the raw deal that she was dealt on the car dealer's lot itself, what a brawl that was, yes, mi bred, I felt it myself." Lots of them were there, chatting amongst themselves about the pair; that cup of blend, dead who'd hopped up on the bed and then fled to the med that was said to be better than hot bread, at the time. As they sat there and said what they had to say to the blind. Backsliding from waving the payment purse at their head by then, eh, swaying away from what they were supposed to do to pay 'em, Ray. First and foremost, yes, of course, that's what they did all around the coast. Those thieves stole it out of the purse first and then sold it to self.

"Oh, please, you mean..."

"Yes, to themselves, of course." That was why they had a lot of it to offer as pay packages when they were to have happened to pounce upon those paupers again, on the course. Those upon whom they'd placed a slaughter and blamed everyone else but themselves after our names. "But of course." We almost lost the very last of them back then. Now they're out to do the same to those who came in after and remained. Just as they did to her when they were trying to get her back to work, the crib mister, on, please, please, and yet more, please. By netted links too, those that they'd plotted and weaved while cursing away at other thieves who... Like, those who were getting busy rolling up their sleeves at the time, you know, to go out working on the long overdue reprieve of mine. Or two, so it would have seemed to some of these, and you?

Meanwhile, let's pay attention to these otherwise old guys, yes, my child. She was very wise at working with the sick and sitting beside the beehives. But she was dragged back to work before she was ready again to thrive, or even to leave the birth house for the outdoor sides, of course. Oh, the multitude of pleas they'd made. They were to succeed as he did, though, at least, for a brief moment in time, and gazed, all because of these. "Should I show them, though?" "Oh, yes, go on and show it to them, so that they may understand the real, reasoned-out reasons, and get to know how it all ends."

However, something else needs to happen before evening. Yes, before that, pouring rainwater fills out the pot cover and the saucer it's sitting in, in the soldering thing, in the basin. However, her husband did it, like so. "Don't believe me?"

"No."

Well, whatever you do, don't go. Don't leave me a loan here to worry and fret, at least, not just yet. Or else you might forget, and then you will be made to pay back that debt with everything you've got on your sweat.

"Or off."

"Oh, yeah, that too, I forgot."

"Here's how it was said to go; he had been carrying around some very potent agents in his backpack kit of late days' ends." So said the widow who was telling us the story of the husband and father to the young maiden. Been carrying it for the last eighty days hence, in some of his overcoat and jacket's pockets, too, (too craven). She'd gotten some of them to open up to her and tell her the truth about him. The compound was what he would use to keep them quiet after the shots he'd fired, would hit hard up against the stinging parts of the liars' hearts. Like that brute, the one who fell upon the point of his pocketknife that he took from the wife of a knight who was lucky enough to have felt the full brunt of the Slim one's wrath when he was seen dropping to a stop on the brier. Was numbered among the first from the last breakthrough. Well, as it turned out, it was the first one, too, yes, the breakthrough of the knight, into the dim light. Slim was just about to wake up from his sleep-in and go take up the night shift at watching over his little girl's turn at sleeping, again. That was when he saw him, sneaking in and breaking into the dim lights of a cabin he thought was occupied by just Kim. A pretty little girl, too scared to even take a walk outside in the dark to go and meet him as per the agreement he thought that she'd signed with him on the walk home from school, and then go babysit his own child. As it pertains to the Slim one and you, though? He was breaking in upon the sharpest truth of the very youth they'd wanted to hunt and shoot, for years, oh. But he did not know, so...

After the breaking of every bone in his body suit was replaced with bits of metal and wood, like this. Lucy Slim was more than prepared for anything the likes of him, such a no-good. (Turned and spit). So, when the time came, that opportune time for him to shine in the realms of the swine stain, he was more than prepared and ready to shine his wrath down on them. His war chips, too, were more than ready to go out and worship who?

"The mayor?"

"Yes, man, at the shrine even."

"True?"

"True." That was what he did, and he was able-bodied. Yes, he was enabled by somebody that he knew and was to come out alive, and that was how he got to show others, such as them, how to live and thrive. Then got back into the acts of showing 'em how he was about to wax and shine their hide, amen.

He fought as hard as a tyrannical eel hanging from the cord over his sleeve, trying to prevent the ordeal. Yes, I'm telling you, man, same as I'm here telling them now, that man fought for real. Attacking such eels as these all on the conceal, but...

When the youngest of the young twin, no less pretty than their mother and him, yes, the "pretty" name tag across the front of the dress she was given to have, belonged to, not just him, but her. Well, the "pretty" part of the name, as it occurred. Yes, you can go right ahead and subtract, or add some, since you don't like the "pretty" part of a name for your man, Mr. Handsome. After all, they were his two baby girls, like beautiful pockets of pearls, but when one of them also died right there by Slim, undressed and deprived of hers, yes, not him. Even her loving mother and the only love of her father, who was not like the others. Those who were in the habit of living too many lives as a farmer, or whatever other titles they may use to disarm her, trying to thrive when not at churches, marrying off daughters as wives as if to take them home and away from their fathers on bribes, as the curse was.

When she also died in the watery wash basin, the father cried again. But then, he dried up his eyes, tear-stained, got up from kneeling where he was beside the dame, and began to fight off their hides from covering their names. Fought it clear from covering over there, with the help of his lone remaining child, who was well prepared.

"Where, fight off the hides from where, exactly?"

"*Yuh mean, yuh nuh knoah*?" From somewhere near and dear to covering the boneheads' brown skin around their backside spheres. Fought it clear from wrapping up their backpack of Pride's lager beer, too.

"Or Brown's."

"You know them, like, better than none, my dear." Those bears that come in off the polar ice-cold rolling tide once a year are usually naked and barely bare.

"Or was... wasn't it nearly?"

"Um, whatever." Well, they might have been bare, but beware! They're not that cold since their coats are warm and well-prepared for such atmospheric alarms, of sorts. Quite unlike how these contrite club-hites with anxious eyes are walking around and watching the guys, whoever they are. Not knowing who to trust anymore with their lives since the advent of the man who is fighting to avenge his wife for what they did to her. But as said before, Father fought it with all that was left within his pot... I mean, pocket, sorry. Everything he had on him was called into the slaughtering. All that was left of his strength and his might in his pocket full to overflowing of blight on sin with cement was called in, too. He answered the call and did what he ought to. Did so until the end came with his own, like…

"What, go-go dance show, I must know, now?"

"No, not that at all, not a blow-wow. But with his demise, in the fall." Well, so they thought, you know. But "he'll soon be revived, one of these days perhaps, to face his cup of tea poured out on him from the hottest of the pots." So they were heard saying to passers-by and people like me, on the lots.

"Or will he?"

"Just wait and see, it will be featured on TV soon."

"Was he, was he really dead?"

"No, no, mi bred." They'd afforded him just the right amount of time he needed to recover and help his other little girl grow older and wiser. It wasn't his fault, though, that she died. But the man could spare just one hand on either side. No surprise there. That just happened to be where they were tied up and left hanging on a string to go help out in feeding, clothing, and caring for him on grass husks and badger's skin, to wear.

"I know, I know."

"Yes, but let me tell you how things got this tough to go slow." Trust had bitten the dust oh, again, due to the current conditions hitting against their names. The child left her seat where he'd sat her down to eat, and climbed back on the inside of it, yes, the washbasin deep and wide as that, and this. Wide as sleet on the meadows covered in ten feet of rolling avalanche tide.

"Or was it, wasn't it a blanket?"

"Same piece of sheet like that, and this." As wide as it was, just like… (oh no, I can't look at it).

"Like what, her mother's gapped teeth?"

"Yes. That's it right there, boldly shown off from the framed smiling head above the chair, you sure are slick this year. She wanted to go practice, probably. Practicing how to navigate and swim the wide-ranging seas within me. Happened when he went into the box of food to grab something for them to eat that was good. You know what I mean, right?"

"Yes, right you are."

"Well, I'll continue to write the tall tales of the stars, because... In the minds of the jet-setting elitist kinds, those up her uppity types of the weak-spined... no, not mine. But those of the jetsetters getting fatter off the stranded and weak, you know, yes, I know I'm right. I mean, as right as — "As right as their two right feet at the dancing feat. Right?"

"Yes, you're right."

"I know I am, like, when they're supposed to be seen coming together to meet up on the streets, cars?"

"Of course, those folks can really bust a dance, Ann, they have no left feet to get in the way of a man and his right hand to throw them off balance if and whenever they do dance, man."

"No?"

"No, it's a joke but..." Those were the same ones who were setting up their kinds of uppity eyelashes while watching the blind, missing all the matches, but mine. As they were accustomed to saying while washing your feet behind the wristwatch swaying at the watch-night meeting services, no?

"No, but..."

"Even better than that show, though, is this." Greetings, Mr. Benbow, here it is."

"What, what is it, are you here delivering the sweater?"

Yes, sir, what do I know about the weather, I mean, you? This is not yours, though, but theirs, because... You were there washing their feet and saying your prayers. Those very feet that they'd considered much better to eat than liver, while dropping off pears like these to deliver.

"What, the pair of sweaters?"

"Yes, sir. Those sweaters are sweeter to eat than meat, so, go on, eat it, since you don't seem to know how to knit it."

"Don't you mean 'me,' instead of 'meat,' can someone eat that?"

"Well, if you feel like it, go right on and wash your feet on the path. Then sit back down and relax as you heat it with the wax, perhaps. Whatever 'it' is, that was how they saw it through, via their eyes getting wetter and quicker than you, oh."

"She must not sleep," they'd said to the weakest of the weekend's wicked. Like. She who was there dying to sleep, with you, yes, so that she may hasten the casket when her man of the latest day gets wind of it, as I'd guessed. She wanted more than anything else at the time to take a nap in the new casket the big man had bought and paid for with a fat dime, for her last hit upon a dying day's score. Had it for weeks, though she didn't know that much about such a practice. "Nor should she stop working, the line, not even for a week," they said. "A day," others say while puckering their mouths at her, okay. At the nanny's back door, too, behind her face, well. That's all that you're going to hear from Gord, no more than me and mine, or Grace's head. "Oh, Lord." "No, not even for bread," they further said. "Not for any reason, so to speak," as was read. Sweet, eh, yes Edith, my Niece, and Mildred, oh...

"No, don't do it. Let's tell the truth-oh, just as a tip. Because that's not really how it goes, we're not related, as you'd supposed."

"I understand, you've got more than a thousand reasons why you'd want to deny even knowing such a man, as this." So, here's what they said further, Moe, I mean, there's more. "Not while the important people of the week are in dire need of your ever-in-demand servicing style list stick habit." Caregiving, you know, with a twisted smile like this, so to speak, of it. TikTok time clock, wrapping up pennies and dimes on that. Sweet as sausage, it was, they had to grab a supporting role in the act, Sis, from above, in the act of trying to hold it all together in control, and rock this, with love.

"For what, man, and, and, for how long?"

"For a week at the very least, so I was told when I asked this. Well, so everybody there was told then." So, she went back to work on the fabric, trying to make a shirt for a jerk like this one that couldn't speak. It worked well for a while. "For a short while," she'd said when she accepted the hard-earned bread in fits of rage. But it was in agreement with their pleading, and yes, pity was wrapped up in it and needed... like, like while kneading out the wheat dough mix. Yes, it was wrapped up in how much they'd begged and spat. She would have done so until she shirked and stopped it.

"Oh, sheet, why, what happened? She'd skipped?"

"No, you know? Well, it wasn't like that, but this; she hit upon a burnout and crashed."

"Oh my gosh. Why would you even think to say a thing like that? She's not a quitter to do them like that on the wicker, is she? Oh, noo."

"No," she said, with a long drawn-out oooo, accentuate...Ted.

"I know, I know, it wasn't that, but it was because..."

"What, because of what?"

Because she dropped plop off her thigh, yes. Just like this orange here, and that rye over there. So, she dropped and died, like, just like those go-go wax-to-a-shine thighs, yes, mi bred, dead. If you want to, you may leave, since you don't believe, but I'll go on and tell it to these guys' sleeves. She died trying to get back up, you know?

To get back up and continue to work, standing on her toes, trying to finish folding the shirt, but she could not, so she lay there till she stopped breathing, and died. Right there on the flat of her belly like guava jelly.

"Where, you mean..."

"Yes, my dear, right there on the job."

"Yes?"

Look at his mouth, open wide as... "Yes, there." Then comes the really big surprise of the year. Hubby had gone nowhere; no, he was still there. Here, take a look through this youth's tube, see? Hobby was always wise. Well, he's Papa too in this leg of the shoe from Bata that's now bouncing on and off their backsides good and proper. But yes, he was wise enough, though not as seen through their uppity eyelashes neatly brushed to go show off to Mister McAnuff. They were closed in, and most of the islanders' time clocks were all but frozen. Those who had already gone the way of the fallen, they too fell to the plague that called them.

"Yes?"

"Yes."

"Where, to hell?"

"True. Well, at least for some of them, not you. You're a Saint as we all already know, so." "Come away from there," was what you heard. So came a voice very serene and clear, as it said to you, "Get out and run for your life" before the full wrath of the plague came storming through that night, and you? Yes, you got up and left in obedience to their begging and pleading. But it was all because of the hellish call that was heard coming through the wall. They didn't want you to be caught up in such protocols.

"So that was how she'd managed to escape the sword at all?"

"Yes. Happened when you'd skipped the hall, she heard and did as you'd said when you'd called, telling her to get out and come with you to survive it all. Hence, you're here with her now and standing tall, to answer the other calls and my talking tales that are so very tall that... no, let's just leave it at that and go back to that shock of a show. You've already gotten the prize that they owed you, you know, so. The cure was almost ready, right?"

"Sure."

So they say to Freddy. And yes, you too, Brice...

"Who are you talking about now, Gord?"

"No, not you now, nor him over there at whom I'm directing this sharp sword. It's to that guy further along over there by the soiled-up style it sticks and is strong, though a bit bored, so. By the time it got there and settled in steadily, though, taking up arms to go playing with new clear and Freddy..."

"Yes, I know, the old one too, no?"

"Oh! Well, yes, couldn't you guess? He wasn't someone known to be giving up on a trusted old friend like you, Tess, just because of the new

Aunt's circumstances. Ants such as that, and this, those that had happened to drop in on the antics at the old boat house in Newlands 6."

"No-o"

"No, and no heavy-handed soothsayer like you was going to make him change his shoe on sheets like these."

"No?"

"No."

"Okay, hold on, because you're leading me off track, man, stop that at once, or else."

"Else what? Go, move your horse, because that one-trick pony of yours doesn't know the first thing about a dance, but it was because this was to prove just as deadly, okay?"

"Okay, so what next did they say?"

"We've got to hold on just a bit longer," yes, that was what they said to everyone, and her. "If we get past this rut of a one-hit wonder..." Hit her hard in the gut down under, you know, yes, yes, Zander, hard enough for someone to bust a sweat to wet way down below their latest odd dress. But "we'll be home and good to go bulk cooking the gander and the food to go with it too, unless..." Okay. We'll leave it at that address and go westward to undress.

"Yes?"

"Yes, just the word I heard them all say at the time, too, as soon as they heard about the undressing parts, and you. 'Yes,' was what they all said to you, Mister Alexander Wood. Would you allow me to say it again, and just as good?"

"Yes, go on, go on, yes, you can."

"Yes, I thank you, Sir. But you can't rest now, sweetie, and she." They were talking about the other lady, the one with the key. The one who was there, pointing the finger back at me at the time, as if she wanted me to go and take her place in the line. "No," they say, that's not good, okay. Not for us, no, not you, "and me," I had to interject this in and agree. Not when we, wonderful people like us and like, like the Anguses, "for the sake of Chru'rice man and those kids, and?"

"And who, the Goods?"

"Yes, she, too, that one door ring woman over there in the trolley made of wood, 'we need you,'" they said. You can't do that to us, not while we need every available hand-me-down thing that we can find on the bus to use as a grip upon the Lot Tory hotline string. Don't forget to remember, you're not doing it for a favor, like, for free, no. You're doing it on fees, in the sweetened-up pots of David's teas." Of morning coffee beans from dried Blue Mountain scenes, too, yes, and the teas that they said were green, but when they gave it to mean in the cup, that was a bit unclean. That was when I'd noticed that it wasn't green, but brownish and... and — "Mean, or me? Don't you mean me?"

"Probably, but they were feeding her the plated plots of..."

"What, vegetarian sardines, ee?"

Yes, you know what? When she responded in the negative on these and turned around to go home and ease herself out of the ordeal, and left to... to go and take a p-p, will you please, please, you know? "Oh, come on!" Was what she heard coming from...

"Who, from whom, them?"

Yes, those were the very words coming from them. They begged and pleaded along yet some more, mi Breda man. Oh, which one are you wearing, a man, or a woman's shoe, my brother from the Netherlands?

"I won't answer that, there's no need to, let's just see if we can tin you."

"Please, allow me some time to feed..." she said, reversing the talking seeds right back at their shaky knees below the head. They wanted to remain as the headship in the fed... Whilst bedding down in their well, combing gowns for the overnight harbor ring ships' kind of welcome. Whenever they come into town to call in sick when the rising hell comes, but she disagreed with it. That was when the guns came into play on her relatives' butt... oh, sheets, no. No naked parts, such as that wart was there to show off, but like, that buttoned-up arm, below the neck, and the head one in command of the buttress' warm, welcoming address. Or something else might have been ringing, like the alarm that was there, wringing bloody red. Yes, the one made of clay, mi Breda dear, was announcing the next one called in sick, as said. Pumped full of bloodshed by the said pop's man and husband, whom they'd already pronounced dead. The announcer himself was the very next one who was to be blown away like puffs of smoke the very next day. He and his clan were chief among the Sayers who did the tell-say.

"You mean, like, like, that one, along with the called-in sick, front desk girl?"

"No, let's leave it that way as it is and go twirl." It was coming from the nose and mouth, okay? Because someone else was seen hiding out there and smoking the regular tar-studded pack-a-day. But her father, and husband to their mother, wasn't like Mister Rose, her legal brother. No, siree, he really knows, and he, too, has one of those. He knew how to use it on whims and fancying the fancier things like those pentalene.

"What's that?"

"Those, you mean... I know, you haven't seen them before... Look, man, look, see those men walking towards her door? They just love to use them. Some new concept armrests that are used these days to get them warmly dressed when they don't want to upset the rest of the jet set. Wink-wink. Don't worry about it yet, we think." But, yes. Father has one of those things for them; he was sure going to use it on them.

"Who, on whom?"

Those who were there, firing off their mouths of talks on and off, things that didn't belong to you, like, like your pops and such other things that, like, those that I'm pointing at, like, him, and her, not me nor you. But, yes, at that same one at whom I'm now turning to aim again, and still pointing a finger ring tool. He'll be the next in line to wear those boots. Yes, father has more than one, as a matter of fact, and was prepared to take a stand with the ax. Standing up to them on that and placing the blame on those fat cats over there, too, those who thought that they knew. Yes, those types of blowers were hanging on his arms, resting on his shoulders too, on the hideout farm. Worse off than that, and you, he knew how to use them; use them was what he was about to do to amuse them. Quick, real quick, boo.

"Put them in their proper order, man, so that everyday Joey kind of people like us may be better able to understand."

"Okay, Mick, my brother. Okay, listen on." He was the very person who ended up raising the two, then one less little girl than you, by himself, days in and out, on and off the mean and lean plates of food coming from you, no doubt. One pretty girl was gone, way too soon; the remaining one was sitting in the room, combing up her curly locks, one cane row at a time. A dress, too, the one that was sent in by way of the car tune, was addressed to them to put on the line, "or to get it shelved on that shelf of a friend of mine." Well, so said the note that came along with it, and took notice of the familiar habits. Like, like, such habits as Clementine's. But didn't say from whence it had come to them to stay that time. The shelf that is, but the dress, it wasn't mine, okay, look nuh, look nuh.

"Yeah, I understand the way."

Happened before he was to exit the door and turned to pop potshots on and off their hide for them to swallow and chew their pocket full of pumps and pride back through the shallow and down inside to go and hide out beside... "Well, do you know what would have caused that?"

"Yes, the periodic surprise attacks, no?"

"Yes." One was wiser than that, wide enough to have known that they were coming in one after another, gunner after gunner, searching for the brother, since they never knew that it was that same brother who was firing back the loads of lead and Copper at the caller.

Lots of gunners were doing it on the roads, even those. Yes, like, runners running in those days called in sick from a stuffy nose. Pretending you know. I wasn't one of those among the six, but I would have witnessed it. But that was that for that rose pot of fire ring sticks.

But we're still talking about the farmer from the former farmyard. Did it up until somebody saw him and quit the scene to go do some telling. (Oh, my Lord, tell me). Yes, but this is off-the-record if you'll agree, okay? I'll tell you some more one of these days, Nellie Hingh. But now this, this was what came after he was done with raising the first hell with it. The one side dead one that was to come when they took away his one door, woe man from here, but then comes the 2nd cup (of coffee). Because, by then, his other bee love... head daughter was also gone up, the grownups slot, to be flirting at being made a goner, by the same pack of crappy big shots.

She was nine going on twelve when she started ringing doorbells. Popping off potshots alongside her "hide-out" pops as well. Slick she was, nobody even knew what she knew. But she had to work for both of them; that was why she went. Yes, to go working off her behind the shelf's kind of nails, all uncontented, though it would have meant, and walking the fine line between dine and some time, oh, well. Like, when walking the dog for Bradley's yard, and crying, loud and hard. While passing by some of them on the road, runners clocking new world records like... it was as if they were flying to get out of the yard, again. Passing her by and crying. What a shame.

"Oh lord, that must have been hard."

"Yes, she called on her too, her God, not you." She wanted her to come to her yard to play with her dad's pack of cards, and to their rescue, that was for sure a truth. All that was to come after she was done with the long walk home, going to and from school, children, or run... like, when doing the running. Yes, my child, and babysitting bratty little pickney, lame and wild.

"Like them?"

"Yes, more of the same. Like, those bad brutes there pointing back at your hair in nets on somebody's brains, yes, out of style again, so I hear." Like, wherever the gig becomes available for fees to share the vegetables, she would go. To gain edible, like these ripe pears, you know, like, money to buy her some food, was what I heard. To keep her fed on chicken feed and bread, and not having to go off popping her pops' pop cho-cho spread for the chow she needed, as she was being asked to do regularly, to feed. All such orders were sent down to her from the king's dread, yes indeed. Good enough to get some of them close to her pap's hideout cave and got sent off to an early grave. Along with the other things, she never told them that she needed to go along with the duck egg. Like, the accumulation of dead-left bullets in her pops' hideout keg, that was all that she could afford not to go out and beg. Just as it was said before. There was much of this type of work available around those parts on the shores by then, though. Yes, Kirk Venable, go.

"Why did they, though?"

"You know, that's a very good question."

"Yes? So, what's wrong with the others, those other questions I've been asking all along these borders, what's wrong with those?"

"No man, you're getting it wrong, that's not what I meant to say, it, it was because." Because listen up, my friend, and just ask if you don't know the real facts of the game. Don't talk so much or you'll tell a lie, on such. Pay attention, and you'll grasp the truth about us. Islanders were wasting very little time down under the firing line, if any at all. Working wonders on the one-door inn line, near the rear ends of the hall, late-night calls were coming into the wards in those times. Nearer to the pillar in the wall, Ted's sweet and sour wines. There were more of such than you could have imagined when you too came to call on them in the mad inn. Offering all that could have been offered off to anything looking like a Mister Manning, even him. By them, yes, while licking and picking off the skin of their sour orange. They were quick in getting back up on the beds near the wall, imagine. The one with the "well, come on in and sit, I'm coming back soon," kind of friendly house call. Such was coming to fall on anyone and everyone. Anyone who was found able and lengthy, long time sin ting something, like he, and he, wanting to be with her lifting... Like, helping her out in lifting her new heavy leggings onto the bedding, first in the bedroom, by the... spreading, of course. Then to the delivery room space, which she ran to in haste. Delivering the straw for a wooding... or was it a wedding? Well, something. I can't remember things that well these days, but as they were sometimes said in a fearful fire ring line when tasting the tar wine that they were mired in at the time. As it sometimes sounded to be when such things are said to mean, and mine. First by them, and then back to me again, to make sure I hear, you know. Since they all knew that I tend to have trouble with the hearing aid, sometimes, ago.

Many people would have died in the plague-stricken bad ride. Sliding in on the blades of the surgeon's knives, and the scientist's bag of pride. So, they were looking way up ahead to get laid away again instead.

"The knives were, right?"

"Yeah, right." I roll my eyes now, too wet from laughing to be bright, wow. As already said, it was happening beside the bed somewhere around there to stay for a long time to come. Whenever they come, not if, notice? Look, they're already coming in, in a Cummings truck. To come over and repopulate the said bordered-up, lump sum of a place called Kingsland, as already said, mi king man. The Kingsland world was about to get a rebirth and to be reborn, of course. So, that was when the decision was made, way back then, as a matter of fact, companion reading, your thoughts.

"When, really, when did it all start to get so fat?"

"From way back then, Neily. Like, it was like they had been sitting and watching fools fighting themselves when it happened, I mean, while waiting for it to happen to them, at the right and proper seasons for it to get out and going." "Amen." Yes, the Cummer truck was quick in coming, too, off the shelf, and into being with you, humming something on your highway through. "This is the time," they said, as we've been seeing the eyeing. As some were beginning to see it all as the dream lines sailing in on all seven miles of the Black Stars, "lined her good and proper mi stars," so they say.

Yes, that was what they would always say in those daily days, but that was when the command came down from the top man's hand-me-down brainy companion, in all his ways. To come looking for more Pum-pum yams to fall on their plate, fei nyam, so that they could eat it, then beat a retreat. But it came to pass that, when it came at the last act, it got them staying closed in and shut down to Rastafar-I Mass Ross

Brown, or was it up? I can't seem to remember a lot these days, my guys, but sit down and don't get back up. Besides, such was going to remain on the pum-pum yam dem, all day long, and night times too. On what was said at the time to be their piece of clay pine, to make a potted brew. That, as it was to have turned out, was to be some kind of tough luck cup of red pea soup to burn out the gas Mama wanted for eating and cooking. Wasted it all, on the rough rock bough, but, but how did they get to the stop on that slippery spot, homey? Only under their jaw, Boney M's original music, singing it in a strange land for us to muse with, and on birthright spills that they were bringing in because they owe me 'em, "remove the wick."

That's what they were saying on the confidence drill, Hingh trick, back then. "All day, all night," just like Miss Miriam, loud and bright like a yam. "Up until — "Wait, seems like a good place to start a foot race to her house, no?"

"Yes, man, go ahead and craft your will."

"Yes, you're right, I guess."

"But why, why would I do a thing like that, my guy?"

"Why not? Why would the top-tiered spy guys over there miss that opportunity to say their goodbyes to the bunch of no-good guys that they'd been keeping under their eyes to stare at me?"

"You mean, they were watching us, and them? How long?"

"From way back?" He wasn't like that; he wasn't accustomed to doing those sorts of mess-ups on anyone's one shoe in the shop, so that was when...

In the meantime, the undefended borders between countries in people's yards, oh, lord, were out of order most of the time. At least one of them was, it was closed to non-essential traffic signs, as was ordered from up above the young master's loins. The orders that followed them in, were ordering such things as tourists and people looking forward to taking risks in sin. Risks like those, and yes, these, too, were going to win. Like some who were shopping for that and these sorts of holey biscuits, and cheese. On which to dine and chew the lickerish ticklish poppies of thieves. This was done to slow it down, the spread, you know, of the curse from the crown, of course. From that thing up ahead of them and the rest of us, or worse. This was about to become the new normal at international border lines, super for her call, gal, and mine. Even at some crossroads, board her crossing her leggings and formal orders.

It formally went into effect one night at about eight, going on to the midnight offering on the plate, or off, what the heck. In effect, it was clocking in on a gated door and locking it up some more. Under the bilateral agreement, as it was signed between him and all the other three men, the rest of them, he meant, you know. Signed with their golden pen, making the glee men, yes, those heathens again, as even as they have ever been, even her more even things than his, was called in. Happened when they were seen signing the decrees on the scrolls of sins. Truckers and workers who were essential to maintaining the supply line, like us, her, and the other gals, my girl. Those types were exempted from the travel orders. The one that says to them, "Tan a yuh yard oh." This means, in delay man's terms, stay in your house and obey the order. Up until the same truckers weren't exempted anymore, Sir. That was when the mad as f... um! Someone with powerful charms became a sucker of the thumb on the wrong right arm. Also exempted were health care professionals aplenty and personnel. Some well-fed personnel and others, too, of the empty and dirty ones. Like, like those who work on one side of the border, gal, but live on and off the other border, at all, with you, my pal. Students who hold valid visas, temporary foreign workers coming in to breathe her as... You know, just like we all knew they would, and aiming to hurt ours, if at all, they could. Along with anyone with valid work responsibilities, they say. Such are the ones who may, of course, go the other way, and come back again on some other day, until they are not. Like, allowed to act like that, anymore. Because their actions, interactions, and reactions were just about to plunge them headlong into the asking parts of the bigger boss man. Yes, these types I'm here looking at may also cross, one day, perhaps, um. "Well, okay," was what I was heard to have said and laughed kikikikiki'i a. Yeah man, I know, that was a bit childish like Pickney, I am. But go, because, as long as what you're crossing to do is of interest to the real boss, "Hi, man." No, not you. You're allowed to pass through.

Time now for a reset and then a restart, no?

"No."

"Who said no?"

"*Mi nuh knoah*. I don't know, and I don't care that much either."

"Okay, we'll do it anyway, just to please her." So. If you were the person in charge of the business's purse strings. Like, strumming hard on the guitar's classic chords and worsened, around these parts in the yard, and bursting. Oh, my king! Make sure you discard that as... As the first thing? While cursing the shirt off others in D chord, for her sin. And let's say it this way. "Let's say you want to run — "What? Oh no! I won't run, yuh moussie mad." You've got to be crazy, my lad.

"Oh no, it's not like that, not to run away from the task at the request of some acting cats at the school of arts, no. Not like they had done." That should be easy to come one day, but not just yet, I'd say, but c'mon. We're talking about the run here, as in, running the business, that is what we're here thinking of singing, "your I-Nez," and to manage it well, too, that is what we're trying now to sell to you. "If so, wouldn't you be there and keeping the hell out of a watchful eye in your stare ring gear — 'Your I-Nez!' While looking at the headlines and worsening there?"

"Yes, mi Breda dear."

But only when not keeping those high things on your business page, shredding the affairs, and cursing the un-toasted bread covering the spread over there, "right?"

"Right."

Or, even whilst you're there doing periodic stocktaking to stay in the clear, thin, or thick air, this won't you? Don't be an ask like that kind of a boss who will not stop and listen to what the chap is trying to tell him fast, and you... And staying safely in. 'Tis a thin line between here and there, no?

"Yes."

"But you're there, and not just hoping. Making a living that's fair and as slick as a token, yes?"

"Yes, Mi slick chick, no sin in so doing, now, let's carry on with it since you're already in."

"Okay, wait a minute. First, do this, go sing and play out a melody on your strings with this, because I'm feeling sick under my skin covered over in ticks, like him and his…"

Anyway, look at this, and let's say. If in your stocktaking, risky habits, and your oversight days as were called in sick. One night, let's say, after you were done with sinning that way, yeah, on the slight of hands sins of Dickson's, that's Mister Dick's sins, not his son's, okay? That's what we're talking about today. Like, on the rough and tough riders mounting up on the best rides of the day. Riding that same rough and rocky road rider away too, to begin with, and getting it right on through, to the victory stick.

"Ride on, my chick."

"Yes, man, on route through, to the golden cupped-up top prize of the week?"

"Yes, man."

While you're there doing these, let's say you would have happened to notice a threatening head rising red with ease and in fig-goh siddung pan his knees. Like, go, over there and sit on it, on the bed of badger's skin, Mildred, and Fitz. Or on any such something, Sin Ting things we dread. Like, on the legs dressed up in leggings, in the middle, without an invite, even as a riddle. Like, (as said before) to get to come and go in peace, just the way you like to do it, however you may like it, please. You know what I mean, right? But after getting the call-in talk show on the radio one night? There it was. Something popped the plumb plum pudding that was just about to cum to the wooding. I mean, wedding, sorry, man. I'm known to always have these sorts of troubles with my spelling, as written on the tongue where I'm dwelling, so, forgive me, I'm begging you, please. But it wouldn't. It wouldn't come. But one day, upon your insights, and with your keen eyes gazing at your hideout, Days Inn plights. That was when you'd noticed it as it began to happen that way more than twice. Like, again, and again. Then, constantly so for the rest of the time as it remained. You know, like, every time you deal with it in one area of the plight pain in the pant he... Sorry, I meant to say pantry. In the pantry kit pair "Yah Suh Missa Morgan," Mick, I swear. Despite it, not just by sleight of hand, yes (yah soh sah), even in there. It pops up in another. Just like that daggering chick over there — "And this one, the other?"

"Yes, my brother, be prepared. What would you do next with it for my father?" Sit, Sir, sit down, and tell me. Would you just ditch on your spit like a speaking addict and throw your hands up in despair and quiver at it? No, mi Breda big boy silver, I don't think so, Trevor "the builder," because one thing is for sure, applause, and clever. The threat will not go away just because you do so and pray like never before. Like, give up and quiver, and pray every day, pray every day, read your — "Oh, heck man, you're leading me astray. Why, *wah mek Soh*. Why?"

Because no. One doesn't become a winner that way, on show, or anything else like so, okay? You keep on fighting away. Now go. *Gwaan, galong man, yuh nuh hae weh mi sey? gweh.*

Let's ignore that and continue to score the chat. Especially if and when you know what you already know, like what you know that you've already got, or have at your fingertips near the heart row, at your command, and at your disposal too. You know who you are, and the company you keep with the other go gal in the car, yes, my star, true?

"Who, what gal are you talking about?"

"She, right there across from you and pouting her mouth at you, and me. Isn't that True, mi B?"

"True."

"Yeah, man, yes, that part, I already know that you knew, but..." Hey you? Listen on, and tell me this truth all the way through, the commons. What if the business we're talking about here isn't the grocery store on the corner by the square, e, mi scout, look, man. Open your doors from the inside nook near the stairs where you are, Bookman. Go, stare out there some more through the bar, and take another wide-eyed look up at the stars. See? Can we now agree? It's not that at all, but the city. The city by the shore is four squares and tall. "It's even said to be pretty —

"Like me?"

"No, not quite like you and me, but like this one right over here, by a waving arm at the cover charging fee, or by the country, gone clear out across the sea as if afraid and running away from everybody." But what if it's the world? But then again, no, my girl, because we all know the cause.

"Which cause, tell me, so that I may go out and support it too, for a fee?"

This, this was what caused all of it. Because the Kingsland world doesn't run like that, gal friend Shelly-Ann girl, nor like a grocery store shop on the bend down twirl, you know, not like a one-man operation and such things more.

"More than what?"

"Them, more than those, but…"

"But, but what?"

What if it is? You know, like, what if that's how it's run in the KDs, like a grocery store shop? Or, what if it's not a one-man operation that we're resting this talk upon, per se? But more like, on a "one kind of man" operation, from among all other men of clay upon the sand on which you stay not so strong, but in shut-down, all day? Or one man over and above all other men, let's say. (Like. Oh, Mister Brown? Alright). Like those other men, some of whom are finally coming into their own again, to play. Coming up with something to stay around and to say, like, when saying whatever they feel like saying, you know, and are now saying such things and more, not just obeying the bore. Like they're now demanding a piece of the auctioned-off Hong Kong pied piper in the down-home way.

"On the ice glazer mainstay?"

"Yeah, there too." Now, do you think that this man right here is going to just slice up the pear, I mean, like, the pair of pies? Round or square and hand it off clear to that manly guy over there, and I? Then laugh ha ha ha haa? And then hand off some more, to you, and me too galore, just because? Just hand it all off to us? We who aren't even that smart, to begin with, the… (Applause). "Hear that?"

"What, the applause?"

"Yes, did you hear it?"

"Yes, but what is it all about?"

"Okay, put it on pause, and let's go out to play with the boys on the boats. Because this is what they're over there laughing about. Surely, they knew that it was not a smart thing for them to place so much trust in folks who were not that smart. Especially those who are not quite as smart as you, like Mark Badaus over there by the walk-pass.

"No, he's not?"

"No. He will not do such, like. Just slice it all up and then…"

"Then what?"

Then give to the other one, too, and so on down your walking shoe, on the path beaten evenly on you. Even down to your boo-boo sons, Cad-Jeru, and Mark junior, e, mister man?

"Phew."

Well, yes, go on. Wolf whistled at the pussycat in a dress on the shelf, for once. Because neither will the new woolly kid on the block himself, he will not, no. He won't stop firing potshots at your baseball cap now, just because he runs into more obstacles than before.

"Than before what?"

"That which he was accustomed to, on the resistance. Tough cow foot of the shoe, like that one out there on the track."

"With a calf? Like, moo-moo, yes?"

"Yes, not cat meow," that won't do a blow-wow. Like, not like you and I, Mister Leow, won't do.

"No, not me, 'it wasn't me,'" as she'd said, "I disagree, so leave me out of this, you see."

"Okay, I'll just say 'He' then. He, there, it's him that we're talking up a pot shot at and laughing hee hee hee anyway, to begin with, or even she, on any given day." No, he won't. He has grown accustomed to those types of challenges to overcome and is about to count his ten fingers down to a bumpy piece of lump, doing so by this time, on de-rhyming oranges sour like lime, yes, somehow, my son isn't even lying. It's what now fuels his drive into the primetime hog sow slot. Tightly panting for the water it wants out there in the penned-in pasture lot.

"As if hot to a boiling point?"

"Sir, sir, look at her."

"Mi blow wow. Bring it in and come. Come with a drink for her, look, she's turning pink and sudden at the tongue."

"Now?"

Yes, now, bring it into the timely beehives with honeycomb. Sweet little thing you, come on home, you sure know the way to overcome, and how to survive by now, on sinew and bones.

So, tell me, what have we got here? Take a look deeper in and stare, see? What is it? What do you see? Yes. Two hard heads are going at it, unfair and unfit. Like, stale bread, too, or three or four, or however much more than theirs and yours put together to try and even up the score, on you and your... "Oh, sheet, don't do it." This is now an all-out war; you already know the way such things are; all is fair in love and war, right? So, everybody is going to fight, using whatever is available to anybody else who's clever and always bright. The other knights, too, who are not always nice, will be in the news too, tonight, yes, them, even. They're going to fight to win the right to the right foot of the shoe, from the brother's ongoing plight of chicken flu. They will win it over you and yours, on every other unhinged door. To try and get a leg up on the other one-eyed girls, or two, no?

"No, no more of this from you, go."

But what the hail are you going to do about it anyway? None of you will be left around here to pursue the last suits you're going to file against the last brute that day, flirting around a win against the one who won the file over you and them. By trampling on those rights, you know, it belonged to you, not them, but then again. Remember what would have happened to the rest of them? "No."

"No? Listen up then, here we go." The constitution was tossed through the loophole that the cast of awe... some blue hole-bleeding bloody killers who killed you off did not bother to contact you. "When we're done," they'd confided among themselves as one, "there will be none of them left around here to take us on; they'll all be done and gone home. So, we've got to be strong and press on towards the end. No matter how hard they may try to push back against us and pretend. We're the ones who've got the 'real power full whack on the bus.'" But let's continue with the old man first and foremost.

What if one of them, just like that man, should wake up one day sometime around ten from the dome house, and let's just take a wild guess and say, realize that he too has got the power to spare, or money to spend on expensive gear. To stop the entire Kingsland world in its tracks, King gears, to stay amends, and ahead of the rest of them and their swords. Still in command, too, in his quest to get the win over the girl and him? For his mom and dad, you know, not you. Just as a present to show them how much he loves and cares about them, it would have meant, of a truth.

"Well, and to have his way over all others."

"Like, those wearing pearls, my brother, them even?"

"But of course, yes." Like, those few other warring brothers over there, or something else, this way, my dear. Yes, I hear, but what do you think he's going to do, Skink, stop the world from coming to tumble down on you? Of course not. Or will he?"

"Would he do that?"

Huh-huh. Pardon me for sounding a bit like that, like, cynical and such the likes. Like, such bad lap topping firing off their shot at you, and you're a ah... some but, but. Has anyone noticed a disconnect? Have such fizzled ends latched on top of your doorstop yet? Look, up above his neck, did you see the sweat sliding down the hanging thread? He's running away from them today, yes, mi bred. From the people he's saving up to save from an early grave, and why. Because folks are beginning to see through the lie. "Oh my, what a boatload of nonsense talk."

"Yes, as said before, word play is the order of the day around here."

16

Billie B Leave and the Wong Brothers

Belive it or not, this was the order of the day on the lot, Tory pot all day long, proper, and yes, night times, too. Brother number one created and wrote the wrong writings of the eighties. Right along he went writing things on the parchment, yes, Papermans bright for the babies, or the big grown-up ones. All are now hinged on the wrong Wong for him tonight in the KDs, where I lived once, it didn't make a difference, though. It was he and only he who was in the "know" and was wise. But bro, brother two reads a lot and tells stories such the likes as these, and those too, to guess who? No, not you, oh please, but to Billie B Leave, his ears are thin, and getting thinner every day, and everybody knows that you're not one of these, "okay?"

"Right."

You're not like those who do as they're told to do because, unlike you, to please is what he always does in the household that leaks like a sieve on people's closeted clothes on New Year's Eve. Quite unlike these strong and bulging arms in your shirt sleeves. Yes, that's what he does. Like, to leave a gaping gal-size hole in the house old dress of yours and his, whether it's on or off his empress's Biz knees.

"Yes?"

"You'd better believe, because... It makes no difference unless she's to be found wearing the bare sleeve with the high heels under your sleeves. No less than these, and no more sheets."

"Oh, please, wasn't it under ours?"

"Man, I don't know about that one, but believe what you want to B Leave. You're quite okay with these. B cause." Even after the eyes of the Kingsland world were open to the latest shows, his remained closed. Increasing the wind on his sleeves, heaven only knows how often he's now seen wiping his nose away from the sneeze. Listen and learn how to blow the leaves around and through the trees. "Boy, the darned thing sure is colder than deep freeze."

"What, the fallen leaves? Or the trees?"

Oh, please, no, but the wind. C'mon, let's go in. Look, the rain is just about to come rolling in. Look but don't touch, they said to us that day, but this is the new mash-up anyway. Breaking hard to a stop at the news coming from the doctor's cup, on replay. Now look up and watch, then tell me if you see those ballroom gowns dressing down to a slut. That was more than enough for those with the realest buffs, until the on-lookers wanted to reach out and touch. The real badass eel had enough oomph from last night's Ted meal to rump up the way he felt. Now the high-riding chapter is getting hotter and out of order. Honk E wanted to step out of order and go across the border, but "Stay in your house, stay in your corner" was the order he heard coming at him through the warner, or sounder, I mean, whatever. That would be the word coming at him from the speaker of the day, okay? Well, here's what they were heard to say, "Look through the glass window post at us, okay." But tell me, what else do you see while you're there, gazing up at the TV properly?

Pretty young girls were winning the Miss Stress of the world, cupped in the palm for a sup at the tea Leigh was bringing to me, yes, yes, my girl. You'll be alarmed too, when you start feeling me this warm, true? "True." Happened while someone was cupping yet more prizes on TV, and why is that a surprise? Close your eyes not even in the least, my guys, if you want to see. You're sure to see more than that, and this Mister Priestly Broad bore, because…

While somebody was walking up to hot, hunky chaps, sporting tightly woven six-packs under their T-shirt of sorts, and matching caps to go with that, as a start. T-shirts that are sometimes called "shut" by folks from over there on the other tarmac in the yard slot. Those who are tightly shut up in a jailhouse (or not). Some are in the hot seat, too, waiting to be mailed out. Yes, my dear, those over there are not you, our e-mail scout. So, remove the frown from your ear, shot, and pass through, on the way out. You've been sitting there alone, and everywhere else are the ones who may choose to turn their head and look around at you, or none.

Spreading everything that they may feel like, like leggings anew if you like, our gnome, and any other such thing that can be spread thinner than you. While hanging out in the news coming from the Bat-Chillers pod, I'm glued tonight. Lusting to be grabbed and held together really tight, to be glad if even half as bright, seen?

"Yeah, man, I see."

Yeah, right. Rolling my eyes, though, like her. Bright, ee!

"On screen, even, and in the bright lights, too?"

"Yuh mussy mad feh true. 'This — is — crazy!'" he said, whilst slapping the freshly smiling parts of his palms down on his leg. Too damn bright, are you?

"Says who?"

"You." You may look as much as you like, but don't get within two meters of touching the plant. Shush, slap that blight.

"That's right, 'Blow,' keep those hands of yours at an arm's length," says Aunt Clore's argument.

"But, but why?"

"Here's what I meant, my guy," she replied. "It's because we don't want any more of such columns and bars moving on up, like, to the stars. We don't want the curved lines to go all the way up on score, to a deluxe apartment somewhere, outdoors. While ringing in the signs and a whole lot more. Not any higher than slant, but before..."

"But before what?"

"Before that comes about, we must not do this thing nor that scout. Because we want to level the curves first and foremost, don't forget to..." Hey. Stop. Look at that, it's almost term-up.

"Yes?"

"Yes, but the frock, look at that." (He's sneaking a peek). But then, after getting it back down to the lowest possible rascal flat, board-walk-able, slow as a mountable dash, he continued with the talks. "We must shift the focus to try and trend it down to the earth's dust, on your account first and foremost. The curve we are speaking of here is the birth rate on the tarmac."

"It is? I thought it was to stop the death of the old and sickies."

"No. Not that, but this, as it is. Well, yes, those were the first on the lists, maybe. But no, kids, don't be deceived by a baby, like this one, your baby, even. Not even on her tantrum-throwing behavior and fits of rage, all evening."

So, I went out on that first date and didn't make it past the girl's front gate. Yes, I got to see the maker's face as fate would have eaten one eighth of her hate away." Taste, hmmm, sooo good. Yeah. But I was forced to stay two meters away from the cake, Sir. Never made it to anywhere near the pum-pum yam from way down in Jah make her.

Yeah man, the one that the Jamaicans ate, at least, they love to nyam it roasted on the plate. With roasted codfish and a cup of hot chocolate, as it states. Never turned out as planned, Sis. So, I thought I'd hide out the one-eyed goat and surprise her with a dash of sanitizer. So, they went about blaming things on either, or Hi-dah. Like everybody else, and wider. Never on him, you know, their god and king. Not on his eyes nor their daddy's backsides still bearing the scar from them skinning the hide off his git ore, within. But why should they? Their gods are okay, wouldn't have done such half-full things to them, eh, after all, he wouldn't have had any reason to cull, I mean, call. Nor to be visiting them with such wicked "e mi fren" sin ting, things such as retribution protocols, not as they are. They're wonderfully good people, and the goodly smart ones so far. All of them over there in the Kingsland-bound vehicle, my star, yes, they are. Like, real superstars.

"Yes, you mean, all of them?"

"Yes, they are, by far, my Breda man." Not like those loose Czars over yonder stars who choose her over "har," the one over there at the bar. Nor the weatherman. Like, like. Those other wicked ones hanging with the nedda one, guys, as was heard coming over the news grammar. Can't say whose they are, I'm hers, playing the guitar to soothe somebody's Grand Mama sometimes, as it occurs. So, blame it all on that other guy behind my bad grammar, as usual. Never on you nor your blue gal mama, she's mine. She who's there singing a new song to soothe them all, from behind. But then again, listen to all of them. They know full well that the trouble will soon come to an end. Just a few more days to labor before we go back to doing business as usual, as ever, amen. Just as we've always done, them.

"Safer?"

"Of course, say 'sure.'" Because great, and even greater things are waiting to happen after we're done with ridding the rotten plague of them. By a slip of the tongue, I mean, I should have said, the pen. "Don't worry, my friend," said some of them, it's just taking a bit longer than them and their long-time gal friend, Sin Ting. Or something longer than expected, for them to awake from their sleep-in. Just a few more people have been infected by some mutated strains of the already inspected and pronounced as injected and thoroughly protected blames.

"Mi gut. 'How is that even possible?'" He'd asked.

"I thought it might be a good prop to wax an ax at this too, because we were home good and comfortable and all that, and you?"

"No, it's not me at all, but I'd like you to tell me some more about it as we go, because it's, it's, I mean, this tale of yours is so tall, that..."

"Yes, I know, now I will, because we've got quite a few more miles to go, you know, before the final call for the kiln comes for us to go. Because we have to go and protect the unprotected with the protection that didn't protect the protected ones, 'so long.' Get a moving man, we can't waste any more time. Go get your protection game on, so that the unprotected such as me and you won't jeopardize the protected ones anymore." Yes, we can. We've got all the ammunition that we need right here in our right left-over hands, and we are offering it freely to you, and them, even for this once. But, as you can see, "this is just some sort of a rut to set us back to rawtid, ee — "What, did he just say that?"

"I guess you're hearing right, he did."

"The solution," they said, "is coming out one day, and it's moving expeditiously along the way, mi bred, has just hit upon a rough spot of war."

"To the skid beyond the savior's star?"

"Yes indeed." When it's all over, we'll be able to discover whoever it was. Like, we're going to do an investigation to find out who the man was. Or call in a woman, in other words, upon an order to go farther outward. Much, much wider than that, to go find out from her the size of her frock, I mean, how to start, how to begin. To try and find out how to begin doing this thing and see if we can get her to find out for us, how it all began to get so out of hand around the bus, stan sin ting. So that we may be able to place the blame where it rightfully belongs, with him. Like, squarely upon the head of that one called Choppan. That bad, bad come, Yunis, man, stop dragging your feet along. Come on nuh, mek weh galang. We're going to find him, the man who we all want to be rid of for 19, however long, years, Hingh.

But somehow, he would have managed to evade us and hang on in the carriage to blow wow and got to become stronger than the caved-up cow and us to rawtid.

"Who? Who is stronger than you?"

"Well, let's just say, 'someone with a noble name like you,' and a far-reaching arms-length too." Okay, Brenton Woo...

"Oh boy! I never knew..."

"No need to repent, I'm almost through." When this investigation is done, it will be plain to see everyone coming to the plumb plum pan tea pudding with red rum. Then, we'll get to find out what went wrong with what he was doing there, wooding on, I mean, doing wrong, what else he was there doing that could be construed as the wrong thing while he was there chopping away at splitting the ax with the wood behind the dragon Blues Inn. The bottom ends were up on the wall, long sin Ting, or something. Like, like when one of them was heard saying. "Long time nuh see yuh, 'buddy.'" He would have managed to get it done subtly, all hinged on you and me. To bring all this nuisance upon everybody. Wright or Wong. Yeah, man, come, let's blame it all on that chap named Choppan. He lives across the pond on the borderland. In the meantime, though, "our economic stick must continue to grow." So, we've got to work on a "stimulotus pack" ages ago, for them and us, and a whole lot more of such gut-busting good luck. But fuss and fore must, as a nation, plus. The two-term house is in a ruckus, the people of Kingsland must become willing-handed enough to bite the bulleting dust, look, it's there upon the notice board where — "Where, where is it?"

"Look, man, look nuh, look nuh. Open your eyes and stare. If you somehow can't see, then listen to what the man said and agree with me on what you hear."

"But, but I can't read that; I don't speak the language act."

Well, I'll tell you, "We cannot go back to business as usual," that's what it says. Like, like, looting like your blue gal, trust me, it's the new gal who'd sinned, as it's become the new thing for them to go raving. A few more gals may become too craven and hence will have to be brought up to the gate and reined in. But just... just a few, and just the way we were going to do before the plague brute thing busted a hit upon a one-hit wonderful one-door ring wanderer like you, and us. This is unsustainable, and it's not good anymore, Mister Wayne Able, hands up. We must not allow ourselves to become like that chap, what's his name again?

"Who, you mean, Choppan?"

Just the same as that clap hands, holey rolling along my brother, rolling along. Yes, we're better than that one.

"I guess."

"Or two?"

"Still no contest."

"After all, we're the mighty people of Kingsland, that's who we are, yes. Shout, Paul Rue." 'Roarrrr,' came the uproar. Now, close the door. Push, hitman, push, push it in the bush, I mean, in... push it in just a bit more. Yeah, that's it. Close the gate, too, then Chew.

"Phew," goes the wolf whistle, again. That was a bit much, though, nuh true mi fren, tell me, isn't it true?

"Yes, it's true."

"Yeah. That's it, that's what I meant to say from the beginning of the practice, okay?" That's what they were there doing, asking for money often, as if they were Foo Hingh or something (coughing) and didn't have any shoes on in the dumb thing. To say it another way, they were stand-up, open-mike comics. "Coming in on comedy practice — "Oh guard dammit, man, are we the only ones, I mean, am I the only one-eyed pride who's tired of hearing you blabbering and going along with lies?"

"No, I don't think so."

"So, stop it then, and let's go, okay?"

"Okay, I will, someday." Because somebody else is in that way and will be made to pay, that same buddy of his is the one who is behind it. It's his buddy's business to go out and find it. So, vomit, if you can't nyam it, I mean, swallow, if you can't swallow it.

"What's that?"

The puke-up you could no longer hold back, look at it, right there in his fist. "Bubbly, eh?" Someone was heard saying this that day. "He is Bubbly, eh?" But, beware, okay?

Well, let's close up this old house and move away.

"But, but why?"

Because they were there teaching you how to take leave of your senses, same as your conscience is, and it's because that was the nonsense that is sitting beside you on the benches. But you choose the one cent,

Sis, the one that makes no sense as it is, so it was to become very easy for them when they were ready to wax you thin, even to a sparkling glow of a shine thence. But, huh, never mind me and my, Um! Wipe that sleazy grin off your frontal face and come. Now, sit and talk to me if you want to see, or go discuss it amongst yourselves about what the other underlying story might have been when it was sold, on or off, you, me, and my... But, but...

17

Die Will is Done

In recent times, the seer types among their kind started seeing the new sign. Whereas those bought and then sold out again, media spheres were being inundated with the musky air. Mouthful of talk in reports of the clever sorts of such things we all hated the most out here. But never thought it could have happened in our house to the kids and us, if you care to hear. Like, the ravages of the current health scare and disadvantages wherever it appears, and the damages, too, weren't theirs, no. The damage done to the plaque by the plague as it was and is, was the last screw that they needed to tighten up on you, and your... as is. To get their cold fingers completely gripping the Holdings' airtight play-by-play commentary down on your screw. "Isn't it true?"

"Yes, I must confess, it is."

Well, nice to see you at this new address, with these because... By then, Kinglanders were being flooded with reports of wives and hobbies down under their busy bodies, tongue-licking their newborn cubbies dry.

"Oh my! Look," they said, "it's so pretty I could cry," but... Let's continue to try and say goodbye, while lashing along with the long-tongued madam about the way many of them were carrying on with the painting up of the plain things rebuffed, and by dying the air curls every day, nothing seemed naturally good enough. Everywhere over there for these to get a lay, they were busily laying it down. Yes, like, Lays potato chips please, with that kind of lying down on tricks, you know. Mostly the old and sickly or those with underlying health scare issues, they say. "Unfair, eh?"

"Like sickle cells?"

"Yes."

"Well, okay, Mae, 'liar you.'"

"Sshee, careful, he might hear you."

Nine times out of ten, though, those reports were coming to us and them at the mouths of those few who were old, and with glaring underlying health issues, passed off as a cold, as such things are always sold together with a wad of paper towel kind of tissue in their hold, yes, always. Even at first glance at the heavy eye bags and dancing along with you, on dabbing a wet kerchief, wrapped up in romance and walking the hallways, hurriedly. Pen in hand and rocking it, the man lied some more, sobbing galore. Yeah, man, sob some more, because... "Wait a minute, was that a sob, or a gut-busting chuckle to grab his attention because you're glad?"

"Mi nuh knoah. Anyway, let's continue to go astray."

This part may not be so obvious, but still, come on, Bob, reach out and touch the silk. "Oh, you already have?"

"Yeah, man."

"Well, now I'm the one who's glad." Anyway, come on, enough of such. What is going on about us, though, is this and that, kind of show. Nonstop, as a matter of fact. All sorts of shows all around the outdoor stops in such circles, as those, and yes, that. Follow my pointing finger with your eyelash, you'll see. There are many more "some" who are, just like those "just comers," in the car. Those who are affected with Urkel as nerdy dust, gnomes' comb crumbs of the worst scar. They are old and blatantly battling their issues galore, but there are many more such things to blame on them and their kings behind the oak doors. Whatever they say and do, or whatever happened to them and you (traditionally), is usually told and retold to the over-told position, Leigh. To get known by everybody in the household, and this one, no, not me, I'm just trying to see. Then sold yet some more on you and your soft soul train walking shoe, yes, that, too, Kishon Glasspoole, as you already knew. Yet, amid all the current happenings. How many of the old, from among the reporters of gold, whom the rest of the reporters are quoting in their reports of new things unearthed from the rotten ends, to get them sold on the rest of us and them? Or even those who those reported stories, as told to us and you hard bodies, are about sometimes, and coming from the most, on time. Those stories tell us of people who are dying like dust. One thing is for certain, all along the roads in and out, those talks of the deaths of the old strings, and those with underlying health issues and threats, who were dying from the household names, yes, were coming to us off them, alright, but...

How many of those elite types of old friendly ends and roosters' cold feet chasing hens to boost her tonight, trying to roost with her? How many of those are there among them in the death toll tallying booster upper kit, and... Miss, yes, you. Am I allowed to ask this bold question: a kiss from you? "Yes?" I like you already. What's your address? Well, I digress. Leave it at that, my empress. Now, back I must go to the plow from this haphazardly friendly mess up of ours. Even when I know that I'm going to miss her like, like, so very much. Tell me. What is the dividing line here and why? Oh, my dear, why? I saw that from the corn... her of my eye, as she was about to turn the corner and pass by. Oh, please, don't cry. But then again. Though the illness is mild in most people, they say, the elderly folks are particularly susceptible to serious symptoms and decay. Those who bear the greatest risk, too, of going away from you, from the Kingsland spheres to some other island inland somewhere else, beyond the blue.

"Well, okay," was what an amazingly good-looking guy looking a lot like you, him and I, was heard trying to say.

"Goodbye, gweh, yuh too damn lie."

"But, but, where are we?"

"There, we're supposed to be there, if you still can see."

"Thank you for bringing the show back on queue for me." Now, look over here.

Once upon a time in the Kingsland kingdom of the KD's, and mine too, yes, the knights and dames lived in peace with the local ladies there, and they made beautiful baby chairs, with too fine a shoe, "fair?"

"Fair."

But then, there arose a plagued baggy bug "out of nowhere," (or so they'd supposed), and nothing has been the same since.

"Perfect remedies," was what popped out of his tooth decay to meet me at the corner and go take a hop-over on somebody that day, trying to disarm her. Well, so it would have seemed to you and me when we took a moment, later on, to go down the avenue and look away. Like, that's how to keep control of the Kingsland world you already got on hold, no? Like, locked up in the home-staying daycare center of your girl, no, I mean, in your grasping grips upon them. Just cry: overpopulation, they say. Then, try the pandemic and vaccines, as the overlay, my son. Overly wise, educated guys and liberated people tried scare tactics and used social distancing axes as their alibi. After all of that and this, it was because of your doings in the first practice, I'll abide. As you and I had said, when we said it in the first place, that's it. That was what had caused that and this escape, nope?

"No."

"No? Go on and say so, if you want, but yes. It was your doing that had brought it about, you know, one shoe in, their mouths, yes. The good and better showing of the show was shoved out on the brothers first. Free body moves, body moves, got in the grooves, and steamed food, too, were removed from their mouths near the bladder. It's only fair to fake that you care and keep on working at it from up there. No?"

"No, no way."

"Well. Okay."

Meanwhile, the old timer's eyes took a flashback to look behind her, where she was over the walls of a time-like circle, far and wider. Those old eyes got wetter at what he saw, looking back at me to get her on the draw. All of the changes, broken promises, and deception he'd had the displeasure to have looked upon. Came looking back at him with a subtle explanation of what the reasoning for it all might have been, kids, listen to your pops, man, and not the wicked. Now look, the good people are in danger of succumbing to the evils of the stranger in their vehicles today. While the benefactor of such a whack attack culture, the eventual gainers of what should have remained ours, and not the vultures', okay? They are the same crooks, psychopaths, and jackals who'd tumbled down on us with the whack attack, old timer thought. He might be a bit used up by now, yes. But "The Doc," as he's known in this abandoned town on the rocks, is trading breathing breath yet, and still mighty blessed. His boys have grown up and left his house now. Not like he'd pictured and planned it a blow-wow, but "out" anyhow, and still going along the rocky road somehow. Or coming back towards his home. "Will my eyes fall upon them at all, ever again?" The old man lodged a new complaint up in Mount Haven. In the meantime, though, I'll continue to walk along, slow, yes, that slowly. Want to stick your neck out some more and follow me through the door, Leigh? "Oh, no."

Miles went out towards the south, southwest. Lucy Slim thinks and agrees with his papa; the proper West would suit his papa best; he was leaning in a bit more towards the west proper. Leaving behind his reluctant and (seemingly) fully resigned to his fate, Papa. "Slim is a tough one," his father knew that much. Also knew what metals he was made of. "He's made of steel," he said, "literally." But now, Miles is sleeping for way too long this evening, again. Started off napping upon his old traveling companion's decision to take off by himself and leave him that evening, on top of the last few. Trying to catch up on his rest, you know, and thinking of you. While sidestepping the gnawing pangs in and around his chest. near the bottom. Somebody has to address this soon. But who ma son, whom?

18

Click This Case, and Step In

His heart wasn't in the decision to go, and everybody knew it. Well, as far as we could see by watching him through this, as the miles disappeared under his feet.

Several miles up ahead, I was looking in on the other Bred. He felt drawn to go back and see the old house over there where they used to live, quite a bit removed from where he now hides out and works his magic in the mined-out pits. Today, though, it's a mimed field for the legs and blasting down to the toes of anyone who will dare to venture on his hallowed territories, uninvited. In his better days, he walked the lands and worked the ground there as a supervisor, minding the family's daily survival. Like, like the real treasures that they are, and were. But what's left of that family now is just Kim and him in the car, as it occurs. It was ages ago when such bad luck came calling, but in his mind, it still seemed like yesterday, in the morning. Looking back at how far they've come, it's outright amazing to them now how they'd managed to keep on going, astray, instead of back home. The woman, his wife and mother to the girls, has been dead for almost two decades, their single remaining daughter has taken up where she'd left off, only because...

But her voice still calls out, and somebody always seems to be eager to obey whatever it says. He couldn't stop himself from going, so he went, even after knowing firsthand the perils that lay in waiting on the way there and back, perhaps. Those mined-out fields are mimed fields today, yes, they are, mi pops. The cold gripping hands of death await you at every step. Not him, though; he's in the know on all those rats' nests, and about where not to stick his toes whenever he takes a step. He's the one who placed them there, the mimes and booby traps. Well, along with his partner in crime, his loving daughter Devine, always coming up a step or two behind his pops, Kim. With a helping hand, just to remind them... So, they both should know, but the boogie man lurks on every corner, and that icy cold hard hand of death is ever reaching out to grab a choke hold on you and your neck, too, at each peeping in at the mouth of a cave. Or at another stranger's attempt at hiding out in a crevice, or a wrong turn of a corner, like this. But a real man has to do what a real man has to do, even when a real man wasn't told exactly what he should do. So, he up and went to his wife's, and long-dead lover's beckoned call, again. "This is probably going to cost me my life, I know," he said, "but I must go."

...

Bad-luck young Nanny is a real scrapper of a hunter and provider for her and the pops man, ee. Yes, but everything she touches seems to turn to trouble. She has no trouble getting other people's children to touch, though, and often falls into more trouble doing so. It wasn't because she was a bad person, no. But even a great, unlucky working woman needs her job to get paid. Even if, and when it puts her charges at risk, and... She tried hard to keep her charges safe and secure while getting it done. But here it comes, trouble won't leave her alone. Even a harmless earthworm like this one right here and looking on, yes, that... Stop asking so many questions and come along, my dear, and watch. Yes, the one that baby girl, like every other girl, likes to play with. When Kim happens to be her latest babysitter, who just happens to be a little bit distracted now, look at her there with the young mister. They're talking away and side-eyed gazing at the lonesome stranger heading on in and towards them, where they are small-talking (or big). That earthworm can easily turn up, headfirst, atop the soil to pack the most venomous and painful punch of a bite out of the little girl's fingers, in the purse. "Yikes!" Yes, that's exactly what is about to happen on Nanny's watch just before dinner. Look. How is she ever going to get out of this one?

Not to worry. Long live her sister. Look, she's coming to the rescue as an uninvited visitor.

Identical twins they were, there was no official word about that part, but... Anyhow, she's the one who, not many people seemed to know or remember about, around these parts. But she and her little sister had little or no trouble finding work on the sister island, where Kim couldn't seem to find an abiding place to settle down and live as normal teenage girls, and boys? Quite another story is coming up in some reluctant eyes.

Nanny Kim knew something few else on the island knew: her sister was known to be long dead, or was she? Ghostly appearances keep popping up at the most inopportune times to look at me.

"And her mama?"

"Come on, man, pay attention, and I'll fill you in on the action calmer."

Medicated at gunpoint, they forced her back to work way too early after she gave birth to twin girls, ee! She didn't survive the ordeal, no, mi pickney. Her husband fought hard to prevent it, but when her youngest of the twins also died right there under his eyes, watching. No, no, don't blame him too much, it wasn't his fault, Martin, but... That was when Father really began to fight, for the chance of survival for what remained of the pack. In the minds of the elites, at the time, she must not stop working for a minute, "not for any reason," they'd said, denying it. "Not while we, the really important people, are in it, like, dire need of your ever-in-demand service," caregiving, you know, with a fake smile like this. So, she went back to work, way too soon, and did so until she dropped out of the room and ended up in the loom. And then...

They were closed in, yes. Most of the islanders' time clocks were all but frozen; many were already gone the way of the fallen, fell to the plague that called them. "The cure is almost ready," they'd said, "We've got to hold on just a bit longer, if we get past this rut of a one-hit wonder, we're home and good." Which "we" were they talking about, Kid Nii? Was that supposed to include you and me? No, no, Siree. It sure wasn't the average everyday Joe sort of working folks like you and me that they had in mind. But Nanny was one such kind of folk as us. Those types were dropping like flies, and fleas were all around the house at the time. But she was still holding on to the job like crazy while crying. Yes, the caregiving types of jobs, ladies, no denying it. Like caring for the important ones, the sick, and the needy, mostly for the sick and their babies. "But you can't rest now," they said, "not while we need every available hand that we can find, coming to our beds for the wet pans and dimes," to take back home, you know. When she responded negatively to what they'd said, the gunny threats came into play. Their guns first, pointed it right at her head, yes, but in vain threats mostly, okay? Of course, just shaking it as a warning in front of her face, ee. Quite unlike her husband and "baby father" Slim Kim Lucy. Yes, he has one of those things, too. Well, quite a few, and he knew how to use them. Using them was what he was about to do to amuse them.

He ended up raising the little girl by himself, alone. Yes, as you'd guessed, I suppose, go home. So, nobody thought much of him when the silent shooter started out working, and the corpse started gathering. He was much too slim and too busy for their first casting of the lots to come falling on him. But he was soon left with no other option but to grab his little girl and go off running under his hunched-over broad shoulders, compared as a fraction. Protection for her, from them and their onslaught, you know? He cradled her and held her. Well, after he got out of their dragnet and heavy-handed grip, with his life still in his pocket.

Many people would have died in the plague-ridden bad ride, and they were looking ahead towards better days, to repopulate the Kingsland world with the proper kinds of inhabitants, as already said. While picking up from where they'd left off, doing their kinds of things again, in their kind of ways, my good friend and boss. Some other types of folks would have managed to live it out, too, without any help from them, and you? But as for them, they weren't about to restart at the same place as the rest of the people, like those over there, and us two. The rich and mighty (for instance) became richer and mightier, by way of conquest and misappropriation of gains and profits on each idea. Those they would have lifted from the poor, like pickpockets, while the poor who would have dared to ask for more were told to get over it and move on. They weren't prepared to do so, Pops man, not without some form of reparations. Come on, we've been sitting on this rock way too long, let's get moving along. So, the fight was on, but it was to be guerrilla warfare from then on, for at least one man. Only the strongest of the strong were to survive, and boy, was he strong. Yes, like, as strong as steel rails down to his underpants. The "strong" we're talking about here may not be the most powerful, as before. As some might have thought while turning up their noses towards the eyelashes, at the bore. Heads were about to roll. Heavily laden crown-covered heads hunched on crown jewel-wearing necks, among them. Some who would have survived the plague by virtue of such power were about to lose it to the weak, unassuming old cowards, and the poor, someone, too.

"Below her?"

"Yes, and you are?"

"Just one of those who had been pushed a bit too far this time."

"Okay then, I see the sign."

...

The young child was in the garden playing, getting her hands dirty in the flowerpots — "Again?" "Yes, as usual, Devin." 'Funny face,' her boyfriend wannabe, was there again that day, arguing with me. No, I meant to say, her, yes, she." He was talking across the fence to sweet Kim-e and fidgeting away. Although she knew that the little girl was always more than safe in her familiar playground garden space, she was busily splitting her attention between both of them. That was when she heard it, the little girl's loudmouthed screaming habits. In a split second, she was by her side, kneeling and inquiring as to why. What was the reason for the cry? Funny-face was there by her side, too. Don't ask me... I don't know how. He must have hopped over the fence because that's the only way he could have made it to get there by the scenes of action so quickly. As seen through the eyes of a caregiving nanny, whose hands were too busy... Hey, look at me, pay attention, and... By the way, your eyes are beautiful, that's why I want you to keep on looking my way, okay? Keep on looking at me, particularly, and... anyway. Whatever the case, he was there and being helpful. He was about to find out how sweet her kisses tasted, yes, he was sure of it. Because, what with all this, his caring, helpful habits, and all? Not too bad on funny faces, chances at kick-starting his reputation, and to get it on with her now... "Is it, I mean, did he...?"

"Perhaps."

She was there, too, yes, sissy was. But Kim was the only one who knew about the girl. Well, except for me and you. "Get him out of here," said the ghostly voice in her ear. "What's he doing here?"

"Go, go, now," said Kim to him.

"But, but...?"

"But nothing, get out of here, stupid." Hesitantly at first, though he was, he turned around and began walking towards the main gate, which was certainly not the way by which he'd come when he first came here. But then, he squelched out an awful wailing sound, yeah, like that one, and took off running as if he had seen a... well.

At the same time, about a stone's throw across town, other ghosts were showing up in the family circle and home. "Get out of here," it said to the pop's man, near his bed. "Now, get moving, man, we've got to go home." Slim got up and took hold of his trusted shotgun, to add to the cult revolver, which was never too far from his arm's reach. It, too, was now caught in his handling grips. Grabbed his shoulder bag also and took the familiar route out of his den. He was on his way across the creek and up the roughest side of the mountain in no time, going towards their old dwelling house, and mine.

...

It's all up to us now, I suppose, said the mild-mannered young man as he eased himself up to the straightened-out position on his walking stick companion. No use sitting around out here moping, no, I've got to keep on moving. So he continued along in the sunrise direction, heading east-northeast, the exact opposite of the way they were going before his no-name companion skipped out on him and me. Leaving him with the added burden of making hard decisions on his own, which he wasn't accustomed to doing up until now. "Might as well head towards the sun," he said. "Nothing better has found me on this trail yet, so... That is the one thing that I'm going to have to decide on. Well, until I got there, to the sunny place I used to call home. This seems like a good place to hunker down for the night and think about it."

The house is in reasonably good condition, the best one he'd seen so far on this trail inward, on the mission. In his mind, he was beginning to prepare for the worst. The stench of rotten flesh salutes him first as he draws near. But so far, so good. None of such unpleasantry as could. Unlike most of the others he'd come across, this one didn't seem like a big coffin full of rotting flesh and old, bony corpses. "For some reason, this person (or family) must have gotten out with their lives still intact". The man inched his way towards the house, but.

...

Kim was sure she knew where her father might be, since he wasn't home when she got there, hoping for warm tea. Of late, he's been itching to go and see the place anyway, so she figured right away that it might be where she'd find him. She grabbed her kit and strapped on her six-shooter, waist first, and then the thigh below her hip. She threw the leather bag over her shoulder, snapped the safety belt shut in place at the waist, and continued around her other thigh, the same as the other little guy, now a bit bolder. After a quick glance back inside to make sure she's got all she needs for the trek. She took the familiar route out, down the trail and across the creek toward the hazardous mountain trail, and...

No man has walked these trails to cross paths with the army of two, Slim and Kim, and make it back out alive, except you. Not since the start of the big manhunt. She was more than half sure about that. Fifteen people were already dead before they'd finally figured out that it was Lucy Slim who was still very much alive and kicking. Well, killing, he was the person behind it all. Not to count those who fell to his blazing guns on the first hunting season near his home, on the wall. He was fighting to avenge his wife, whose death they'd caused, no surprise. There was no doubt in his mind that his little girl would still be here, too, if they hadn't interfered in his family life. And you?

They quickly assembled a hunting party and went after Slim with all guns blazing. The verdict was indecisive as to what they thought might have happened to him. "He's dead," some were quite sure; no mortal could have gone through such a hailstorm of bullets raining down on them and gotten out alive. Others weren't so sure because the rumors were floating around out there that most of his body was encased in metal. Therefore, they wouldn't put it past him to defy a hail of bullets and make it out alive, to raise hell. However, these doubters also knew about the reputation of the mine pits, even before the team of two would have gone in and added more fuel to gaslight somebody's toe below the armpits. They were in no hurry to go risking lives and limbs for the proof that they wanted. Furthermore, as times and circumstances would have dictated, everybody had far more pressing needs to tend to at the time than they did. Their very own survival was hanging in the balance, on a thin line.

...

Slim saw him coming along the winding trail, picking his way around the mines, explosive "mimes," and booby-traps as if he knew they were there. Or, perhaps he, too, was hearing voices; kind, caring voices like yours, guiding him away from trouble, by the score. "Can't be too quick on the draw here," he said. There was something about this one that spoke to him, you know. "Perhaps he's bringing good tidings," so he's sitting and watching.

...

Kim knows better than to let her guard down, so she's making slow but steady progress home; she'll be there in no time. Her ears and eyes are as sharp and focused as a beast from the wild. Look at her, she heard something coming, that's why her back is now resting against the tree trunk, legs pulled in to make herself as small a target as she may need to be. But it's coming still, whatever "it" is. Gun in hand, and leaning to look behind, from this side of the tree trunk, and then that, to see who, or what, it is that's coming her way. "Is he drunk?" She's as quiet and stealthy as a preying cat, on the hunt for dinner today. After all these years, they still won't leave her alone. Now that she has blossomed into a beautiful specimen of a young woman, all roads seem to be leading to her door. Even when and where there are none, neither roads leading to her home nor doors hinged on as comely a home as they might have thought in their knuckleheads, badly needing a comb. So here he comes, just another of the many who have walked the path towards her domicile. The same fate is awaiting this one, too, as has befallen the others who had dared so to do. "Come to Mama, she said. Well, that's as close as you are going to get, Mister." Bang, bang, two shots rang out, down goes the stranger, bleeding profusely from the side of the head, nose, and mouth.

Oh, Jesus chru-ice, no, no, no! No-o-o, you can't. But he was already gone. Miles was already dead, two bullets masterfully planted in his head. Just a short distance away from reconnecting with his long-lost beloved brother and his daughter. A niece he had not yet met, and the alarm clock came chiming in "ding," chalking up another bright soul on the glory train that evening. But thank God, the guardian of the gods, he was converted.

Oh! What a shame it has been, though, quite another heated pot of cold, slow to go over and stir up fast for them, yes, those meow-wing pussycats, yes, my friends.

...

Look, take a glimpse across the ages, can you see it? Murphy is doing his sheet again, wiping his feet upon them, and playing with his sweet tooth in the weekend legal games. The results are coming out just the same. After all, Murphy is his name. So, these things are always turning out wrong. Why? Because, like always, they cannot seem to get over the Murphy guy, in his better days, but that was then, though; this is now. Again, we say. Oh. Stop asking around, man. We're all good and done, go on through. *Gwaan, galong nuh man.* Oh, yeah, man, that's the show. Yeah, of course you may. Like, stick a fork in me and take a bite, on your way out. I'm that much done, alright. Or am I?

Extras

Like I've always done, I've inserted a bit of the next-in-series project that I'm working on into the current book, which in this case, is this one. If you have not yet done so, be sure to read book number one, New Hiking Trail Cast Shadow on the Tattooed. This, and many of my other works, are now available on Amazon Kindle, Barnes & Noble, Kobo, or wherever books are sold. Go take a look and see if you, like me, want to find the way out of the swindle. "Oh, I'm sold."

Here's an excerpt from book three, just for you. And you are?

Beam Weavers and Puppeteers.

Those were the good old days. They were living fair and sitting in their swivel chairs. That was the order of the day over there. But as for him, he was not going to be there. Even though he was, in fact, a square. It was a rare situation where he used to sit atop the mountains up there. On top of the world, and not even seeing a girl that would, or could love him good, just like she already knows that she should.

"Oh no, that's not good."

"Yeah! I know, I know," but still, that was how it was going to be, for sure. But he stared out the window with his Bungie eyes now cleared, as he looked out and over the whole Earth sphere. That's when and where he started seeing things and what they might be worth to them, and to him. In seeing, he was about to see. Almost everything that was there to be seen he would have seen, and even greater seeing there was to be, of the things to get. Because there was much more out there and over the other "there," yet, he knew it. Quite unlike the other dimwits. Yeah! That side of the green pasture was rare. There was much to be seen by eyes that were keen, and looking in. He knew that much. If he didn't see them yet, he knew he would come to see them later, you bet. Or he would go out to see them if and when he could, and he did, yeah man, that one was his, Wood. He went out and about, manipulating things with his long eye-reach and very powerful arm strings. Soon afterward, everything was taken and gone away from them, like. From every other man round and about, they were going to him and to feed the rest of their mouths.

Gone were they, further along to the other "them" also, like, to the squares and their kings. As such, things were just about to become the regular happenings. Although that was not his plan in the beginning. He did not include anybody but his Bungie in his first scheming. Yeah, that would have been him and him only. No one else was pictured on his pony. Nor in his planning session, reasoning, Tony. But then came the intermission when, out of the hiding place, there in his stalls. Like, in the stalls up there on the square, where for a million years came the lusting calls. (They started the call way up there, you know.) Then came the tumbling downhill-fall flow that was to (eventually) have them squabbling among themselves over tiny things, great or small. "No!"

"Yes, but," loud and forceful came the whoring call. Came it not at them, bursting out from under the rug's sprawl, and as loud as the stink of a thousand what?

"Mothballs?"

Yes, that, Paul. As for the others? Like the rest of the earth and the Hugh man's all, the whole of the earth's habitations worth. They were about to fall and feel the greed under his right-handed need, of course. Upon his coming in, you know? The arrival thing? He would have been bearing heavy-duty, beaten steel. Metals of mass destruction in the deal, dealing it down upon them, each and every one. He was never alone, though; it was he along with the Bungie one flow. It wasn't just them who were in on the meager, like, on the plan. They were to have all the blessings of the squared ones, those who were sitting up there in the whole chains of commands, even. After they were done beating up on the rest of them, you know them. Those who were near them were even found to be akin to their bloodied, squared-hue vein. They would have managed to get that far, ably aided along by the weight of Kingsley's weaponized bar, used as the tools of liberating fools such as you are, no? Yes. But that would have been after the siren had sounded the alarm. Outing Bungie and all his ambitious qualms and carryings-on, as well as putting up with his greed and eccentric charm. Kingsley wanted in on all of the hauls, as was to be seen happening over by the falls. As to how this, all of it would pertain to the conquering calls and exploits. It meant winning the Kingsland world of all its might, and all other things such as the likes. So, the word would have gotten out of someone and hopped into the hearing aid of Kingsley, the King's commands. That was when he'd sent for him to come to them, and to meet up with them to plan. "To fine-tune and to make the mission strong," he said, "for everyone, and our benefit." They were all to be part-takers partaking in all of it. That was it, Bungie couldn't quit, or could he? Well, whatever there be or may yet come to be, we'll soon see. It was to be the beginning of the end for all of them and of the other men, too. Like, those who weren't with them, mostly them, even those of the neighborly den, yeah man, you know them. They, as well as all the circular men and their times, must all come to an end. Their endings had begun right there and then.

They went out on the road again. The high seas were to walk the board with them. With tons of heavy loads bearing on them, my friend. They would have been wielding swords; destroyed were the many who were to come upon any of them on the journey of those globetrotting men of the lords. Those roaming, wandering, thieving squares, and then, "Oh lord!" Gone were all the precious corn and the most valuable ears. No longer feeding the Hares, but gone, from here, there, and everywhere else. Gone over to those squares over there, to go and prop up all of their shelves, and soiling up the cups that were piling up on the gears on top of the Tupperware.

In each of those destructions, the many culling events and other fan customs he meant. Squares would have proposed to leave at least one. Just one of them was alive as it was to cross their eyes. If only to go tell the tidings to other tribes around and about the drive-in, driving the fear of the gods of squares freely. The god of the squared king really, driving it into them, all of them. Such was coming to be passing through the thoughts of his heartstrings, breaking and aching him, because he thought to himself. If they would just go away and die of fear. Or vice versa, die of fear first, then go away later. That would have been greater for those roaming crop takers. Half the squares' work would have been done more safely, sparing him a lot of "not." You know! Like, not having to do any of that for himself, or by himself. Not having to waste precious resources on those wasted waste people are reclusive. But a mangy dog, they say, is better than a dead lion right away, and that is the better option for them on any given day. Every Lar, too, being a person of war, Sue. Small and insignificant though those wars of theirs might have been in the grand and ultimate scheme of worldly things to do. Lars knew such things. Lars and some of those very squares were to become friends here because they were to join together to beat back the Kingsley bunch. They'd met and gotten together over lunch, and that was where the intermarrying came into effect, too. Upon the joyful bites of the crispy crunch, and over more sweating of brows over the drinking of warm, steamy brew. So, by the time Kingsley and his men got to them, they went in and did them in the same manner as they did to the squared one and his friends. Every one of those escaped Lars survivors would have purposed to stay aliver. Yeah! I hear you again, this, too, you say, is wrong, my friend, but is it? Let's carry on with bringing in this sheet. All that was done per adventure, there should come another way someday thereafter. A day when and where Lars, just like squares, will also have their time of fun in the sun, a time in the sunbaker as they would have been thinking sometime later, on. After "sacking" them down, way down under the ground. But will that day ever come, and what will be the ultimate outcome? Leave it up to none, I mean, to none of them, like, those numb scums. But leave it all up to the readers and writers, and the righters of wrongs, and then some. Leave it up to such to decide thereupon, probably. Just an excerpt from book #3, in the series, it's coming soon. Thank you.

E Lloyd Kelly is an Author, Poet, and songwriter.

Other works by E Lloyd Kelly are available on the Author's page at Amazon.com/author/elloydkelly, or https://www.amazon.com/E.-LloydKelly/e/B01G7NYWL6

E.K. would like to hear from his readers. Email him at contact, elkthepoet@gmail.com.